spy school
PROJECT
X

Also by Stuart Gibbs

The Spy School series
Spy School
Spy Camp
Evil Spy School
Spy Ski School
Spy School Secret Service
Spy School Goes South
Spy School British Invasion
Spy School Revolution
Spy School at Sea
Spy School the Graphic Novel

The FunJungle series
Belly Up
Poached
Big Game
Panda-monium
Lion Down
Tyrannosaurus Wrecks
Bear Bottom

The Moon Base Alpha series
Space Case
Spaced Out
Waste of Space

The Charlie Thorne series
Charlie Thorne and the Last Equation
Charlie Thorne and the Lost City
Charlie Thorne and the Curse of Cleopatra

The Once Upon a Tim series
Once Upon a Tim
The Labyrinth of Doom

The Last Musketeer

STUART GIBBS

spy school

PROJECT

A **spy school** NOVEL

Simon & Schuster Books for Young Readers

New York London Toronto Sydney New Delhi

SIMON & SCHUSTER BOOKS FOR YOUNG READERS
An imprint of Simon & Schuster Children's Publishing Division
1230 Avenue of the Americas, New York, New York 10020

For information about special discounts for bulk purchases, please contact
Simon & Schuster Special Sales at 1-866-506-1949 or business@simonandschuster.com.
The Simon & Schuster Speakers Bureau can bring authors to your live event.
For more information or to book an event, contact the Simon & Schuster Speakers
Bureau at 1-866-248-3049 or visit our website at www.simonspeakers.com.
Interior design by Hilary Zarycky
Endpaper art by Ryan Thompson
The text for this book was set in Adobe Garamond Pro.
Manufactured in China
0522 SCP
First Edition
10 9 8 7 6 5 4 3 2 1
Library of Congress Cataloging-in-Publication Data
Names: Gibbs, Stuart, 1969– author.
Title: Spy school project X / Stuart Gibbs.
Description: First edition. | New York : Simon & Schuster Books for Young Readers,
[2022] | Series: Spy school ; 10 | Audience: Ages 10+ | Audience: Grades 4–6 | Summary:
"Superspy middle schooler Ben Ripley races against time and across state lines—traveling
by car, train, boat and plane—to track Murray Hill down before Ben's cyber enemies can
find him"— Provided by publisher.
Identifiers: LCCN 2021050878 (print) | LCCN 2021050879 (ebook) |
ISBN 9781534479494 (hardcover) | ISBN 9781534479517 (ebook)
Subjects: CYAC: Spies—Fiction. | Adventure and adventurers—Fiction. | Friendship—
Fiction. | Schools—Fiction. | LCGFT: Spy fiction. | Action and adventure fiction.
Classification: LCC PZ7.G339236 Spp 2022 (print) | LCC PZ7.G339236 (ebook) |
DDC [Fic]—dc23
LC record available at https://lccn.loc.gov/2021050878
LC ebook record available at https://lccn.loc.gov/2021050879

For the fabulous Kate Grant

Contents

spy school
PROJECT
X

To: My Evil Friends around the World
From: Murray Hill

If you are receiving this email, then things have gone horribly wrong with my most recent evil plan. I set up my account to automatically send this email to all of you today unless I stopped it from transmitting. And since I haven't stopped it, that means we have a problem.

Yes, I said "we" there. Not just me. *All of us* have a problem.

His name is Benjamin Ripley.

I know Ripley is only a teenager, but he has already helped thwart many of your brilliant evil plans—and if he hasn't thwarted yours, then you certainly know someone whose plans he has thwarted. Frankly, I'm sick of it.

If it wasn't for Ripley, a lot of us would be very, very rich. But now, we're not. And to make matters worse, other bad things have befallen us. Some of us have been captured. Some have lost body parts. Some have very nearly died multiple times.

This has to stop. I have talked to all of you about Project X before. The time has come to initiate it.

If you are reading this email, consider yourselves activated.

May the best person win.

Your friend,

Murray Hill

P.S. Ben Ripley sucks!!!!!

June 10

From: The Principal
To: Benjamin Ripley

Benjamin—

I need to meet you at 1200 hours tomorrow. This is URGENT. And also REALLY IMPORTANT. The meeting will be in my office in the Hale Administration Building. (The office that you blew up at the beginning of the school year.)

I know that you will be busy with your final exams, but it is critical that you attend. Your life depends on it.

This meeting will be top secret. Tell no one about it. And destroy this message after reading it.

—The Principal

SELF-PRESERVATION

Lyman Gymnasium

The CIA's Academy of Espionage

Washington, DC

June 11

1200 hours

I had an emergency meeting with the principal.

As if finals at spy school weren't stressful enough.

I used to go to a normal middle school, so I'm aware that exam weeks everywhere are difficult, but ours was brutal. Not just mentally—but often physically as well.

For example, an algebra exam in regular middle school might have a few questions on working out parabolas—while an algebra exam at spy school entailed having live grenades lobbed at you. The grenades were loaded with paint instead of explosives, so they would merely color you blue, rather than blow your limbs off, but still, the test was so traumatic, it frequently left students gibbering in fear. I'm lucky enough to be gifted in mathematics, and yet, there's a very big difference between doing a complex equation in a nice, quiet classroom as opposed to a muddy foxhole with paint-filled explosives raining down on you.

And that was one of the easier exams.

The most difficult was in Advanced Self-Preservation. It also happened to be the most painful.

Well, it wasn't painful if you were *good* at self-preservation. In that case, the exam could be rather hazardous for your instructor. But I wasn't good at self-preservation at all.

Everyone has their strengths. Mine happen to be more cerebral. I'm quite skilled at deducing what bad guys are plotting and then figuring out how to defeat them. This wasn't only in a classroom setting: I had faced *actual* bad guys a surprising number of times, given that I was only in my second year of spy school. Due to some extraordinary circumstances, I had managed to prevent evil organizations from dismantling the planet's electrical grid, destroying the Panama Canal, assassinating the president of the United States, and melting Antarctica. And that was just in the spring semester.

Unfortunately, at spy school, we didn't get good grades for successful missions. In fact, we still had to make up the homework we missed while we were away.

To be honest, I've gotten much better at self-preservation since coming to spy school. I could probably defeat the average person in a fight. But when you're a spy, you don't get attacked by *average* people. You have trained killers come after you. And so, to properly prepare us for the field, the exams in Advanced Self-Preservation were extremely difficult.

The final involved a little-known Tibetan style of martial arts known as Nook-Bhan-San, which loosely translates as "Wow, That *Really* Hurts." Each student had to fight one of the academy's many martial arts instructors. If we could defeat them, we would get an A. Personally, I felt that was highly unlikely. The best I could hope for was a D, which involved losing the fight, but not getting sent to the school infirmary.

I would have been nervous enough about the self-preservation exam on a normal day, but the impending meeting with the principal made everything worse. The principal had two basic personalities, angry and incompetent, and he tended to swing back and forth between them without any warning at all, so being with him was never a pleasant experience. He also had said that my life depended on this meeting, which made me even more anxious.

Then, to top things off, Professor Crandall had been late for the exam. Crandall was an elderly and doddering instructor with a big secret; in truth, he was very aware and capable, but only pretended to be in decline to throw off his enemies. (I was one of the few people who knew this, having learned of it during my first mission, and had sworn not to tell anyone.) Crandall was exceptionally good at the doddering act, and his lectures were famous for being incredibly boring and only vaguely coherent. In his final class of the semester, he had rambled on for a half hour about how to protect yourself against Vikings, even though the last time they had been a threat was 1000 AD.

The exam took place in the school gymnasium. Two students at a time were paired with instructors to fight. Crandall sat in the stands, ostensibly watching the proceedings, although he seemed to keep nodding off. (Like I said, he was a very good actor.) Normally, I would have been in no rush to get my butt kicked, but I was hoping to go early so that I could still make my meeting with the principal.

Instead, I was placed in the final pairing.

By then, I knew there was very little chance that I would get to the meeting on time, which would certainly incur the wrath of the principal. I never enjoyed incurring wrath, but the only way to be punctual would be to throw my exam. That would be extremely painful, and I enjoyed pain even less than wrath. Also, I didn't want to get an F in self-preservation and have to take the course over again the next semester.

So I tried my best.

The student who was selected to compete at the same time as me was Zoe Zibbell.

For much of my time at spy school, Zoe had been my closest friend, although we had recently hit a bumpy patch. Zoe had thought that one of our fellow students had switched to working for the bad guys and had gone behind my back to try to have them arrested. Her intentions were good—although she was wrong about the other student—but I had felt betrayed. Zoe had apologized profusely, and I knew she meant it. Yet things were still awkward between us.

Zoe didn't look impressive physically, being small and slight of build, but she was a formidable fighter. Plus, her size sometimes worked to her advantage. Her opponent, a wiry, muscular instructor, had certainly been told not to underestimate her—and then he did it anyhow. In under a minute, Zoe had him pinned to the mat and howling in pain, an A-plus performance for sure.

My own exam didn't go nearly as well. I was matched against a young woman with muscles so taut, they looked like iron bands. I started out decently well, employing a Nook-Bhan-San move called "Fast as Lightning." This wasn't really an attack. Instead, I just darted about quickly in an unpredictable pattern, hoping that my opponent might grow tired of chasing me around before she got the chance to hurt me. It wasn't the sort of technique that earned you an A, but then, it was a lot less painful than staying put and getting punched in the nose.

Unfortunately, my opponent responded with a move called "Even Faster Than Lightning" where she simply moved quicker than I did, then locked her hand around my wrist with the Grip of Extreme Stickiness and unleashed the Ordeal of a Thousand Smacks to the Face. I managed to slip free of her grasp with the Greased Snow Monkey, although my attempt to counterattack with the Fist of Annihilation failed miserably when she executed a perfect Evasive Yeti Maneuver and all I ended up punching was air.

But then, to my surprise, my opponent made a mistake. She shifted into the unmistakable stance of Pangolin Death Strike, for which the proper response was to drop to the floor and implement a Golden Jackal Leg Sweep. So I did it. In fact, it was the finest Golden Jackal Leg Sweep I had ever performed. There were sixteen separate movements, and I made each one of them perfectly.

Only, it didn't work. My opponent didn't perform the Pangolin Death Strike at all. Instead, she nimbly leapt out of the way of my leg sweep and dropped on top of me, driving her elbow into my solar plexus.

One moment, I thought I was about to win the match—and the next, I was pinned.

Professor Crandall came down from the stands, clucking his tongue in disappointment. "Oh, Benjamin, you walked right into that one. In dropping to the floor, you left yourself wide open for the lethal Here Comes the Avalanche move."

"But you never taught us about the Here Comes the Avalanche move!" I protested. "That's not fair!"

"When you're on a mission, the bad guys are rarely going to play fair," Crandall informed me. "You need to be prepared for *anything*. I'm afraid I'll have to give you a D minus for that performance."

"But . . . ," I spluttered, peeling myself off the floor. "That was my best Golden Jackal Leg Sweep ever!"

"Perhaps so, but this is Advanced Self-Preservation, not Interpretive Dance. In a real-life fight, you don't get points for style. And if you lose, you end up dead. Oh goodness, there appears to be a slice of cheese in my pocket." Crandall removed what was, in fact, a slice of cheese from his fleece vest and looked at it in wonderment, as if its presence was one of the great mysteries of the universe.

At this moment, I began to question how much of Professor Crandall's doddering act was an act and how much was actual doddering.

I really wanted to stay and argue that I deserved a better

grade than a D minus, but I reluctantly had to admit that Professor Crandall had made a valid argument about what real-life fights were like—and I was now late for my meeting with the principal.

"I have to go," I said.

"Have a nice summer!" Crandall told me cheerfully, then nibbled the cheese he'd discovered and exclaimed, "Ooh! It's Havarti! My favorite!"

I grabbed my backpack and headed for the door, moving a little slower than I'd intended, as I was still aching from the Here Comes the Avalanche.

Zoe dropped in beside me, doing her best to act like her extremely supportive pre-betrayal self. "That was really uncool of Crandall just now. You performed one of the best Golden Jackal Leg Sweeps I've seen all semester!"

"Maybe, but Crandall's right about what it's like in the field."

"Yeah. I guess you would know." There was a great deal of jealousy in Zoe's voice. She had recently managed to land an internship with the Double Agent Detection Division, which hadn't turned out to be nearly as exciting as she'd hoped. "While I was stuck working for DADD, you got to go to Central America and prevent a cruise ship from exploding."

"I nearly got killed on that mission," I reminded her. "Multiple times."

"I know. You're so lucky." This statement wasn't said with the slightest bit of sarcasm. Zoe really meant it. "Was this your last exam?"

"Yeah."

"Mine too. Are you heading back to the dorm to pack for spy camp?"

Normally, that's what I *would* have been doing. We were scheduled to begin our summer of wilderness training in a few days. However, I couldn't tell Zoe about my meeting with the principal, as it was classified. All I could say was, "In a bit. But I have to do something else first."

"Like what?" Zoe asked suspiciously.

We exited the gymnasium into Hammond Quadrangle. It was a glorious late spring day. The sun was shining, and yet, there wasn't a trace of the usual wilting humidity that Washington, DC, was famous for. The lawn of the quad was lush and green and fringed with flowers. Many of our fellow students were reveling in being done with their exams—playing frisbee, kicking soccer balls, or basking in the sun.

"Just a meeting," I said. "With an adviser."

Zoe gave me a doubtful look. "What is it really? A top secret conference? Are you being sent on *another* mission?"

"No! I swear."

"I bet. You're probably going to get air-dropped onto

Mount Everest to defuse a nuclear bomb or something amazing like that."

"Defusing nuclear bombs isn't amazing. It's terrifying."

"Well, I wouldn't know, would I? I haven't ever gotten to do it. But you have. Like four times."

"Only two of the bombs I defused were nuclear."

"Do you even hear yourself? Do you realize how fortunate you are? Most students don't get to defuse a bomb until their sixth year here—and those are just pretend ones for class. On your last mission, you got to disarm a real nuke, go undercover in exotic locations, *and* chase a speedboat on a WaveRunner! That's awesome! All I ever get to do at DADD is staple expense reports together."

I was about to counter Zoe's argument, but didn't for two reasons.

First, that WaveRunner chase had actually been pretty cool.

Second, the principal was coming across the quad toward me.

It was easy to see him approaching, as all the other students were giving him a wide berth. He looked even angrier than usual, so everyone was behaving as though he was radioactive, hurrying out of his path.

In addition, he hadn't bothered to put his toupee on properly. Even on good days, his hairpiece looked like a mangy badger camped out on his head, but today it seemed he'd forgotten it even existed, so it was completely askew, leaving a good portion of his bald, sweaty brow gleaming in the sunlight.

"You!" he exclaimed upon seeing me, and then pointed a thick, meaty finger my way. "You have a lot of nerve, Ripley!"

All around the quad, I noticed my fellow students experiencing dual emotions: genuine concern for my well-being—and relief that the principal wasn't angry at *them*.

While I had feared the principal would be upset at me for being late to the meeting, the level of fury in his eyes was far greater than I had expected. Still, I did my best to explain as he approached. "Sir, I'm very sorry that I kept you waiting. My exam in self-preservation went long . . ."

"That's true!" Zoe added, even though she knew this was risking the anger of the principal. "You can ask Professor Crandall yourself! He's right over there!" She pointed back to the gymnasium. Crandall had just exited the building, although he seemed preoccupied, clutching a kosher pickle with bemusement. I suspected he had recently discovered it in another one of his pockets.

"What are you even talking about?" the principal snapped at me. "I'm not angry about you being late! I'm angry about *this*!" He thrust a handwritten note in my face.

It read:

> To the principal,
> You are a jerk, a buffoon, a
> numbskull, a dolt, and a fathead.
> Also, you smell like a diseased
> pustule on the butt of a wildebeest.
> I'll be in the quad if you'd like to
> discuss this further.
> Sincerely,
> Ben Ripley

Many things were strange about this letter, but the most startling to me was that it was in my own handwriting. If I hadn't known better, I would have believed that I had actually written it.

"This was wrapped around a rock and thrown into my office five minutes ago!" the principal proclaimed.

It usually would have been quite difficult to throw a rock into the principal's office, as it was on the top floor of the Nathan Hale Building, five stories above the quad. However, the exterior wall of the office was currently missing, having been demolished the previous September by an errant mortar round. (I was the one who had fired it, although it wasn't really my fault; still, the principal remained annoyed at me for it, which was compounded by the fact that red tape had prevented any repairs from getting done, leaving a gaping hole in the building for the entire school year.) But while this made it *possible* for someone to throw a rock into his office, it still wouldn't have been easy; if I had tried to do it, I probably would have missed the fifth floor entirely and put a rock through one of the lower-level windows instead.

"I checked our handwriting database!" the principal continued indignantly. "This is your handwriting, isn't it?"

"Er . . . yes," I admitted. "But someone must have forged it! Why would I write something like that?"

"Because you're an insolent little pip-squeak!" the principal shouted. "I have half a mind to boot you out of this school!"

"You only have half a mind, period," Zoe muttered under her breath, too low for him to hear.

"This doesn't make any sense," I said to the principal. "I was coming to see *you* for our meeting. So I wouldn't have—"

"What meeting?" the principal demanded. "I didn't schedule any meeting with you today!"

I took a step back, confused. "You didn't send me a message about it yesterday?"

"Absolutely not! And if I *was* going to meet with you, it certainly wouldn't be in my office!"

"Why not?"

"Because you destroyed my office!"

"That wasn't Ben's fault . . . ," Zoe began.

The principal ignored her and kept glaring at me. "Because of you, I have spent the last eight months working at a desk made of two sawhorses and a piece of plywood! But I was finally able to requisition a *real* desk. It was delivered yesterday, and it's beautiful. It's big, expensive, and expertly crafted—and I'm not letting you anywhere near it, Ripley. You're a menace! If you got anywhere near that desk, I'm sure it would catch fire or explode or get eaten by a shark!"

"I think that's all highly unlikely," I said.

"*I* don't," the principal declared. "Not only are you insubordinate, you're also a walking disaster area."

"That's not true," I insisted.

At which point, the principal's office exploded.

EMERGENCY PROCEDURES

Hammond Quadrangle

Academy of Espionage

June 11

1215 hours

The explosion was as loud as a rocket blast.

An enormous ball of fire erupted from the principal's office. A large, dark flaming object sailed through the place where the wall should have been, tumbled through the air, and then thudded into the center of the quadrangle, leaving a crater the size of a small car.

"My new desk!" the principal shrieked.

A few seconds earlier, it had probably been as beautiful and expertly crafted as he'd claimed. But now it was battered, broken, and on fire. The principal and I both stared at it in horror, although for entirely different reasons.

The principal was upset because his cherished new desk was ruined. Whereas I was concerned because if I had been on time for my meeting, then both the principal and I would have been in his office during the explosion, rather than out in the quad. I quickly calculated how large a blast was needed to hurl a heavy desk such a great distance and instantly concluded that there was no way we would have survived it.

Zoe seemed to be thinking the same thing. "Looks like someone's trying to kill you," she told me, sincerely worried, then thought to add, "Again."

Alarms began wailing all around campus. There was an elaborate emergency evacuation system at the academy, which we had to practice with regularity. While my normal middle school had occasionally run fire drills, spy school had drills for fire, poison gas, aerial assaults, insurrections, coup d'états, and bombings. Each had a different pattern of alarms, which signaled how students were to evacuate. The current pattern, two short bursts, followed by two long ones, indicated a bombing.

My fellow students at the academy were, for the most part, exceptionally intelligent and competent. They responded to the alarms quickly and capably, doing exactly what was mandated: evacuating the school buildings and heading into the quadrangle.

The reason for this course of action was sensible: In the case of a bombing, it was dangerous to be indoors, as buildings could collapse, while the quad was a large, empty space, easily accessible from all parts of campus. Within seconds, students and faculty poured out of the buildings and onto the lawn—and then gaped in surprise at the flaming desk in the center of it.

With one exception. Professor Crandall tossed his pickle aside and quickly headed down a path that led away from the quadrangle.

Something strange was going on, and it seemed to me that Crandall was connected to it. It was highly suspicious that the principal and I had received contradictory messages from each other shortly before the explosion, and now Crandall, apparently thinking no one was watching him, had completely dropped his doddering act. He strode away from the quadrangle briskly and purposefully, rather than with his usual shambling gait.

I went after him.

Zoe followed me, intrigued, while the principal also followed, still angry at me.

"What's going on?" Zoe asked me, at the same time that

the principal said, "Not so fast, young man! I'm not done with you yet!"

I ignored the principal and tried to deflect Zoe's question. "Nothing's going on."

"Don't lie to me, Ben. Someone just tried to blow you up and now you're fleeing the scene. Tell me what's happening. I can help."

Before I could respond, three more friends of mine emerged from the growing crowd of students on the quad. Mike Brezinski raced toward us from Armistead Dormitory, clutching a gas mask, while Chip Schacter and Jawa O'Shea came from the mess hall.

Mike was my closest friend from *real* middle school, who had grown wise to the fact that I'd been recruited to the Academy of Espionage, even though it was supposed to be a secret. That, combined with Mike's tendency to think outside the box, had earned him not only his own acceptance to spy school, but also a spot on my most recent missions.

Chip was a few years older than me, a student more recognized for his brawn than his brains; it was often useful to have some muscle on a mission, although Chip was also capable of having surprising insights now and then. Jawa was the best all-around student in my class, extremely adept mentally and physically. He should have been the student going on missions, rather than me, but life had simply worked out differently.

"What's happening, Ben?" Chip asked.

"Yeah," Mike echoed. "How are you connected to the explosion?"

"What makes you think I'm connected to the explosion?" I asked.

"You're connected to *everything* weird that happens around here," Jawa said. "Ergo, if someone blows up the principal's office, you must be involved somehow."

"Exactly!" the principal agreed. "I'm holding you personally responsible for that desk, Ripley!"

"Why are you carrying a gas mask?" Zoe asked Mike.

"I got the alarm bells mixed up," Mike replied. "I couldn't remember if that was the alert for bombs or gas attacks, so I figured, better safe than sorry."

"It took me eight months to requisition that desk," the principal was grumbling. "It had custom detailing and built-in cup holders for my coffee . . ."

"So why are we leaving the quad?" Chip asked me.

I thought about making up a lie, but then decided against it. First of all, I hated lying to my friends. Second, Zoe had been right—they could help. After all, someone had just tried to kill me. It was probably better not to be on my own. Plus, I had lost track of Professor Crandall.

We had arrived at the edge of the quadrangle, between the armory and the chemical warfare building, only to find that Crandall was nowhere in sight.

"We need to find Professor Crandall," I told the others. "He just came this way."

"Crandall?" Chip asked disdainfully. "What do we want with that old coot? Last week, in the mess hall, I saw him putting oatmeal in his hat."

"He's not as senile as he seems," I said.

"You think he's behind the bombing?" Mike asked, sounding worried. Quite a few students at spy school had turned out to be double agents, so it was certainly possible that a faculty member could too.

Of course, none of them knew Crandall the way I did. I would have bet that even the principal wasn't aware of Crandall's facade—although, the principal wasn't aware of much in general; he didn't even notice that his toupee had migrated halfway off his head and now looked like a large rodent clinging to his left ear.

"I'm not sure *what* to think," I said. "That's why we need to find him."

While we had been talking, Jawa had dropped into a crouch and was inspecting the ground closely. He had been the best student by far in our Tailing and Tracking class and was now obviously looking for clues as to where Crandall had gone. "Got him!" he announced triumphantly. "There are slight indentations in the grass indicating someone walked across here only moments ago. The pattern shows someone moving at a swift pace, and there's a faint odor of salami and liniment."

"That's Crandall, all right," Zoe agreed. "The man has a salami sandwich for lunch every single day. Where'd he go?"

"This way!" Jawa sprang to his feet, following the trail, which led across a grassy expanse to a large grove of trees alongside the school artillery range. As we ducked into it, we could hear Crandall's voice. "All right. I'm here. What have you got?"

Since Chip and Jawa were the best athletes, they reached Crandall slightly before the rest of us. He was at the base of an extremely tall elm tree, speaking into a radio microphone and seeming far more lucid than usual—although the moment he saw Chip and Jawa, he went right back into his doddering act. "Skip and Yaya! Thank goodness you boys are here. I seem to have lost my way to the bathroom . . ." He trailed off as I arrived with the others and suddenly became cogent again. "Oh, fiddlesticks. Hello, Benjamin."

"What's going on here?" I asked.

"And who is going to pay for my desk?" the principal added.

Crandall gave me an annoyed look. "I really wish you'd come alone."

"And I really wish you'd told me what you were planning before I nearly got blown up."

"Wait a minute," Chip said to Crandall. "You're not a loony bird? That was all an act?"

Crandall ignored him to answer me. "Keeping you in the dark wasn't my call. That was up to the leader of the operation."

From the way he said those words, I instantly knew who he was talking about.

Erica Hale.

Erica was by far the best student at spy school. Next to her, even Jawa didn't stand a chance. But then, Erica had been training to be a spy much longer than any of the rest of us; it was her family business, going all the way back to the Hales of the American Revolution. Most of her direct ancestors had been spies for America, while her mother was an agent for British MI6.

Erica was also the fellow student that Zoe had mistakenly suspected of being a double agent. Which made things prickly between them.

And she was my girlfriend. Sort of.

I had been smitten with Erica from the moment I met her. She had not felt the same way about me, believing that relationships were a mistake in the spy business—and that I was a buffoon. However, after nine missions together, I had managed to change her mind on both counts. Erica had finally agreed to try dating—although that was tempered by the fact that she didn't know a thing about romance. The first time we had gone out, which was just a walk to get ice cream, I had tried to buy her a rose from a street vendor, and Erica had promptly cited the poor woman for operating without a proper florist's license.

"Where is she?" I asked Crandall.

He pointed directly up.

The elm we stood beside towered high above the canopy of the other trees around it. I immediately realized that a person situated in its upper branches would have a clear view of the entire campus—and possibly the surrounding city as well.

The thick foliage of the trees surrounding the elm hid Erica from view. If Crandall hadn't tipped me off, I would never have known she was there.

"What's she doing up there?" Mike asked, tilting his head back in an attempt to see her.

"Hunting the hunter," Crandall replied dramatically, then looked to me. "Yesterday, Erica received a tip that your life might be in danger, so she came to me . . ."

"Why didn't she come to *me*?" I asked, failing to keep the panic from my voice.

"To avoid this very reaction, I believe. She didn't want to upset you if she didn't have to. She presumed that anyone targeting you might have access to your email, so she concocted the plan to arrange a fake meeting for you and the principal and then asked me to make sure you were late. Then she forged the note from you and threw it into the principal's office to get him to leave, just in case there was an attack."

"She couldn't think of another way to handle this?" the principal groused angrily. "A way that didn't involve destroying my new desk?!"

"This way worked," Crandall said calmly. "And better yet, it's allowed Erica to potentially track the assassin."

"Through radio frequencies!" Jawa exclaimed knowingly. "If the assassin used a radio to trigger the bomb, then Erica could track the signal from up there and pinpoint the location it was transmitted from!"

"Correct," Crandall said.

The loose end of a climbing rope suddenly plunged through the canopy above us, followed by the sound of someone crashing through the branches. We all stepped aside as Erica rappelled down the trunk of the elm at top speed. She was dressed in her usual garb for action, a form-fitting black outfit accented with a utility belt, although at the moment, she also had green greasepaint on her face to camouflage her from view.

She didn't even bother to say hi to any of us—or to ask me if I was all right, given the latest threat to my life. There wasn't time. "I've determined the assassin's location," she said. "But there's a problem."

"Besides the fact that an assassin is targeting me in the first place?" I asked.

"The radio frequency is still live," Erica said.

She didn't say it in a particularly ominous way, but it was frightening anyhow, because we all understood exactly what that meant.

After triggering the bomb, the assassin would have known the radio frequency could be traced, so they would have shut it down immediately. There was only one reason not to . . .

"There's another bomb!" Zoe exclaimed.

And we all had a very good idea where it would be. If someone was trying to kill me, then it made sense to put the second bomb exactly where I should have been after an explosion: in the quadrangle. Only I wasn't in the quadrangle anymore.

But the rest of my fellow students were. As was most of the faculty.

"We need to evacuate the quad immediately!" Crandall announced.

"I'm on it," the principal said with a confidence and calm

that caught the rest of us by surprise. He tapped the screen of his phone a few times, activating a new emergency alert. The alarm pattern promptly changed to a series of constant, urgent whoops.

This was known as the Omega Alert. We had all been taught that it would only sound in the case of extreme emergencies, and that if we heard it, that meant things were very, very bad. The proper response was to get as far away from campus as fast as possible.

Our fellow students and the faculty responded in exactly the right manner. They promptly evacuated the quad. Within seconds, everyone came streaming through the gaps between the buildings, sprinting for the campus exits.

Aware this was taken care of, Erica announced, "I'm going after the assassin," and bolted across the school grounds.

The rest of us followed her. No one hesitated for a moment, not even Professor Crandall, whose very first lesson of Introduction to Self-Preservation had been "Assassins are dangerous"—or the principal, who ran with impressive speed for a man who, as far as I knew, hadn't done a lick of physical activity in the past year.

I wasn't the only one stunned by the principal's sudden burst of competence. Zoe was staring at him, wide-eyed, as she ran, as though suspicious that our usual moronic principal had been replaced by an impostor. "That was quick thinking with the alarm," she told him.

"Of course it was!" the principal replied curtly, showing a hint of his usual irritable self. "Contrary to what all you little ingrates think, I'm extremely capable, qualified, and— oof!" He was so focused on Zoe, he had forgotten to watch where he was going and run straight into a tree.

And then the second bomb went off.

TARGETING

Academy of Espionage

June 11

1230 hours

The second explosion was far bigger than the first. In fact, it seemed more like a series of explosions in rapid succession, with multiple bombs detonating. An enormous column of smoke and fire erupted from the center of the quadrangle, sending dirt and debris careening through the air.

Even though we were quite far away, the ground beneath us shook as though an earthquake had struck. The buildings around the quadrangle trembled so violently that parts of them collapsed. Gargoyles snapped off the Hale Building and shattered on the lawn, while an entire wall of Bushnell Hall was sheared away. I was too far to see the full extent of the damage, but it appeared that a massive crater had been gouged in the center of campus.

I had witnessed a surprising number of explosions in my life, but this was easily the most frightening. Not only was it big, but it was smack in the middle of the place that had come to be my home—and that of my friends as well. I gasped with horror as it happened, and I heard everyone else around me do the same.

Even Erica, who usually wasn't very emotional, seemed distraught—although she quickly shook this off and replaced it with a steely resolve. I knew her well enough to recognize the look: She was determined to find out who had done this and make them pay.

Thanks to the principal's quick action, no one was badly hurt (although, I would learn later that Professor Kuklinski was brained by a piece of flying sod and spent much of the afternoon thinking that he was a platypus). But still, the damage to the campus was extensive and infuriating. I wanted to find whoever had done this just as badly as Erica did. Even though I was still aching from my self-preservation exam, I did my best to keep up with her.

Erica was running toward the eastern perimeter of campus. Despite occupying a large parcel of land in northwestern

Washington, DC, the academy kept its true purpose a secret. It had its own alias, St. Smithen's Science Academy for Boys and Girls, and was surrounded by an imposing stone wall that kept the curious at bay. The wall did a good job of keeping the students on campus as well; it was tall and difficult to climb, so most people just went in and out through the main entrance. But I had no doubt that Erica was heading for some hidden route to get over, under, or through the wall. Erica knew the secrets of campus better than anyone.

She gave me an annoyed glance as I came up alongside her. "Stand down, Ben. Let me handle this."

Despite her curtness, I knew Erica was concerned for me. Sure, it would have been nice for her to express a bit of joy to see that I was safe—but then, I was safe *because* of Erica. If it hadn't been for her plans, I would have been flambéed. And now she was looking out for me once again. After all, I didn't have nearly the self-defense skills that she did. But I ignored her order to back off. First, it seemed that staying close to Erica might still be safer than remaining on campus. And second, I wanted some answers.

"What's going on here?" I asked. "Who is trying to kill me? And why?"

"That's what I'm trying to figure out. But it will be a lot easier to apprehend this assassin without you in the way." She looked toward Mike, Jawa, Chip, and Zoe, who were running alongside us and said, "That goes for all of you. Stand down. I've got this."

"We can help," I told her. "All of us. How did you know I was in danger today?"

Erica frowned, obviously frustrated by my persistence, but then gave in. "My grandfather tipped me off."

"Cyrus? How did he find out?"

"He wouldn't say. He wasn't even sure it was credible, which was why I didn't tell you. I wanted to confirm it first."

I glanced back toward the smoking crater in the center of campus. "Looks like it's confirmed."

"Yes." There was a hint of sadness in Erica's voice, although I couldn't tell if she was sad about me or what had happened to the school. I suspected it might be some of both. "This assassin obviously knows the campus well. They were able to infiltrate the principal's office to place the first bomb, and the second wave must have been set in the service tunnels underneath the quad, the existence of which is a highly classified secret. Plus, they've accessed your email."

We arrived at the edge of campus. Erica had led us directly to a gnarled old oak tree that grew at an angle, so that its branches dangled over the perimeter wall. Without slowing for a moment, she ran right up the tilted trunk, then expertly monkeyed through the canopy and dropped to the ground on the other side. Obviously, she had done this before.

The rest of us couldn't follow quite as fast. Plus, we could only scale the tree one at a time. Chip muscled me out of the way to go second and did a decent job of staying relatively close behind Erica, although he slipped at the end and landed straddling a branch with a squeak of pain that indicated he had just severely impacted his private parts.

Jawa, Mike, and Zoe followed in quick succession, and then Professor Crandall went. Despite his years, he moved through the tree as nimbly as a squirrel. I brought up the rear. (The principal was still doggedly following us, but he had fallen very far behind after his run-in with the tree back by the quad.) By the time I dropped to the sidewalk on the opposite side of the perimeter wall, Erica was well ahead of me, although I could tell which way she had gone by the trail of people following her.

The Academy of Espionage was mostly surrounded by residential streets lined with nice family homes, and that was what I found myself on now. Normally, the neighbors probably went about their day without giving much thought at all to the school across the street, but now they had certainly heard the explosion—and possibly even felt it shake their homes. People were gathered on their front porches or clustered in their yards, all looking warily toward the campus. The small parade of us leaping over the wall and then dashing along the street piqued their curiosity.

"Excuse me," a skittish-looking woman said to us. "What happened over there? Should we be worried about it?"

"Not at all!" Mike said very convincingly. He had been an adept liar long before coming to spy school. "There was just a little mishap at the physics lab. One of the proton accelerators exploded. It's nothing to worry about."

"Then why are you running *away* from the campus?" a nervous man asked in the concerned tone of someone who had seen far too many Godzilla movies and had entirely the wrong idea about what could go wrong in a physics lab.

"We're the cross-country track team," Mike replied, then pointed back toward Professor Crandall. "And that's our coach. He thinks simply running isn't challenging enough, so he makes us climb trees and jump over walls."

"Enough chitchat, Brezinski!" Crandall snapped, doing a very good impression of a middle-school PE coach. "Move your butt or I'll kick it!"

The neighbors now seemed far more worried about Crandall than they did about the explosion, as though he had tapped into their own latent fears of middle-school PE coaches. Several of them quickly ducked into their homes as he ran by.

Erica had already rounded the corner far ahead.

Behind me, the principal tumbled out of the tree onto the sidewalk.

I reached the corner and saw where Erica was heading. There was a small commercial strip close to our school, with a few cafés, banks, and clothing stores—and a staggering number of coffee shops. Most of the buildings were only one or two stories tall, but there was a solitary six-story office building.

If the assassin had used radio waves to trigger the bombs on campus, they would have wanted to do it from as high a point as possible nearby. The top floor of the office building would have been perfect—or perhaps the roof.

By now, I had a decent idea as to what Erica's plan had been. She had lured the assassin into coming after me at an exact time, then positioned herself to pinpoint their location. Now she planned to get the jump on them before they could vacate the premises. It hadn't been that long since the second wave of bombs had been triggered, but time was certainly of the essence. Erica was sprinting as fast as she could toward the office building.

Jawa, Chip, and Mike were close behind her, although Zoe and I were flagging. Our self-preservation exams were really wearing on us. Professor Crandall was slowing down too, which was understandable, given his age. So the others made it to the office building well ahead of us.

The four of them split up to cover more ground. Erica and Chip went through the front door of the building while

Mike and Jawa circled around to the rear entrance, just as we had learned in our Securing the Premises seminar.

Which was why none of them were outside when the assassin jumped off the roof.

Zoe and I were just approaching the office building when it happened.

The assassin was wearing a harness attached to a long bungee cord, which snapped taut when he was halfway down, then stretched out, slowing his descent. He alighted gently on the sidewalk ahead of us, then deftly unclipped the cord before it could yank him back up again. Free of his weight, the bungee shot back to the top of the building with a loud twang.

The assassin started to flee down the street, but froze when he saw me.

We both stared at each other in astonishment.

His surprise appeared to be due to the fact that, after two separate sets of bombs had been triggered to kill me, not only was I still stubbornly alive, but I was also standing directly in front of him.

Whereas I was astonished for a very different reason.

I had met the assassin before.

INTERROGATION

It wasn't like the assassin and I were long-lost friends or anything like that.

He had tried to kill me once before, on my very first night at spy school.

He had snuck into my dormitory room, rudely woken me with his gun, and then asked me a lot of menacing questions that I hadn't known the answer to. Luckily, I had managed to knock him out with a tennis racket, but before I could bring anyone to my room to help me deal with him, he had regained consciousness and escaped without a trace. Some people—such as the principal—had thought I'd made up the whole event.

During the ordeal, it had been dark and shadowy in my room, and I had been terrified, so I hadn't been able to get a good look at the man. But now that I was seeing him in broad daylight, the events of that night came flooding back to me. It was like a switch had been thrown in my memory. I could suddenly recall him clearly as he loomed over my bed, with his thin lips, his beady eyes, and the large collection of scars on his face (one of which I might have made myself, across the bridge of his nose, thanks to my tennis racket). And so I was instantly sure that this was the man who had come to kill me before.

Although, if I'd had any doubts, those were quickly put to rest when he immediately tried to kill me once again.

Usually, when you run into someone you haven't seen in a long time, even someone you don't know very well, you generally say something like "Hey!" or "Hi!" or "How have you been?"

The assassin merely whipped out a gun and tried to shoot me.

He might have been successful if Zoe hadn't been by my side. I had honed my ducking and hiding reflexes since coming to spy school, but I was so astonished to have recognized the assassin, I wasn't at the top of my game. Fortunately, Zoe's reflexes were good enough to save both of us. Before the assassin could get off a shot, she tackled me.

Despite her small stature, Zoe knocked me off the sidewalk and into the landscaping in front of the office building. We toppled over a small decorative hedge and plunked into the mud.

Thanks to Zoe's quick action, the assassin missed us with his first shots. But he quickly recovered. He spun toward us, ready to fire again . . .

. . . when a trash-can lid suddenly came flying at him like a giant metal frisbee. It clanged off his skull, sending him reeling. His gun tumbled from his hand, clattered into the street, and fell through a sewer grating.

This upset the assassin quite a bit. He wheeled angrily on the person who had thrown the trash-can lid:

Professor Crandall. Although Crandall had already shifted back to his fake, doddering persona, and now looked about as threatening as a newborn fawn.

"Did you just throw that trash-can lid at me?" the assassin demanded.

"You were threatening those children," Crandall said somewhat absently. "I did what I had to do."

"You just made a big mistake, Gramps," the assassin sneered. "That was my favorite gun." He touched his forehead where the lid had left a small gash. "And you've given me yet another scar. So now I'm gonna teach you a lesson about sticking your nose where it doesn't belong. In fact, I might just take that nose of yours right off your face." He removed two gleaming knives from a sheath on his belt and whipped them around expertly.

"You're welcome to try." Crandall continued shambling toward the assassin, keeping his eyes locked on him the entire time. "But I think it's only fair to warn you that you'll regret it."

"Regret it?" The assassin burst into laughter. "Maybe you could put up a decent fight back in the Civil War, old man, but you have no idea who you're talking to."

"Actually, I know *exactly* who I'm talking to," Crandall replied. "You're Sal Minella, also known as 'Sal the Knife,' 'Sal the Blade,' and 'Sal who's about to get his butt kicked by a man three times his age.'"

The assassin stopped laughing and now looked perplexed. "How did you . . . ?"

"I make it a point to study up on all professional assassins, so I can know their trademark moves and preferred fighting styles in case I ever need to face one in combat. Although, truth be told, I made up that last nickname right now, just to unsettle you a bit."

"Who are you?" Sal asked, and then gaped as Professor

Crandall removed a pair of nunchucks from underneath his cardigan. "And why are you carrying *those*?"

"To teach whippersnappers like you a lesson," Crandall replied. "Now, are you going to be sensible and give up right now? Or are we going to have to do this the hard way?"

Sal opted for the hard way. Although he didn't say it. Instead, he suddenly lunged at Professor Crandall, trying to catch him off guard.

He didn't. In fact, Crandall appeared to have been waiting for Sal to do this.

The fight lasted even less time than my final exam in self-preservation had. Crandall moved with grace and speed, whipping the nunchucks like a master. They flew about so quickly, I couldn't see them—although I could *hear* them. There was a series of whacks and cracks as they hit Sal in multiple places in rapid succession, each followed by a yelp of pain from Sal himself. Within seconds, Sal's knives had fallen from his hands, and the assassin was curled up in the fetal position on the sidewalk, wailing, "Okay! I give! Please don't hurt me anymore!"

It was an impressive performance. Maybe I should have been taking advantage of the distraction to run away, but it seemed that Crandall had things under control, and Zoe and I were both transfixed by his skillful attack. We weren't the only ones. A few passersby had stopped to watch, probably thinking that they were seeing an old man get the better of a mugger. At the end of it, they applauded.

Crandall calmly tucked his nunchucks back under his sweater, then told Sal, "How much more pain you endure is up to you. I'd like to know what your business is with Benjamin." There wasn't a hint of menace in his voice. He sounded like my own grandfather offering to take me to the candy store. But given the whupping that Crandall had just handed out, Sal was understandably shaken.

And yet, the assassin held firm. He blinked away his tears, fixed Crandall with his beady eyes, and said, "I don't know what you're talking about, Gramps."

"Ah," Crandall replied. "Well, let's see if *this* jogs your memory." He took Sal's hand in his and twisted it.

If you have ever seen a spy movie, there is often a scene where someone bravely holds out under torture, refusing to cough up any information despite a staggering amount of pain.

That rarely happens in real life.

Crandall wasn't even hurting Sal that badly; I knew that, if the professor wanted to, he could have easily dislocated Sal's arm. Or removed it entirely from his body. But Sal, like many bullies, turned out to have a very low tolerance for suffering.

"Ow!" he cried. "Jeez, that hurts! Okay, okay! I'll talk!"

Crandall released the pressure on his hand, but not completely, just so that Sal would know he was only seconds away from another severely painful experience.

"Murray Hill initiated Project X," Sal said quickly.

Murray Hill, I thought. *Of course.* Murray was my nemesis. He was only a year older than me, an ex–spy school student who had gone to the dark side. Despite his young age, he had already managed to be involved with several extremely devious plots. In the past, he had always worked for large evil organizations, like SPYDER, but for his last endeavor, he had struck out on his own, creating a small evil start-up called SMASH.

"And what is Project X?" Crandall asked Sal. "A plot to kill Benjamin?"

"That's part of it," Sal replied. "I don't know what the rest is, though. Murray didn't tell anyone. The piece I know is that he put a price on Ripley's head. As of noon today, the first person to take out the kid gets twenty million dollars."

"Twenty million dollars?" I repeated, unable to stop myself.

"Whoa!" Zoe looked to me with respect. "That is a ridiculous amount of money."

"Who did Murray make this offer to?" Crandall asked Sal.

"Everyone," Sal replied. "The message went out to every assassin, hired killer, thug, and lowlife on earth."

This was very bad news.

I felt as though a thousand ulcers had sprouted into existence in my stomach at once. My legs went weak, and I sagged against the office building.

A hand suddenly grasped mine. To my surprise, Erica was standing beside me.

I had been so focused on Sal, I hadn't even noticed that Erica had emerged from the building. So had Mike, Chip, and Jawa.

But while I normally would have found it reassuring to have Erica at my side, holding my hand, this time it wasn't. Because I saw the look on her face. She had heard what Sal had said—and she seemed scared by it.

Erica didn't get scared often. I had seen her defuse a nuclear bomb while perched on the edge of a steep mountain chasm without breaking a sweat. But now there was fear in her eyes.

She was scared for *me*.

Not far away, Mike, Chip, and Jawa also had the same look. And so did Professor Crandall. He met Erica's eyes and said, "Get Ben out of here. *Now.*"

"Right." Erica kept her hand tightly clasped in mine and raced down the street, dragging me behind her. My friends joined us. Without discussing it, they formed a protective circle around me as we ran, as though they were trying to shield me from any other attacks.

Behind us, Crandall called out, "I'll wrap up everything here and be in touch!"

"Thanks!" Mike yelled back, then asked Erica, "Do you have a plan? Or are we just running?"

"Of course I have a plan," Erica said.

"Would you care to tell all of us what it is?" Jawa asked.

"Sure. Just let me deal with the other assassin first," Erica said.

"What other assassin?" I asked, terrified—at the exact same time that Zoe, Mike, Chip, and Jawa asked the exact same question.

Tires screeched. I glanced back to see a sports car swerving into the road behind us.

"That assassin," Erica replied.

At the curb, a man with an armful of groceries was climbing into his minivan. In one graceful maneuver, Erica pulled him aside, swiped his keys, and leapt into the front seat. "We need to commandeer your vehicle," she told him.

"Our friend has to get to the hospital," Zoe added, pointing to me. "It's an emergency."

I did my best to appear desperately ill, which wasn't so hard, since I really was feeling sick to my stomach, given the circumstances.

I must have looked really bad, because the man quickly

stepped aside and waved me into his van. "I hope you feel better," he said.

"Thanks," I told him. At other times, I might have felt bad about taking his van. But discovering that you are the target of multiple assassins tends to shift your morals. We quickly piled into the vehicle. Chip took the front passenger seat while the rest of us buckled up in the back.

The sports car was barreling down the street toward us.

Erica hit the gas before we even had the sliding doors closed. I was about to shut mine when the principal dove through it. He landed across our laps as we sped away from the curb.

"You're not ditching me that easily!" the principal announced, as though he had just caught us playing hooky. Although, in his defense, he had missed all the revelations as to what was really happening. He was red-faced and panting with exhaustion from his run to catch up to us.

"Want me to toss him back out?" Chip asked Erica.

Erica paused for a moment before answering, as if seriously considering that option. "No," she said finally. "He might actually be helpful here."

She raced through a red light. Cars swerved to avoid her, skidding across the intersection. Somehow, the sports car managed to slalom through all of them without a scratch and stay right behind us.

I glanced out the rear window to see who was driving it. The assassin at the wheel was a middle-aged woman with long dark hair and an eye patch.

"What's going on here?" the principal demanded. "Where's the jerk who blew up my academy?"

"Back with Professor Crandall," Jawa explained. "But he's not the only one after Ben. Murray Hill put a price on his head, and now every assassin in the country wants a piece of him."

The principal fixed me with a hard stare, as though this was somehow my fault. "This is all about *you*?"

"Who'd you *think* they were trying to kill in your office?" Zoe asked. "You?"

"I *am* the principal of the academy. It's completely understandable that someone would want to kill me and not a student."

"I guess that's true," Mike said. "I can think of plenty of students who've wanted you dead."

"I'm not talking about students!" the principal snapped, offended. "I mean professional assassins! I have an awful reputation in the evil community."

"And it's even worse in the espionage community," Erica muttered under her breath, then took a corner so quickly that the principal rolled off our laps and fell onto the floor.

We had left the small commercial district behind and were now speeding through a residential neighborhood.

While the downtown section of Washington, DC, was generally choked with bumper-to-bumper traffic, this area was quiet and suburban, with narrow streets and manicured lawns. Erica was driving at three times the speed limit; the sports car stayed glued to us.

"This is awesome!" Chip shouted. "We're in an honest-to-goodness car chase!"

"With someone trying to kill Ben," Zoe noted.

"I know!" Chip exclaimed, missing the point. "We're confronting assassins too! Best day ever!"

Beside me, Jawa appeared equally enthusiastic. I understood why. Both he and Chip had enrolled at spy school hoping for action and adventure, but over the past few months, Erica, Mike, Zoe, and I had seen lots more of it than they had. Now their wishes were finally coming true—albeit at my expense.

Zoe shifted her attention to me, as though something had been nagging at her for the past few minutes. "Why *does* Murray want you dead?" she asked.

"Because I thwarted his evil plans in Central America," I replied.

"You've thwarted his plans plenty of times," Zoe said. "And he's never targeted you for assassination before. Why now? Did something happen between you two on this last mission?"

"I think he's just getting really tired of me thwarting him."

"You also tricked Murray into thinking Zoe had a crush on him," Mike reminded me.

"What?!" Zoe exclaimed, suddenly looking very upset.

"We *had* to," I explained quickly. "He couldn't remember his password to turn off the detonator for the bomb. An entire cruise ship full of innocent people was about to explode. So I told Murray that you would go out with him if he stopped being evil—and that jogged his memory."

As I said this, the finer details of that day came back to me. After I'd tricked him, Murray had been much angrier at me than ever before. "Murray said that I had made this personal," I recalled. "And that I would rue the day that I'd met him."

"He also said he would destroy you," Mike put in. "I thought he was just being dramatic, but I guess he really meant it." As evidence, he pointed out the rear window at the assassin pursuing us.

At that very moment, the assassin rammed us from behind, throwing us into a skid. We sideswiped a line of parked cars, shaving the rearview mirrors off all of them, but Erica managed to otherwise keep us under control.

"I need you to take the wheel," she told Chip.

Chip looked as though someone had just told him he'd

won a free trip to Hawaii. "You want me to drive in a car chase? Oh man! I've dreamed of this day!"

"Stop dreaming and start doing. Right now." Erica unbuckled her seat belt and slid her seat back, even though we were hurtling down a residential street at sixty miles an hour.

Chip reacted quickly, scooting out of his seat and into Erica's while she squirmed out of the way. They managed it with only some minor banging into the cars along the street.

"What do you want me to do?" Chip asked.

"Take the scenic route," Erica told him.

Ahead of us lay Rock Creek Park, a wide strip of forested hills that wound through the city.

"Got it!" Chip exclaimed, then cut across traffic onto the park road.

Once again, cars screeched and swerved to avoid us. And once again, the assassin stubbornly avoided smashing into any of them and stayed right behind us.

Erica was now standing in the space between the front seats, facing backward, so she could observe the assassin through the rear window. "That's Myrtle Combat," she observed. "One of the best hired killers on earth." She shifted her attention to the principal and said, "I'm going to need your toupee."

The principal immediately turned red with embarrassment. "What toupee?" he asked weakly, even though the toupee in question was barely atop his head anymore. "I don't wear a toupee!"

Erica sighed. "Fine. Then I'll need whatever this thing is." She tore the toupee off the principal's head.

It made a ripping sound as it came off, as though it had been attached with some kind of adhesive, revealing the principal's gleaming bald head in its entirety.

The principal squawked in surprise, and then his embarrassment grew even greater. "All right. I suppose I might have a slight hair-loss problem," he admitted.

The park road snaked through a forested canyon in the middle of the city. Myrtle Combat kept trying to pull up alongside us, but Chip was preventing this by expertly weaving back and forth across the road. While most normal high schools offered defensive driving classes, spy school had *offensive* driving classes. Chip had performed among the best in his grade at those. Behind us, the assassin seemed to be frustrated by her inability to get beside the van.

Zoe asked, "Her name can't *really* be Myrtle Combat, can it?"

"Of course not," Erica replied. "Her real name is Prudence Buttercup, but that made her sound more like an interior decorator than an assassin. So she changed it. Lots of female assassins have pseudonyms: Dinah Mite, Barb Dwyer, Kay Ottic." She looked to Chip and said, "Let her pull even with us."

"What?!" Chip momentarily took his eyes off the road ahead to give Erica a look of befuddlement. "You do know she's trying to kill us, right?"

"She's not trying to kill *all* of us," Erica said calmly. "Only Ben. And I have a plan to save him. Trust me."

Chip stopped swerving and let off the gas ever so slightly. "This better work," he grumbled.

Myrtle Combat instantly shifted into the oncoming traffic lane and gunned the sports car's engine, pulling up alongside us. At the exact same time, Erica flung open the van's sliding passenger door and leaned out into the breeze.

At the wheel of the sports car, Myrtle was holding a gun, trying to draw a bead on me—although Erica's behavior distracted her attention. She swung the gun toward Erica instead.

Erica flung the principal's toupee at the sports car. As usual, her aim was impeccable. The hairpiece hit the front windshield with a *thwack* and stuck there, thanks to the adhesive that normally kept it gummed to the principal's head. It instantly blocked Myrtle's view of us and the road ahead—and since it looked like a large rodent of some sort, it startled the assassin as well. Quite likely, she thought that some unfortunate, butt-ugly woodland creature had just been pancaked on her windshield.

Myrtle lost control of the car. It was only for a few

moments, but at the high speed she was traveling, it was enough. She squeezed off a shot, but it went far wide of me, hitting the van's engine instead. Then the sports car slewed off the shoulder on the far side of the road, clipped a tree, and went into a spin, whirling like a top in the middle of the road. Still, Myrtle was an accomplished driver and managed to recover—only to find a semi truck bearing down on her.

Myrtle had no choice but to bail. She dove from her car just as the truck smashed into it. The sports car crumpled like a used tissue, tumbled into the trees, and promptly exploded.

"Whoa," Jawa gasped. "Talk about a bad hair day."

On the shoulder of the road, Myrtle stood, battered and bruised but still alive, glaring after us with the flames of her totaled car flickering behind her.

Everyone in the van whooped and cheered with relief, then congratulated Chip on his driving and Erica for her fine toupee-flinging skills.

"That's why I wear a toupee in the first place," the principal informed us proudly, as though he had somehow played a larger role in our escape than simply being a bad-hairpiece delivery system. "I don't really need it, of course. But I shaved my head to give me an excuse to carry that, just in case I ever found myself in a situation like this."

Under his breath, Mike whispered, "Next thing you

know, he's gonna claim his toxic bad breath is to fight off bad guys too."

I kept staring out the rear window as we sped away, watching the assassin silhouetted against the flames. My relief at escaping her didn't last long. She was still alive and well, and would probably be coming for me again. And with twenty million dollars at stake, others certainly would be coming for me too.

I turned back to Erica, who was sliding into the passenger seat as Chip continued down the Rock Creek Parkway. "Back before the car chase, you said you had a plan?"

"Yes."

"What is it?"

"Isn't it obvious?" Erica asked me. "We need to find Murray Hill."

PLAN OF ACTION

The Metro

Washington, DC

June 11

1330 hours

We had to abandon the minivan.

High-speed car chases tend to attract the attention of the police. We could hear sirens wailing in the distance, indicating law enforcement was on its way. Plus, the van's engine, having been shot by Myrtle Combat, was making funny sounds and belching smoke.

"The last thing we need right now is to get arrested," Erica told us. "Any decent assassin will be monitoring the police radio frequencies. If we get hauled into a police station, we'll be sitting ducks."

Traffic was already backing up on the other side of the Rock Creek Parkway due to the wreck of Myrtle Combat's car, which was blocking the road behind us.

Erica directed Chip to leave the park at the nearest exit. As we did, several police cars flew past us, bubble lights flashing. We found a parking space close by and left the van there.

It wasn't until we got out that I realized how banged up the van was from our chase. The sides were scraped raw and covered with more dings than a golf ball, while the rear bumper was mashed and both rearview mirrors dangled from their wires. Between all the damage and the smoking engine, we would have been lucky to get another few blocks before the police pulled us over.

There was a subway station close by. All spy school students always carried Metro cards, so we headed that way.

Merely walking a few blocks through the city was now terrifying to me. I feared that assassins could be lurking in every doorway, or hiding behind each lamppost or tree. The only thing that made the journey possible was knowing that Erica and my friends were there to protect me.

The presence of the principal wasn't quite as reassuring.

He stayed with us, apparently unaware that he was useless. I got the sense he felt it was his duty to look after all of us. The principal had actually been a field agent at one point in his career, but he hadn't been a very good one—and now he had grown rusty after years in an office. He was even more skittish than I was, flinching every time a car honked or a pigeon took flight.

Still, we made it to the subway station without incident, descended underground, and caught the first train we could.

As it was the middle of the day, the train wasn't too crowded. We found a car with only a few other people in it and clustered at one end so that Erica could explain her plan.

"Since Murray ordered the hit on you, he's the only one who can remove it."

"I get that," I said. "But why do we have to find him in person? Couldn't this be done with a phone call?"

"Would you trust Murray to call this off just because we asked him nicely?" Erica asked me.

"I guess not," I admitted.

"The only way he's going to work with us is if we force him to. We need to be there, making sure it actually happens—or there's no way to guarantee your safety."

I sighed, realizing Erica was right as usual.

"So where *is* Murray?" Zoe asked.

"Falcon Ridge federal penitentiary," Erica said. "It's a

supermax prison in rural Pennsylvania, about a hundred miles north of here."

"Supermax?" Chip repeated. "I guess Murray's proved too much trouble for juvenile hall."

That made sense to me. The government had already tried incarcerating Murray twice before. Due to Murray's young age, he had been sent to lower-security facilities, but he had managed to escape each time.

Supermax prisons were reserved for criminals that the federal government considered exceptionally dangerous. The security at them was extreme.

And yet, for the first time I could recall, I found myself doubting one of Erica's plans.

"You really think he'll be there?" I asked. "You don't think he's figured some way out again?"

"Not this time," Erica assured me. "My grandfather personally delivered Murray to Falcon Ridge. No one has ever broken out of that place—and Murray isn't exactly Houdini. He never engineered his escapes before. SPYDER did it for him. He's still there. I guarantee it."

But despite Erica's confidence, I wasn't convinced. And it turned out, I wasn't the only one with misgivings.

"I'm with Ben on this," Jawa said. "How could Murray even initiate a plot like this from a supermax prison? All his communications must be monitored. There's no way he'd be able to contact all these assassins from inside."

Erica bristled. She wasn't used to having her leadership questioned and obviously didn't appreciate it. "We can ask him how he did it when we get there."

"No you won't," the principal said. "Because none of you are going."

We all looked to him, surprised.

"I know you have all ended up on multiple missions," he told us, "but the fact remains that you are still agents-in-training. The CIA has plenty of actual agents who can handle this. *They* should be going to deal with Murray Hill, not you. I'll notify headquarters, and then we can all return to the safety of campus while the professionals take care of this."

"There is no safety of campus!" Erica exclaimed. "Sal Minella blew a crater in the middle of it—and Myrtle Combat wasn't far behind." The principal started to argue, but Erica cut him off. "Face it, the academy is compromised. Its existence is no longer a secret. Which means it's not just unsafe for Ben . . . It's unsafe for *all* of us. Honestly, I'm not sure we can *ever* go back."

A tense silence fell over everyone as Erica's words sank in. On this point, she was undoubtedly right. And the truth was unsettling.

"So what does that mean?" Zoe asked quietly. "That there's no more spy school?"

"I don't know," Erica replied. "But for the moment, we have other things to worry about. I'm not willing to trust anyone else to handle this . . ."

"Not even your family?" I asked. Erica had several relatives, like her mother and grandfather, who were exceptionally accomplished spies. (As well as at least one, her father, who was a not-very-accomplished spy.)

"No, we can trust them," Erica assured us. "In fact, they're already aware of our mission. Mom helped me put all the pieces together last night. But in the meantime, Ben, it's best for you to stay in motion. It's a lot harder to hit a moving target than a stationary one."

I nodded agreement, as did my friends. I still wasn't convinced that heading to Falcon Ridge was the right idea, but I believed Erica about staying in motion. With so many assassins coming after me, it was hard to imagine any place safe enough to ride out the storm.

Mike asked Erica, "Do you have a way to contact your parents?"

Erica held up a mobile phone. "My mother lent me this. It's MI6-issued, so it can't be tracked."

Most phones had chips in them, which allowed almost

anyone to pinpoint your position. For this reason, we rarely carried phones at school. Non-traceable phones were standard-issue for most spies, like Erica's parents, but for spies-in-training, they were very expensive. Even a student as talented as Erica could hardly ever get one.

Around me, my friends had grown sullen. The excitement of being on a real mission had worn off. Now, in addition to being concerned for my safety, there was obviously something else bothering all of them as well.

Chip was the first to put it into words. "I can't believe spy school is gone."

"It's not," the principal said, clearly in denial. "This was just a minor bombing. In a few days, we'll be able to patch up the hole in the quad, buy me a new desk, and then get right back to your regular schooling."

"It's been eight months since your office blew up and you still don't have walls," Jawa reminded him. "It'll take *years* to repair the damage that Sal Minella did. Maybe decades. And even if the campus wasn't gutted, we couldn't possibly resume school. We already had a bad mole problem—and now Murray has probably leaked the school's purpose and location to every assassin on earth."

The principal gasped as the reality of the situation dawned on him. "So . . . I'm not getting another desk?"

"I don't think so," Zoe said.

The principal made a small whimper and sank down into a seat.

While I was certainly upset about what had happened to the school, I was far more upset about what had nearly happened to *me*. If it hadn't been for Erica, it would have been me who had been blasted out of the principal's office, not just his desk.

The discovery that I had been made a target was extremely disturbing. My hands were trembling, my knees wobbled, and I couldn't help but fear that any of the other passengers on the subway might be an assassin, waiting for the right moment to attack me. I knew this was paranoid, and yet, I had a perfectly valid reason for paranoia: People really were out to get me. Plus, one of the other passengers, an elderly woman, had been stealing wary glances at me for the past two minutes.

This wasn't my mind playing tricks on me. She had definitely recognized me somehow. She had originally been knitting, but since noticing me, she hadn't done a single stitch. I was too much of a distraction.

Beside me, Mike said, "How does Murray even have twenty million dollars to pay an assassin?"

"The guy's a criminal," Chip said.

"A criminal whose plans Ben has repeatedly thwarted," Mike corrected. "Maybe if one of those plans had succeeded, Murray would have that kind of cash, but if anything, he ought to be broke, thanks to Ben."

"Mike's right," Zoe agreed. "Plus, Murray only cares about getting rich. If he *did* have that kind of money, he'd spend it on mansions and yachts and private islands, not assassins. There's no profit in having Ben killed."

Jawa said, "I guess he's really, really, really angry at Ben."

Our subway train glided to a stop at the next station. A few passengers got off while others got on.

The elderly woman knitting stayed put and continued stealing glances at me.

The train's doors slid shut and it started moving again.

I lowered my voice to a whisper and said, "I think that old woman over there might be an assassin."

Everyone shifted their attention toward the old woman at once—except Erica, who knew that this would alert the old woman that we were onto her.

Sure enough, the old woman grew even more agitated.

Chip laughed. "The old lady? Seriously? She doesn't look the slightest bit like a professional assassin."

"Any decent professional assassin probably doesn't look anything like a professional assassin," Zoe told him. "Otherwise, everyone would know they were professional assassins."

"But she's old," Chip explained. "And frail. I'll bet she can't even open a jar of peanut butter, let alone kill someone."

"Professor Crandall also looked old and frail," Jawa countered. "And that turned out to be a ruse. It could be the case with her, too. Maybe the moment we drop our guard, she'll try to disembowel us all with her knitting needles."

"Well, whoever she is, she's definitely watching Ben," Erica said. "And she has been for the past few minutes."

I looked to Erica, surprised. Her back had been to the old woman the whole time we had been on the train. Then I realized that she had been watching all the other passengers in the reflection of the windows. As usual, nothing escaped Erica's attention.

"The guy in the red baseball cap has been watching you too," Erica informed me. "He's just been much more subtle about it."

I hadn't noticed the man in the red baseball cap, even though a red baseball cap was among the most noticeable articles of clothing a person could wear. I had been too distracted by the old woman. Now I shifted my attention to him. He was muscular and physically imposing. He was sitting toward the far end of the train, reading something on his phone.

As I watched him, he looked up. Our eyes locked.

The guy was startled for a moment, appearing embarrassed to have been caught staring. And then his eyes narrowed, like he was angry at me.

I quickly turned back to Erica. "Do you think *he's* an assassin?"

"I don't think so," Erica observed, "and I don't think Granny is either. But something strange is going on."

"I wonder if it's the other part of Project X," Zoe said.

"What do you mean?" Mike asked.

"Sal Minella said that the price on Ben's head was only part of it," Zoe replied. "Well, now random people are staring at Ben. I assume that's also related to Murray's plans."

Chip looked at her blankly. "You think that, in addition to offering money to have Ben killed, Murray is offering money to people to stare at Ben?"

"Er . . . no," Zoe said.

The guy in the red baseball cap had returned his attention to his phone. He looked at something on it, then glared at me even more angrily.

"I think you're all blowing this out of proportion," the principal said dismissively. "People stare at me all the time, and it doesn't mean someone's plotting against me."

"People stare at you all the time because your toupee looks like a diseased wombat," Mike informed him. "They think it's attacking your head."

The principal turned slightly reddish, although I couldn't tell if this was due to embarrassment or anger.

The subway train slowed as it approached the Union Station Metro stop.

"We're getting off here," Erica announced.

"Why?" Jawa asked.

"To catch a train, obviously," Erica replied. Without another word of explanation, she headed for the subway door as it slid open.

The rest of us followed her out onto the subway platform.

Most of the world's subway systems are warrens of narrow tunnels, but the Washington, DC, Metro system is open and airy. Each station is a cavernous space with high, vaulted ceilings. At the far end of the train platform, a bank of escalators headed up to the ticketing area, beyond which a second bank led into Union Station. We headed that way.

The principal nattered on as we walked, still stubbornly trying to convince us he knew what he was talking about. "You might all *think* you know what's going on here," he lectured, "but you're still young. I've been a spy since all of you were in diapers. I saw plenty of action in my day. That's why I was put in charge of your school. I know what I'm doing. And therefore, I can assure you that those people back on the train are no danger to you at all. They're simply normal citizens. I'll stake my reputation on it."

The speech was confident and self-assured. It was almost even convincing . . .

Except that the moment the principal finished giving it, the man in the red baseball cap attacked me.

CONSPIRACY

Union Station Metro Stop

Washington, DC

June 11

1400 hours

I was about to step onto the escalator when the man grabbed me from behind and yanked me away from my friends. His hands clamped onto my arms like vises while he stared me right in the eyes.

"I know who you are," he said ominously. "And you won't get away with your evil plans."

After two separate attacks by assassins that morning, I was prepared for another. My fighting skills weren't as good as Erica's or Zoe's, but I was at least familiar with Ponti's First

Maxim of Self-Defense: Even the toughest, most dangerous man on earth can still be brought down with a kick to the crotch. Thus, I had my leg poised and ready to inflict maximum pain.

But there was a strange look in the man's eyes as he spoke to me. He was angry at me—and he truly seemed to believe that his anger was justified. I had faced a disturbing number of professional killers in my young life, and they were never angry. Assassination was just a job to them; if anything, some of them had even seemed kind of bored by it. This man didn't want to kill me—although I had no idea what he *did* want. So I refrained from punting him in the soft bits and asked, "Er . . . what now?"

"You and your kind will not succeed!" the man declared. "The Brotherhood of Truth is onto you! Now show yourself!" With that, he grabbed my right ear and yanked hard on it, as if he was trying to rip it off.

As much as I wanted to understand what this man was talking about, I also wanted to keep my ears attached to my head. So I decided it was time to put Ponti's First Maxim into action after all.

But before I could kick him, Chip, Jawa, Zoe, and Mike counterattacked from all sides at once. It was not a coordinated assault. In fact, it was about as uncoordinated as assaults could be. Each of them was rushing to my aid at once, and in their haste, not only did they take my attacker down, but they took each other down as well. They ended up in a pile on the Metro platform, with the big man writhing angrily beneath all of them. "You might be able to overpower me!" he cried. "But you will never defeat humanity!"

"What are you talking about?" Mike asked, confused.

"Your day of reckoning will come long before ours does!" the man proclaimed.

Before we could press him for more answers, Erica waded into the fray and tried to pry my friends off the crazy man. "We have to go," she hissed. "*Immediately.* You're all making a scene. And we want as little attention as possible right now!"

"This guy started it," Chip said, pointing accusingly at my attacker.

"We need to get to the bottom of what's going on here," Zoe told Erica. She had an arm locked around the big man's neck and was refusing to let go.

"I already know what's going on," Erica informed her.

Jawa looked up from pinning the man's arms behind his back. "You do? Why didn't you say anything?"

"Because I only learned a few seconds ago," Erica replied. "I can explain everything on the train. Now, let's go before this turns bad." She nodded down the platform, where a small crowd had gathered to watch us.

The old lady who had first noticed me on the subway was at the forefront of them all, glaring at me and clutching her knitting needles in a menacing way.

Mike reluctantly released the big man's legs, got to his feet, and asked, "Which train?"

"The one we're taking to Philadelphia," Erica said, as though it was the most obvious thing in the world. Then she grabbed me by the arm and hustled me onto the escalator.

The others joined us, leaving the big man free once again. He pointed after me, yelling, "Police! Help! Stop that kid before he gets away!"

Two Metro police officers were posted near the top of the escalator I was on. They were looking over the railing at the man, regarding him warily. As Metro police in Washington, DC, serving at the subway station closest to the US Capitol, they were probably all too used to encountering crazy people spouting nonsense. Still, they shifted their attention to me as the escalator brought me closer to them, as though they were wondering if I was a credible threat.

Before they could do anything, the principal, who was a few steps ahead of me, flashed his official CIA badge at them. "Thanks for your concern, officers," he said. "But I have this all under control."

The police officers now appeared surprised that the CIA was involved. They approached the principal as he got off the escalator, took a closer look at his badge, and recognized it was genuine. "All right," one of them said. "What should we do about the lunatic down there?"

"Let him be," the principal said. "The last thing we need is a nutjob like that thinking the CIA is involved in a conspiracy." He then clutched my arm tightly as I stepped off the escalator, as though he were taking me into custody.

The police nodded in agreement, then stepped aside to let us pass. "Can you tell us what this is all about?" the first asked.

"Sorry, no," the principal said. "It's classified." Then he hustled me toward the escalator that led out of the Metro.

The rest of my friends followed us, and we rode the moving steps up into Union Station. The train station was one of the great, beautiful buildings of Washington, DC, made from glistening white marble with a soaring arched roof.

Erica reached into her utility belt and removed a thick wad of cash. I knew from experience that Erica was always prepared for emergencies; in addition to cash in multiple currencies, her utility belt also held mace, lockpicks, and a variety of other tools and weapons, as well as snacks, because it was never a good idea to confront danger on an empty stomach. (Erica's mother had given me a utility belt as well, but I wasn't nearly as good as the Hales at keeping it stocked with emergency supplies; I wasn't even wearing it at the moment, having left it in my dorm room because utility belts weren't allowed to be worn during exams.)

Erica quickly pressed the cash into Jawa's hands and said, "Get tickets for the next train to Philadelphia. Ben and I will meet you down on the platform."

This provoked a quick barrage of questions.

"Why are we going to Philadelphia?" Mike asked.

"Why aren't you coming with us?" Chip inquired.

"Why does Jawa get to buy the tickets and not me?" the principal demanded. "I'm the adult here. I ought to be paying for things."

Erica quickly responded to each of them in order. "Because Murray Hill is being held in the Falcon Ridge federal penitentiary, and the closest train station to that is in Philadelphia. Because every assassin in America is looking for Ben, so I don't want them to see him heading to the train. And because I need to make sure we actually get tickets for the right train, and I trust Jawa to do that, not you. I don't want to end up in Canada."

Everyone looked as though they had a dozen more questions, but before they could ask a single one, Erica dragged me away from them all.

In the station, there was a large board that marked the arrivals and departures of each train. Washington, DC, was one of the main hubs for train travel in the United States;

from there you could head south through the Carolinas to either Miami or New Orleans, or west to Chicago and ultimately, Seattle or Los Angeles. But the most popular route by far was the northeastern corridor, heading through Baltimore, Philadelphia, New York City, and Boston. At least one train an hour came and went from that direction. The arrival-and-departure board showed that the next train heading north, the Carolinian, was due in the station on Platform 4 in twelve minutes.

Erica deftly swiped a dull gray baseball cap from a souvenir stand and plunked it onto my head. "Here," she said, pulling the brim down low to cover more of my face. "This ought to help hide you from potential assassins." Then she led me out the front doors of the station.

The grand entrance fronted Columbus Circle, which wasn't a circle at all. It was only a semicircle, with a fountain in the middle of it. From there, it was a straight shot up Delaware Avenue to the US Capitol, whose great white dome gleamed in the sun. It briefly occurred to me that had it not been for Erica and me, the view would have been very different. Only two months before, we had stopped an attack that would have destroyed the building—and wiped out most of our government as well.

The next thing that occurred to me was that we were heading in the opposite direction from all the trains.

"How are we . . . ?" I began.

"This way," Erica said before I could even finish the thought, then led me around the corner of the station. Directly across the street was a large government building that housed the main US Postal Service in the city, as well as the National Postal Museum, which was very likely the least popular branch of the Smithsonian. Although both Union Station and the post office building were beautiful and impressive from the front, they were dreary and down-to-business in the rear. The road between them was narrow and cast in shadow, and it angled downward to provide access to the basement levels of both buildings. It was as though we were dropping into a man-made canyon. This section of the train station wasn't made with polished white marble, but instead dull yellow blocks of stone that looked like a child had stacked them.

Halfway through the canyon was a truck entrance for Union Station, a large rectangular gap in the yellow blocks. As we approached, a semi truck rumbled out, bearing goods that had just arrived by train.

Passengers certainly weren't meant to enter the train station this way, but Erica and I acted like we were supposed to be there and faked it with confidence. We walked right in and no one said a word to us. It was quite likely that no one even noticed we were there.

The entrance led to an immense space underneath the train station. The station was actually built above ground level: The trains passed underneath the building, and so the boarding platforms were down here. We could see them in the distance, although the area we were in was for moving cargo. Up until that point, I had always thought the trains at Union Station were only for passengers, but now I realized that a staggering amount of other things came to Washington, DC, on them as well.

For example, a great deal of mail. Hundreds of carts full of letters and packages were being wheeled back and forth from the trains to the post office and vice versa. In addition to that, there were thousands of other items, ranging from high-priced electronics to fresh produce, all being shunted about in large crates and containers. Forklifts and trucks rumbled past us. The entire section of the building was dark and dingy, lit by ancient fluorescent lights. Throughout it were thick steel columns supporting the station above, stained black by a hundred years' worth of smoke and diesel fumes. We worked our way toward the boarding platforms, dodging the trucks and forklifts.

"What was going on back in the Metro?" I asked. "What did that guy want with me?"

I knew that Erica had said she would explain everything on the train, but I couldn't wait any longer.

Still, Erica told me, even though she would probably have to do it all again in a few minutes. "Zoe was kind of right. It had to do with part two of Project X. Crandall got Sal Minella to tell him everything and then texted me."

"So what is it?" I asked, more impatiently than I had intended.

"Murray started an internet conspiracy theory about you."

"That's all?" I said, feeling relieved. "Compared to sending assassins after me, that's not so bad."

Erica gave me a look that seemed half-pitying and half-annoyed that I hadn't fully grasped the situation. "Actually, I think it might be worse."

"Worse than having every assassin in the world wanting my head on a stick?"

Erica slipped past a forklift carrying a large pallet of cabbage. "There really aren't that many professional assassins in the world. But there are *millions* of people who believe in conspiracy theories. Maybe billions. And with the internet, those theories can spread like wildfire. Think about it: Murray didn't initiate this very long ago, and there were already at least four people on that subway train who were looking at you funny."

"Four?" I repeated. "There were only two. The old lady and the guy who accosted me . . ."

"No. There were two others. I just didn't want to alarm you by pointing them out."

I frowned, upset at myself for missing the other two people. And, more to the point, I was now growing increasingly worried about Murray's plans. "What does this conspiracy claim?"

"That you're a key player in a clandestine plot to overthrow the government. Murray took everything good you've ever done and turned it on its head. Like, when you saved the president's life, but for a while everyone thought you had tried to kill him . . . ?"

"Murray's saying that I actually *did* try to kill him?" I finished, growing annoyed.

"Yes."

"That is so uncool!" I exclaimed, unable to control myself. "Murray's the one who was part of a top secret plot to overthrow the government! I stopped him! And now he's pinning everything he did on me?"

"More or less. He's leaked all sorts of evidence that would have implicated him, but he's altered it to make it look like *you* were the one who did the dirty deeds."

We reached the area where the boarding platforms began. Each was a long, raised strip flanked by train tracks on both sides. Passengers would descend to them from the station above, while the trains themselves entered from the side of the building at ground level. Since passengers weren't allowed down to the platforms until their trains were arriving, most were empty, although at the far side of the station, the 2:15 Capitol Limited from Washington, DC, to Chicago was boarding. Erica and I scurried across the closest set of train tracks, hauled ourselves up onto the platform beyond them, then dropped down onto the tracks on the far side.

I was steaming mad now. "Can't we beat this by posting evidence that Murray's the *real* criminal here? He's been arrested three times! That ought to make people stop believing him!"

Erica shook her head sadly as she climbed up onto the next platform. "Murray isn't posting all this as himself. He's pretending to be a mystical top-level agent at the CIA known only as 'X.'"

"And people actually believe him?"

"There are an awful lot of people who will believe almost anything they read on the internet. In fact, I haven't even told you . . ." Erica trailed off, looking ahead of us.

We were almost to the platform for our train, which was on the other side of another set of train tracks. The other passengers were arriving on it via the normal route, an escalator down from the station. Mike, Zoe, Chip, Jawa, and the principal were among them. My friends were all looking about nervously, most likely watching for assassins or wondering where Erica and I might be. The principal, meanwhile, seemed to be far more concerned with trying to remove a long trail of toilet paper that was stuck to his shoe.

Our train was coming into the station, slowly approaching along the tracks.

Erica's eyes were locked on the other passengers funneling onto the platform.

"What's wrong?" I asked.

"Nothing," she said. "I thought I might have spotted an assassin, but it was just a normal person."

"You're sure?"

"Yes. But he looked bizarrely similar to Hugh Gingery. I wonder if they're cousins."

"You were starting to say something else just now. Before you got distracted."

Zoe spotted Erica and me. She quickly pointed us out to the others, who looked relieved to see that I was safe. Although they still weren't fully at ease, given that they were on the alert for potential assassins.

"Oh right." Erica took my hand and jumped off the platform. We raced across the train tracks toward our friends. "I haven't even shared the craziest part about all of this."

"What's that?" I asked.

Chip, Jawa, and Mike helped us scramble up onto the next platform as our train arrived.

"Brace yourself," Erica warned me. "It's insane."

RESEARCH

Aboard the Amtrak Carolinian

Northeast corridor Amtrak route

June 11

1515 hours

"They think I'm a lizard?" I exclaimed.

"Not a lizard," Erica corrected. "A lizard-like alien that has shape-shifted into human form in order to plot the overthrow of our civilization."

"Oh yeah," I said sarcastically. "That makes a lot more sense."

"I warned you it was nuts," Erica said.

We were on the train, speeding through the countryside northeast of Baltimore, Maryland. Small towns, farms, and occasional patches of forest flashed past the window. The scenery was quite beautiful, but for most of the trip, we had been riveted to Erica's and the principal's phones instead.

Erica and I had encountered no issues boarding the train. We and the others had found a group of seats that faced each other at the forward section of one of the cars and gone to work, learning what Murray had done.

He had started his campaign of disinformation two weeks before, posting on websites known for spreading conspiracy theories. There were a surprising number of these, and many of the theories they championed had staggeringly large groups of followers. There were groups who were sure that the Apollo moon landing had been faked, groups that thought world governments were controlled by secret societies, and even a disturbingly large group that somehow believed the earth was flat. Murray had targeted the government-conspiracy groups and begun posting his evidence against me.

I had to admit, he'd done a very good job. Since Murray had eagerly participated in several evil plots for nefarious organizations, he already had plenty of evidence at his disposal, most of which should have incriminated *him*. But, like Erica had said, he had manipulated it so it appeared to incriminate *me*. For instance, Murray had snapped plenty of photos on his evil missions, posing with stolen nuclear missiles and atomic detonators, like a morally bankrupt tourist. He had then altered these by digitally inserting my face in place of his. In addition, it turned out that he had covertly filmed me doing the occasional incriminating act, like breaking into the British Museum and subsequently destroying some of the antiquities there. (I had only done this because enemy operatives were trying to kill me at the time, and I felt terrible about it, but it still made me look bad.) Altogether, it really did appear as though I had been repeatedly involved in attempts to cause chaos and mayhem, rather than trying to stop them.

To make matters worse for me, a few months earlier, SPYDER had framed me for trying to assassinate the president. Even though the Secret Service had ultimately declared me to be innocent, many conspiracy theorists had never believed it. So I already had a presence in the online wacko community. Now Murray had fanned those flames. As the mysterious X, he had quickly gone from having only a few dozen followers to having millions—and those followers hadn't merely spread the word; they had often embellished the conspiracy with their own bizarre alterations to the story. Like the lizard thing.

It didn't appear that Murray had come up with that. Instead, there had already been an active conspiracy theory claiming that shape-shifting reptilian aliens from the planet

Flumbo were secretly taking the place of normal human beings. The Flumbonians had been accused of being behind everything from crashing the stock market to rigging the Super Bowl to ruining the last season of *Game of Thrones*. It hadn't taken long before the Flumbo conspiracy met up with the Project X conspiracy.

All of which might have been somewhat amusing if the conspiracies hadn't been about *me*.

"I hate to admit it," Zoe said, "but Murray has been awfully clever this time. He hasn't just put a price on your head; he's also created a network of millions of people who are looking for you. These sites are already reporting that you were in the Metro at Union Station." She held up the principal's phone to display a video where the big man with the red baseball cap was stating his version of the events. It had been posted to a website called The Truth.

"I nearly caught him in the Metro," the man was saying, "but he had backup. Two dozen of his fellow Flumbonians jumped me. They probably would have eaten me alive if I didn't know kung fu. But by the time I fought them all off, Ripley had escaped."

Jawa looked to me sadly. "With our help, I figured there was a chance you could elude all the assassins, but with millions of conspiracy theorists on the lookout for you, it's going to be almost impossible to escape detection."

Even as he said this, he glanced around the train, keeping an eye out for any potential conspiracy theorists.

Thankfully, the train wasn't that crowded, and our fellow passengers seemed to be far more interested in working on laptop computers or playing games on their phones than they were in looking for space lizards posing as humans.

"How is Murray even doing all this?" Chip wondered. "He's in jail!"

"Maybe Falcon Ridge has a computer lab," Mike suggested. "Like, as a reward for good behavior. Murray wouldn't need too much time there. Part of the brilliance of this conspiracy thing is, it doesn't require much more than an internet connection. It probably only takes him a few minutes to post, and then the conspiracy nuts do the rest."

"Or maybe Murray has someone helping him on the outside," Zoe said. "Someone he gave all this disinformation to before being captured."

I forlornly skimmed through a post by someone named SuperPatriot863 who was accusing me of being responsible for the Bay of Pigs invasion, even though it had happened several decades before I was born. "The real question is: How do we put an end to this?"

All my friends reflexively looked to Erica for the answer. The principal immediately got upset.

"Why are you all looking at her?" he snapped. "I'm the

adult here! Don't you think I have some ideas as to how to fix this?"

"No," we all said at once.

The principal flushed bright red. "Well, it just so happens that I do! To stop this, all we need to do is post a series of reasonable responses on these websites, explaining the truth of what is going on here."

Mike rolled his eyes. "There are people on these sites who believe that space lizards are controlling their minds through microwave ovens. I don't think this is the sort of group that is going to listen to rational arguments."

"The internet is the place where reason and logic go to die," Jawa added. "There's plenty of good information on it, but there's also a tremendous amount of disinformation. And the problem is, lots of people can't tell the difference. They think that the people who are telling the truth are lying to them and that the people who are lying to them are telling the truth. Like Murray. He's spewing lies, but all these people believe him. And once somebody believes something, getting them to admit that was a mistake is extremely difficult."

"It's called confirmation bias," Erica said. "People tend to look for information that backs up what they already believe and reject anything that says the opposite. So even if you try to tell them the truth, they'll ignore it. Or interpret it as an attempt to deceive them. Even though they've already been deceived in the first place."

The principal blinked at her and Jawa. "How do you know so much about this?"

"There's a whole class about it at spy school," Jawa reported. "Methods of Mass Manipulation. Don't you ever read the course guides?"

"Er . . . ," the principal said weakly. "I've been very busy lately."

Zoe said, "The CIA pretty much invented the disinformation campaign. I'll bet Murray learned everything he needed to know about this scheme at school."

The principal grimaced.

Jawa turned to Erica. "So what's the plan?"

"We have to deal with this the same way we were going to handle the assassins," Erica replied. "We have to go right to the source. The only one who can put an end to this is Murray himself. His followers won't believe any information unless it comes from him."

"But he's been lying to them all along," the principal said.

"They don't know that," Erica countered. "They *think* he's been telling them the truth—and one of the lies he has told them is that anyone who tries to tell them the truth is lying. Therefore, any truth we tell will be regarded as lies, while any lies Murray tells will be regarded as truth. And so the only way to get the truth across is to have the liar tell it."

"Ow," Chip said. "Your logic is making my brain hurt."

"This is one of the great ironies of conspiracy theory," Erica went on. "The theorists think that almost everyone is lying to them—the media, the government, the scientific community—and that only they can figure out the truth. And yet, the one person they truly believe is the very person who is really lying to them."

"But what if Murray *isn't* at Falcon Ridge?" I asked. "Then we'll have wasted a huge amount of valuable time."

"That's a good point," Mike agreed. "Maybe we should split up into two teams. One would go to Falcon Ridge while the other would look for Murray somewhere else."

"There's just one problem with that plan," Erica told him. "It's terrible. There's nowhere else to look for Murray, because he's at Falcon Ridge." She took my hand before I could protest and looked me in the eye. "I know you're having doubts, but you have to trust me on this. Murray's there. So going there is not a waste of time. In fact, it's our only play. Now, the prison is in the countryside north of Philadelphia. I was planning to take the train to Philly and then find some alternative transportation, but we're going to have to change that."

"Why?" I asked.

"Because there's an assassin on this train," Erica replied.

EVASIVE ACTION

Aboard the Amtrak Carolinian

Northeast corridor Amtrak route

June 11

1545 hours

"We have to move," Erica announced, then snapped out of her seat and started down the aisle in the center of the train.

I followed right on her heels and everyone else stayed right behind me—except for the principal, who had been distracted playing a game called Flapjack Frenzy on his phone. It took him a few seconds to realize we had left, and then he sprang to his feet and huffed after us.

Like all trains, ours was separated into multiple cars; the

Carolinian mostly consisted of passenger cars, which simply had rows of seats, although somewhere along its length there were also sleeper cars with small rooms, a restaurant car, and several cars at the rear holding freight. The passenger cars were grouped toward the front of the train. Erica threw open the door at the end of ours, and we quickly passed through the junction between our car and the next.

The movement of the train had barely been noticeable while we were seated, but it was far more pronounced as we moved through the junction. This area wasn't air-conditioned or soundproofed, so it was hot and loud, and the cars were shifting on the tracks independently of one another. It could be hard to keep your balance when merely walking through the junction, but running through it was like trying to use a treadmill during an earthquake.

The next car was another passenger car. We quickly hustled down the aisle between the seats.

I risked a glance back, but since the junction was now blocking my view of the car behind us, I couldn't see any sign of the assassin.

"Are we being followed?" I asked.

"I presume so," Erica replied.

"How did you even know there was an assassin on the train?" Chip asked. "Did you see them?"

"No," Erica said. "I *smelled* them."

"Smelled them?" Jawa echoed, astonished. "How?"

At times like this, I realized that the others didn't know Erica nearly as well as I did. For much of her time at spy school, Erica had believed that friends, in addition to relationships, could be a liability for a spy, rather than an asset, and so she had been aloof and standoffish around her fellow students. The only reason I had come to know her was that I had been thrust into multiple missions with her, which had allowed me to learn about her incredible abilities—as well as other things she would have preferred to keep secret, like her fondness for posters with photos of adorable kittens.

"Everyone has a distinct scent," Erica explained to Jawa. "For example, you smell like cardamom and hair gel, Ben smells like Irish Spring soap and fear, and the principal smells like bad breath and body odor."

"Hey!" the principal cried.

Erica ignored him and continued. "One of the people coming for us smells like greasepaint and way too much Savage Steel cologne."

"Oh no," Zoe said suddenly. "Warren Reeves is after us?"

Warren had been a classmate of ours at spy school before defecting to SPYDER. He wasn't talented at much spycraft, but he had been an expert at camouflage, which explained the greasepaint; he would use it on his skin to help blend into his surroundings, and even when he wasn't trying to hide, he usually had a few residual blotches of paint on him that he had failed to fully clean off. As for the Savage Steel, he had always worn it, hoping to impress Zoe, whom he'd had a massive crush on. The crush had not been reciprocated—Zoe had secretly liked *me*—which had driven Warren to working for the bad guys instead.

"Yes," Erica answered, leading the way through another junction between cars. "He's probably two cars behind us."

"You can smell Warren from two train cars away?" Mike asked, astonished.

"He wears *a lot* of that cologne," Zoe said. "He bought it by the gallon. He thought it made him smell manly. But it didn't. Instead, he smelled like a wet dog who'd eaten too many beans."

We headed into the next passenger car.

When we had boarded the train, I had made a point of counting the cars. There were twenty. We had been in the ninth from the front. Which meant that relatively soon, we were going to run out of train.

Erica said, "Obviously, Warren doesn't have the spy skills to track us down on his own. So I presume he's working with someone else."

"Joshua Hallal?" I asked. If Erica thought I smelled like fear normally, now I must have been reeking of it.

"That'd be my guess," Erica confirmed. "Although

I haven't smelled him yet. He's still too far away. For the record, Joshua smells like sassafras and WD-40 machinery lubricant."

That would have been because Joshua was no longer entirely human. He was also a spy school student who had turned traitor, although he was several years older and significantly more competent than Warren. He had been a key member of SPYDER and very respected in the organization. However, Joshua had suffered some serious injuries when I'd thwarted SPYDER's plans and, at last count, he had a cyborg-like prosthetic arm and leg. None of that had really been my fault, but Joshua still blamed me for it. He had been intent on killing me even before Murray had put a price on my head.

The last time I had seen him had been a few months before, in Paris. I had escaped by knocking Joshua off the Eiffel Tower. Apparently, the fall hadn't killed him, which would mean he was now even angrier at me. And possibly even more cyborg than before.

We passed through another junction and into the sixth car from the front of the train. I asked, "Erica, what's your plan for when we get to the engine?"

"Oh, we're not going to get to the engine," Erica said calmly. "We're going to double back after this car."

"Double back?" I repeated worriedly. "How are we

supposed to do that? There's only one aisle inside the train. We'll run right into Joshua."

"That's why we're not going to double back *inside* the train."

I felt my stomach twist into knots as I grasped what she meant. On the other hand, Jawa and Chip were absolutely thrilled.

"We're going to run across the top of a moving train?" Chip exclaimed.

"Awesome!" Jawa proclaimed, sounding like a kid who had just been told he would get to skip school for the next week and go to Disney World.

"Ooh!" Chip cried out. "Maybe Joshua will catch up to us and we'll get to have a fight sequence up on the roof!"

"That would be amazing!" Jawa agreed.

"Actually, it wouldn't," I told them. "Joshua can shoot grenades out of his prosthetic arm. It's very dangerous."

This did nothing to dampen Jawa's and Chip's spirits. In fact, it amped them up. They now looked like they had learned that, in addition to going to Disney World, they were going to be allowed to have ice cream for every meal.

"Fighting a cyborg on top of a moving train!" Chip exclaimed. "This day just gets better and better."

Erica led us into the next junction. This time, she did not continue into the preceding car. Instead, she started dismantling the lock on the door that led to the exterior of the train.

Passengers normally got on and off the train at the junctions—although for safety reasons, most only did this when the train was stopped. So the exterior doors automatically locked during transit.

"We're not going to fight Joshua on the roof of the train," Erica told Chip and Jawa. "Because if we do this right, he won't notice that we've doubled back."

"We're not going to do *anything* on the roof of the train at all!" the principal announced. "As the head administrator at the Academy of Espionage, I cannot condone such reckless behavior on a field trip."

"This isn't a field trip!" Zoe told him. "It's a life-or-death situation!"

"And the 'death' part is what concerns me," the principal replied. "Do you have any idea how much trouble I'll be in if I let a student fall off a moving train?"

"Not quite as much as the student who fell off the train," Mike pointed out.

"Er . . . yes," the principal admitted. "But I'd still have an awful lot of paperwork to fill out."

Erica finished dismantling the lock and yanked the door open. A massive gust of air burst into the junction with such force that we were all nearly knocked off our feet. Between the roar of the wind and the clatter of the train on the tracks, it was so loud, we could barely hear Erica as she shouted, "Follow me!"

With that, she disappeared out the door.

For a moment, I thought she had jumped. But then I realized that she was climbing up the side of the train to the roof.

Zoe nudged me forward. "You go next!" she yelled.

That didn't seem chivalrous at all. So I yelled back, "No! You go!"

"No one's trying to kill *me*!" she hollered, and then shoved me to the open door.

I grasped the doorjamb and peered out. The wind created by the train's movement was so strong that my eyes instantly began watering, making it hard to see. However, I was still able to spot a series of metal rungs built into the side of the train, designed for accessing the roof. It was a struggle to even reach out against the wind and grab the first one.

I estimated the train was hurtling along the tracks at around a hundred miles per hour. The ground beneath me was a blur as it rushed by.

I pulled myself out the door of the train and started up the ladder. The wind pummeled me, trying to tear me off the side, but I clung on tightly and climbed as fast as I could. It was only a few feet up to the roof, where Erica was waiting.

She was on her hands and knees, as standing atop the train in the wind would have been difficult even for someone as athletic as she was. She helped me clamber from the ladder onto the roof.

I scuttled to the center of the train. From there, it was eight feet to either side, so it felt safer than being close to the edge. Not a *lot* safer, but still, it was something.

The train was now passing along the upper reaches of the Chesapeake Bay. To the east, what looked like summer vacation cabins dotted the forested banks, with the water glistening in the sun beyond them. To the west was a large swath of forest that was probably part of a state park.

It was a warm spring day, and the metal roof of the train was broiling in the sun, so it was hot to the touch, while the wind was chilling the rest of me. It felt as though I was in a snowstorm with my hands on fire.

Within only a few seconds of my arrival, Zoe appeared at the top of the ladder and then climbed onto the roof.

Erica grabbed my arm and yanked me to my feet. "Let's go!" she yelled.

"But the others . . . ," I began.

"They'll catch up!" Erica firmly pulled me with her, heading along the roof toward the rear of the train.

With the wind at our backs, we moved very quickly. In fact, the real challenge was to slow ourselves down, so we didn't lose control and run right off the side of the train. Erica also made a point of stepping as softly as she could, not wanting to make any noise that would alert Joshua and Warren that we were on the roof. I tried to follow her lead.

Behind us, all the others made it to the roof. Even the principal. Then they followed us along the top of the train.

Erica and I reached the next junction. Erica paused atop it, stopping me as well, and cocked her head to the side, like she was listening to something.

I put my mouth right next to her ear so I wouldn't have to shout and asked, "What is it?"

She responded in kind. "I think I heard Joshua and Warren pass into the car we just ran over, but I'm not sure."

Behind us, the principal tripped and fell.

Even with the wind and the clatter of the tracks, I could hear the thud as he hit the roof.

After which, I heard the distinct sound of Joshua Hallal's prosthetic arm warming up. A second later, a grenade blasted a hole in the roof two feet from where the principal had landed.

"Holy crabcakes!" the principal exclaimed, and sprang to his feet.

"Yeah," Erica observed. "Joshua's definitely in that car. Run!"

There was no longer any point in treading softly. Erica fled along the roof of the train, dragging me with her.

My friends came up with the exact same plan. It didn't take them long to catch up to us. Even the principal was moving with the speed of an impala.

I could only assume that Joshua Hallal was now heading back through the train as well. But with the junction doors in his way, he would be moving significantly slower than us.

Still, he knew we were on the train. Literally on top of it. There was nowhere to hide up there, and there were only thirteen cars left until we would reach the end.

The sound of the train on the tracks suddenly changed. It was no longer as loud, as if the noise wasn't being bounced back up to us anymore.

We had passed onto a bridge. Below us, an arm of the Chesapeake Bay cut west and we were crossing over it. I looked back in the direction the train was heading. The bridge was quite long, at least a mile. Although at the speed we were moving, it would be less than two minutes until we reached the far side.

There was now water on both sides of us. We were at least ten stories up.

Erica stopped by the next junction and stared down at the bay.

My stomach twisted even more. Because I knew what she was thinking.

"We have to jump," she said.

"No!" I exclaimed. "I *hate* plummeting!"

In my defense, Erica had forced me to make death-defying jumps several times before. I had leapt off an abandoned trestle into a raging river in West Virginia, sprung from a cliff into the rapids of the Potomac, and even fallen through the glass floor of the Tower Bridge in London into the Thames.

Jawa and Chip, who had never done any of those things, were naively excited by the prospect.

"Yes!" Jawa exclaimed. "This is going to be epic!"

"Everyone else at school is going to be so jealous!" Chip added.

"No!" I said again. "This is much higher than anything we've jumped off before! The fall is going to be awful, and landing is going to be even worse!"

"I'm with Ben on this one," Mike agreed. "Even if we survive, we'll end up soaking wet and my underwear's going to be riding up my butt all day."

Zoe looked at him like he was an idiot. "That's your major concern in all this? Wet underwear?"

"It chafes," Mike informed her.

There was an explosion in the next junction forward. Joshua had blasted the exterior door off the train. It sailed away like a piece of crumpled tin foil and plunked into the bay far below.

"They're coming," Erica told me. "We *need* to jump."

"There must be another way," I pleaded. "If we jump off this train, it could add another day until we reach Murray, which is another day I'll have assassins and conspiracy theorists chasing me all over the countryside."

Erica started to argue, but then paused, as though she'd realized I'd made a good point.

"You're not afraid of jumping, are you?" Jawa asked me tauntingly.

"What are you, chicken?" Chip teased, then flapped his arms and clucked a few times.

Even with our lives on the line, he was still finding time to bully me.

Erica looked me in the eyes. "There's no other option," she told me. "We have to go."

Although there was something odd about her voice as she said it.

"I don't think this is a good idea either," the principal cautioned. "Dangerous behavior like this is definitely not sanctioned for agents-in-training. . . ."

"If we don't jump, we die," Erica said.

"Oh," the principal said, turning pale. "Well, in that case, I suppose we can make an exception."

At the other end of the train car, I could see Joshua Hallal's metal hand clamping on to the rungs as he climbed toward the roof.

"Last one into the bay is a rotten egg," Chip announced.

"Jump!" Erica yelled.

But as she said it, she grabbed on to Mike and Zoe's collars.

Chip, Jawa, and the principal leapt off the train.

The rest of us did not.

The other three screamed at the top of their lungs as they plummeted down off the bridge.

No matter how brave you are, *everyone* screams while plummeting. It just happens. The same way everyone screams on roller coasters. Plummeting is scary, and your body's response is to make noise. Very loud noise.

(Well, *almost* everyone screams. Erica didn't. I had plummeted beside her a few times, and she had always been bizarrely calm. If she'd had a book handy, she probably would have read a few pages on the way down. But then, Erica wasn't like most people.)

Jawa, Chip, and the principal were loud enough to even be heard over the roar of the wind and rumble of the train. Especially the principal. He screamed so loud, people in Philadelphia probably heard him. It certainly grabbed Joshua Hallal's attention. Instead of pulling himself up onto the roof of the train, he turned to watch the others fall.

An interesting thing about plummeting is how time stretches out when you're doing it. Whenever I had dropped from great heights, the fall had always seemed to take forever. I had plenty of time to imagine how terribly it was going to hurt when I landed, or to see my life parade before my eyes. But now that I was watching other people fall, I realized that the event was surprisingly quick. Within less than three seconds, Jawa, Chip, and the principal had plunged into the bay, making enormous splashes.

This all worked to the advantage of those of us who hadn't jumped.

Joshua was clinging to the edge of the train and being buffeted by a gale-force wind, which was certainly making his eye water and blurring his vision, the same way it had done to me. (Joshua only had one eye, having lost the other as a result of all the injuries he had suffered, so in addition to having his vision impaired by the wind, he also had really bad depth perception.) Plus, due to the great speed that the train was moving, we were quite far from the others by the time they hit the water. Since everything had happened so fast, Joshua probably couldn't tell exactly what had occured, other than that several people had jumped from the train and into the bay. It would have been difficult to determine exactly how many people had jumped—or who they were.

Still, to play it safe, Erica dropped to the roof of the train and flattened herself against it.

Mike, Zoe, and I instantly followed her lead.

This hid us from Joshua's view, although we could still see his metal hand clamped on the top rung of the ladder in the distance, glinting in the sun.

It stayed there for a few seconds, as though Joshua was watching the bay below and considering whether or not to jump.

Erica slithered to the opposite side of the train from Joshua and climbed down the ladder by the doors.

Once again, Mike, Zoe, and I followed her lead.

Two sets of rungs flanked the doors on the junction. There was just enough room for the four of us to cling to the side of the train, out of sight of anyone on the roof. The idea was that, should Joshua decide to check the roof of the train—just in case he suspected that we had only tricked our friends into jumping off while not actually jumping ourselves—he wouldn't be able to see us.

I was clinging to the ladder above Erica. The wind was pummeling me so hard that my cheeks flapped. From my position, I could see a tiny sliver of the interior of the passenger car ahead of us through the window.

After thirty seconds, Joshua Hallal stormed into the car from the junction.

It was hard to tell, given my angle and my wind-blurred eyes, but he looked really annoyed.

There were two other people with him.

Not surprisingly, one was Warren Reeves. Warren wasn't camouflaged, which made sense, as there was little point in blending into the background at the moment.

The other person was Ashley Sparks.

I had first met Ashley on a mission at SPYDER's evil spy school. At the time, she was training to be a SPYDER agent, having turned to crime after missing the cutoff for the US Olympic gymnastics team by a thousandth of a point—due to a deduction she believed was unfair, by a judge who mistakenly believed she had not stuck the landing on a quadruple-flip dismount from the uneven bars. Ashley still dressed somewhat like a gymnast, in form-fitting athletic wear covered with sparkles, and had a penchant for combining two words into one. When she was happy, she preferred the word "swawesome," a combo of "sweet" and "awesome," although when she was annoyed, she preferred "jidiot," a combo of "jerk" plus "idiot." (I had heard the latter directed at me quite a lot.)

It wasn't much of a surprise to see Ashley there. She had teamed up with Joshua before, and had a tempestuous romantic relationship with Warren. But still, I was disturbed that all of them had united to come after me once again.

Now that I knew they had given up the hunt, I scrambled back up the ladder to the roof of the train so they wouldn't notice me through the window. This time, Erica, Mike, and Zoe followed *me*.

We then lay on the roof of the train.

"What now?" I asked Erica. "Do we just stay up here for the rest of the trip?"

"I think that's our safest option," she replied.

The train continued heading north, whisking us toward Philadelphia.

EMOTION

Atop the Amtrak Carolinian

Moving through southern Philadelphia, Pennsylvania

June 11

1630 hours

There's a reason that passenger trains don't have rooftop viewing decks.

Being on top of a train, exposed to the elements, is not fun. We spent most of the trip lying on our backs to keep out of the wind, but the sun continued to roast us—except for a brief thunderstorm around Wilmington, Delaware, which drenched us. After that, even though the sun came back out, the wind on our wet clothes made us cold—and, as Mike had warned, our underwear started to ride up and chafe our nether regions.

Also, every time I sat up, several bugs smacked into my face at a hundred miles an hour. I made the mistake of saying "Yuck" after getting pegged in the forehead by a high-speed grasshopper and had a moth promptly fly down my windpipe, which left me gagging for the next five minutes.

So by the time we arrived on the outskirts of Philadelphia, I wasn't feeling so good.

The fact that every assassin on earth was hunting for me, and a significant portion of the country thought I was a shape-shifting lizard alien trying to destroy human civilization, didn't help.

"When your father recruited me to spy school, he said it'd be dangerous," I told Erica, "but he didn't say it'd be *this* dangerous."

"He couldn't have possibly known what was in store for you," Erica replied. "Although my father doesn't really know much of anything. He still can't even operate the toaster."

We were lying beside each other on the roof. Mike and Zoe were splayed out a few yards away. The train had slowed to maneuver through the city, but it was still so loud that the others couldn't hear our conversation.

The train tracks wound between a series of oil refineries and the Schuylkill River, whose banks were choked with garbage and the occasional gutted car. It wasn't a particularly auspicious way to enter a city.

"I'm only a few days shy of fourteen, and I already have a nemesis who is willing to send assassins after me," I muttered. "It's not fair."

"It's not," Erica agreed. "I've done just as much to thwart Murray as you have. You'd think he would have put a price on my head too."

"I meant it was unfair that I'm being targeted at all," I told her.

"Oh," Erica said. She lay beside me silently for a while, then added, "I know this must be really scary for you."

"It's worse than scary. It's absolutely terrifying. I mean, I know you're not afraid of anything, but normal people like me are and—"

"I get scared," Erica said suddenly. "In fact, I've been scared plenty today."

I sat up in surprise to stare at her, even though this put me right back in the wind again. "You were? But you didn't show it."

"Well, I didn't want you to get even more freaked out. The truth is, you're kind of right. I didn't used to be scared. Grandpa trained me to push the fear away and not think about it."

"What changed?" I asked.

Erica looked at me like I was a moron. *"You."*

A junebug splatted into my forehead so hard that it exploded on impact. I wiped it off and lay down again.

Erica said, "Remember how, back when we were getting to know each other, I told you that relationships were dangerous in the spy business? Well, now you and I have one, and I'm worried about you. It turns out, you can feel a lot more worried for someone you care about than you can feel for yourself. It's really unnerving."

"Sorry," I said.

"Don't be." Erica rolled over on her side so that she could look at me. "I'm not upset at you for it. I just feel bad that I've let you down today."

"Let me down? You saved my life several times over."

"I still should have done better. I haven't been at the top of my game. It can be hard to concentrate when you're worried or scared."

"You being slightly off your game is still a thousand times better than most other people on their best day. I'm glad you're here."

"So am I." Erica smiled at me.

Despite the assassins and the bugs and the fact that both of us looked like we had spent the last few hours in a wind tunnel, it was sort of a romantic moment.

Although it only lasted for half a second.

"We have an idea!" Zoe announced. She crawled along the top of the train to my side, with Mike right behind her. "We know how to stop this conspiracy theory!"

"We already have a plan to do that," Erica said, sounding slightly annoyed. "We're going to Falcon Ridge . . ."

"Which is dangerous and time-consuming," Zoe responded. "And possibly a waste of time. Like Ben said, Murray might not even be there."

"He's there," Erica said curtly.

"Even so," Mike told us, "I think this might be worth a shot."

Erica and I propped ourselves up on our elbows to give them our attention.

Zoe said, "All we need to do is go online and do the same thing to Murray that he's done to Ben. . . ."

Erica shook her head. "I already told you, that won't work. These people won't believe the truth."

"Who said we'd be posting the truth?" Mike asked.

That caught Erica by surprise enough to silence her for a bit, giving Zoe a moment to launch into her explanation.

"You're right, these people won't listen to the truth. So if they're primed to believe conspiracy theories, then let's give them the biggest one of all time. Let's make it look like Ben's just a pawn—and that the *real* bad guy behind all this is Murray."

"But they trust Murray as the source of all their information," I pointed out.

"No," Mike countered. "They trust *X*. They have no idea who Murray Hill even is."

"We've got access to plenty of info and photos of Murray in our school accounts," Zoe went on. "We can take all that and doctor it and then go to these exact same sites that Murray has been using and flame him."

"Right," Mike agreed. "We fight fire with fire. We say he's not just a Flumbonian lizard person. We say he's the *king* of the Flumbonian lizard people. We say he has a giant space laser that can make hurricanes, that he likes to find the most adorable dogs on earth and eat them, and that he has an evil plot to destroy all of the world's ice cream."

"That's completely ridiculous," Erica said.

"So is the fact that Ben's a shape-shifting alien reptile," Zoe countered, "and all these wackos believe *that*."

Erica looked like she was about to argue against this, but I cut her off before she could. "It couldn't hurt to try, could it?" I turned to Zoe. "What would you need to do this?"

"Not much," Zoe replied. "Just a portable computer and a good internet connection."

The train's brakes suddenly made an ear-piercing screech. Our car jolted hard enough that my elbow slipped and my head bounced painfully off the roof.

Erica sat up quickly, scanning the area around her.

The train was coming around a tight bend in the Schuylkill, which had forced it to slow down. We were past the refineries and now approaching 30th Street Station in downtown Philadelphia. The river cut straight through the city. The opposite bank was lined with skyscrapers and condo complexes. On our side, the railroad tracks were flanked by a beautiful park filled with ball fields and jogging trails. The city was starting to look a lot nicer.

However, Erica appeared upset with herself. "We need to get off the train," she announced.

Mike, Zoe, and I sat up, concerned.

Zoe said, "Isn't it generally a good idea to wait until a train stops before getting off it?"

"Yes," Erica admitted. "But not today. It'd be bad to get off in the station right in front of Joshua Hallal."

"Right," Mike said. "Because you used to like him, but now you're with Ben, so the whole thing would be really awkward."

I gave him a sharp look. "And because Joshua is trying to kill me."

"That too," Mike agreed.

Erica was already on the move. She went to the closest junction between train cars and started down the metal rungs.

The three of us followed her.

Even though the train had slowed considerably, it was still moving at least twenty-five miles an hour, which was not exactly a safe speed to jump off. But we did it anyhow. Our momentum carried each of us forward a bit, stumbling before we caught our balance—except for Erica, who nailed the landing perfectly.

There was only a spindly chain-link fence between the train tracks and the park. We easily hopped it, landing on a jogging path that arced around the ball fields. In the distance, up a hill, was a grand brick football stadium that looked to be well over a century old.

"Where are we?" I asked.

"The University of Pennsylvania," Erica replied. "The oldest university in America, founded by Benjamin Franklin in 1740. My grandfather went here—and so did his father and his father and *his* father. As well as some of the finest middle-grade novelists in America."

There was an explosion behind us.

We spun around to see that another train door had been blasted out of the junction. It sailed through the air and clattered across the ground.

Joshua Hallal stood in the doorway with Warren and Ashley at his sides. They had spotted us.

"Unfortunately, there's no time for a campus tour," Erica said, breaking into a sprint. "Let's go!"

Zoe, Mike, and I raced after her along the jogging path.

Joshua, Warren, and Ashley leapt off the train. Ever the gymnast, Ashley executed a perfect flip before sticking the landing. Warren fell right on his face.

"Hey!" Joshua yelled. "Wait!"

"Yeah!" Ashley echoed. "Wait, you jidiots!"

We didn't listen to them. Instead, we ran away as fast as we could.

A branch of the jogging path angled up a long ramp to a bridge that spanned the river. We went that way.

Even though he was running, Mike still tried to adjust his underwear. "I *hate* damp undies," he muttered. "Just like I said, it's chafe city down below."

Behind us, Joshua, Ashley, and Warren jumped the fence onto the jogging path. Ashley did yet another flip. Warren got his pants caught and flopped on his face. Again.

"This is exactly what I was talking about," Erica grumbled to me, sounding extremely angry at herself. "I'm off my game! I got distracted talking to everyone when I should have been more focused on the mission."

"This isn't your fault," I told her. "If you hadn't gotten

us off the train when you did, we'd be in deep trouble."

"And if I'd gotten you off the train even earlier, then we wouldn't be running for our lives right now."

We arrived at the bridge. Erica ran directly in front of an empty cab, forcing the driver to skid to a stop. He promptly unleashed a string of obscenities at us, which, I would later discover, was a very common occurrence in Philadelphia.

Mike, Zoe, and I piled into the back seat while Erica got into the front beside the driver.

"Drive!" she ordered. "Now!"

"I'm not taking you losers anywhere," the driver replied gruffly.

"Have it your way," Erica said. "I'll drive."

Before the driver even knew what was happening, he was out on the street. Erica slid over into his seat, stomped on the gas pedal, and sped away.

The driver shouted even more obscenities at us.

We roared across the bridge and into downtown Philadelphia.

Behind us, Joshua Hallal also stepped into traffic and forced a cab to stop. He didn't even wait to see if the driver would agree to take him. He simply yanked the man out of the car and stole it. Warren and Ashley hopped into the back just as Joshua hit the gas.

Even though Philadelphia is one of the largest cities in

America, its downtown turned out to be surprisingly small, the same concise grid of streets that had been laid out by its founder, William Penn, back in colonial times. It was only twenty-four blocks across, and we moved through it quickly.

Perhaps if Erica had been following the rules of the road, it might have taken a bit longer to cross downtown, but we had no time for that. Erica was breaking almost every traffic law there was, sometimes violating half a dozen at once. She ran red lights and stop signs, veered onto sidewalks, and obliterated the speed limit. She clipped other cars, flattened road signs, sideswiped hot dog carts, and left hundreds of angry drivers and pedestrians in our wake—all screaming obscenities, of course.

Joshua Hallal was doing the exact same thing. If there was a street sign we didn't knock over or a hot dog cart we miraculously avoided, he took care of it.

Mike, Zoe, and I clung to each other in the back seat, cringing at each close call.

Zoe asked, "Erica, just out of interest, where did you learn to drive like this? Did your grandfather teach you?"

"He taught me the basics," Erica replied. "But mostly, I'm making this up as I go. Hold on."

We smashed through a pretzel vendor's cart and barreled across Broad Street, a crowded six-lane thoroughfare that marked the center of the city. Cars slammed on their brakes to avoid us, setting off chain reactions of fender benders. We got grazed by a bus, spun in a full circle, and narrowly avoided three more near-death collisions before making it to the other side of the street.

"It's a good thing my pants were already wet," Mike said. "Because I think I just peed myself a bit."

Joshua Hallal tried to follow us across Broad Street, but his cab got caught in the massive pileup Erica had created. Four different cars slammed into it, trapping it in a sea of wrecked vehicles. Joshua clambered out and roared with frustration as we left him behind.

But there was no time to relax. We now had a new problem: The police were coming for us.

Erica's reckless driving had drawn plenty of attention, and several squad cars had taken up the chase. Every time we flew through an intersection, another dropped in behind us, sirens wailing and bubble lights flashing.

Erica didn't slow down. She kept hauling through the streets.

"Why are we running from the police?" I asked. "Shouldn't we just stop? If they take us into custody, we'll be safe from Joshua."

"If they take us into custody, you're dead," Erica corrected. "Every assassin will know exactly where to find you."

"Oh," I said. "Good point."

"Don't worry," Erica assured me. "I have a plan."

Two blocks ahead of us, more police cars raced into the road, forming a barricade.

"Is your plan 'Make the taxi fly'?" Mike asked. "Because otherwise, we have a problem."

"Be ready to get out," Erica replied. *"Fast."* With that, she pounded the brakes. The taxi slewed wildly, jumped the curb, and skidded to a stop only a few inches away from a brick colonial building with a distinctive white clock tower.

We had nearly crashed into Independence Hall.

Erica sprang from the cab and fled. Mike, Zoe, and I were right behind her.

We were in the center of Philadelphia's tourist district. Across the street behind us, a glass pavilion held the Liberty Bell, while in front of us, Independence Hall spanned an entire block. It was actually three separate buildings, connected by arched colonnades. We raced beneath one of these into Independence Square, a small, tree-filled park that had been there since well before the Revolutionary War was fought.

The police cars that had been following us screeched to a stop in the street. Then dozens of police officers jumped out and pursued us on foot.

It was nearly five o'clock, the end of visiting hours. The final tours of the day were filing out of Independence Hall. Since the site was part of the National Park Service, each tour was led by a park ranger in an official uniform with a Smokey Bear hat.

The square was packed with tourists. There were lots of families with kids our age, so it wasn't that hard to blend in.

A young park ranger was holding open the door to the main building, making sure that everyone on her tour had left. Once they were all gone, she exited herself.

Erica deftly caught the door before it locked, then waved the rest of us inside.

"Hey!" the park ranger yelled. "You can't go in there! It's closed!"

Erica slammed the door in her face and locked it.

We were now in a central foyer with a grand staircase that led up to the second floor.

Outside, angry park rangers pounded on the door.

"Not to question your plans here," Zoe said to Erica, "but how does breaking into a national monument get us into *less* trouble?"

"Just follow me," Erica said.

She led us into the Declaration Chamber, the very place where the Declaration of Independence had been debated, presented, and ultimately signed back in 1776. The room had been preserved to look almost the same as it had back then. In a sense, it was a smaller, cozier version of the Senate chamber in the US Capitol. Along the far wall was a raised dais wide enough for five people to sit upon and preside over meetings, while much of the rest of the space was devoted to seating for the other representatives. A low railing cut through the room, dividing it into the historic section and the viewing area where tourists gathered. Erica hopped right over the railing and entered the historic section.

Back in the entry foyer, I could hear the door that we had come through being unlocked, followed by the sound of footsteps pouring into the building.

Zoe and Mike gave me worried looks. The Declaration Chamber was a dead end. We were only seconds away from being caught.

I flashed them the most reassuring smile I could muster, figuring that Erica knew what she was doing.

As it turned out, she did.

She went directly to the raised dais, reached under some decorative molding, and flipped a hidden switch.

A trapdoor that had been concealed in the front of the dais dropped open.

It was only two feet tall and four feet wide, and it led to a pitch-black space that smelled of musty air. But Mike, Zoe, and I didn't complain. It was a way out.

We quickly slipped through it, one after the other, into the small space.

Erica was the last one through. She lifted the trapdoor

back into place behind her. A split second after it clicked shut, I heard several people enter the Declaration Chamber.

"This room's empty," said one of them. "They must have gone upstairs."

Then I heard most of the people leave, although two remained. "We should probably search here anyhow, just to make sure," one said.

"All right," the other agreed. It sounded like the young park ranger who had allowed us to enter the building, although I couldn't see a thing from the dark space where we were hidden.

Erica, Mike, Zoe, and I froze and held our breath, not wanting to make a sound that would give us away, while the park rangers searched the room above us. It didn't take them long. There weren't many places to look—and they seemed to be unaware of the secret space we were hiding in.

After less than two minutes, the rangers left the Declaration Chamber. Then came distant voices in the foyer as people gathered to figure out where we could have gone. One person reported that we weren't in the chamber on the other side of the foyer; another said we weren't in any of the rooms upstairs. Other people suggested that maybe we had gotten into the clock tower, or gone out onto the roof, or passed straight through the foyer and right out the front doors of Independence Hall. Someone else proposed that maybe we hadn't even come into the building at all.

No one suggested that maybe we were hiding in a secret passage dating back to colonial times, because no one knew it existed.

No one, that is, except for Erica Hale.

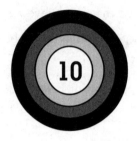

REVOLUTION

Independence Hall

Philadelphia, Pennsylvania

June 11

1700 hours

It took a few more minutes before the police and the park service left Independence Hall, scratching their heads in befuddlement and wondering where we could be.

Once they were gone, we felt it was finally safe to speak, which meant asking the question that was on three of our minds. Mike got it out before Zoe or I could:

"Erica, how did you know this hidden room was here?"

"My grandfather told me about it," Erica explained.

"And it's much more than a room." She removed a flashlight from her utility belt and flicked it on.

For the first time, we were able to get a good look at our hiding place. The space underneath the dais was only a small antechamber. From there, a set of stone steps wound downward into the earth.

Erica started down them. Since the rest of us did not have flashlights, we stayed close behind her.

"And how did *your* grandfather know about this?" Zoe asked.

"*His* grandfather told him," Erica replied. "One of my ancestors, Elias Hale, was involved in constructing this in the first place. He thought that the Founding Fathers of our country needed an emergency escape route out of Independence Hall. After all, they were risking their lives when they met in this building. Drafting and signing the Declaration of Independence was an act of treason against the British. The punishment for that was death."

The stairs ended twenty feet below the floor of Independence Hall. From there, a tunnel stretched onward into the darkness. An ancient oil lamp hung from a wooden support beam. Erica lifted it off its hook and shook it.

We heard liquid slosh inside.

"Sounds like there's still oil in here," Erica observed.

"Think it still works?" I asked.

"Only one way to find out." Erica plucked a match from her utility belt, struck it, and placed it to the wick. The fire sputtered but then caught. The light from the lamp filled the tunnel with a warm glow.

We could now see how the tunnel had been constructed. The walls were rough-hewn rock and dirt, as though the passageway had been hacked out with picks and shovels. A framework of wooden beams shored up the ceiling. Even though they were more than two hundred and fifty years old, they still looked strong and well-preserved. The tunnel was much longer than I had expected, stretching off into the darkness, the other end too far away to see. "Whoever built this did a good job," I observed.

"Of course they did," Erica said. "Thomas Jefferson designed it and Benjamin Franklin oversaw the construction. I hear Franklin even invented a new kind of sealant to protect the beams against rot. Although that's not surprising. Barely a day went by without Franklin inventing something or other." She started down the tunnel.

Mike, Zoe and I followed her. Our fear of being captured had faded, as we were now in awe of our surroundings. Even though Erica and her family had shown me several hidden places inside national landmarks, it never stopped being astonishing. One of the reasons that Independence Hall was such a popular attraction was the chance for people to be in the very spot where history had happened. And so there was something extraordinary about discovering that the building concealed secret histories too.

"Did the Founding Fathers ever have to use this tunnel?" Zoe said.

"Yes," Erica answered. "When the British invaded Philadelphia in 1777, some of the founders escaped through here. If it hadn't been for this route, they would have been hanged. But I've heard that Franklin liked to use the tunnel for non-emergency situations as well. He was like a rock star in colonial Philadelphia, you know. He couldn't go anywhere without fans wanting his autograph or for him to sign their copies of *Poor Richard's Almanack*. This route to Independence Hall was a lot more discreet."

"Benjamin Franklin had groupies?" Mike asked, astonished.

Erica said, "The man invented the lightning rod, bifocals, and swim fins, discovered the jet stream, created the first library in the colonies, founded the University of Pennsylvania, contributed to the Declaration of Independence and the Constitution, and started a volunteer fire brigade. If anyone deserved groupies, it was him."

Despite the awe-inspiring historical significance of the tunnel, it was still kind of spooky. Except for the glow of the oil lamp, we were enveloped by darkness. The musty air gave the sense of being in a crypt, and we kept hearing strange, eerie noises. The tunnel wasn't far below the streets of Philadelphia, so we could hear the muted thump of cars on the road above and water gurgling through nearby sewage lines.

Of course, I was already on edge, given what had happened that day. It didn't seem unreasonable to fear that another assassin might pop out of the shadows at any moment.

"No one else knows about this tunnel?" I asked warily. "Not even Joshua?"

"Why would Joshua know about this?" Erica responded.

"I thought you might have told him, seeing as you were . . . well, close. Back before he became a traitor."

"We weren't that close. It was more like I had a schoolgirl crush on him."

"I still can't believe that," Mike said, sounding slightly disgusted. "You're the last person I'd expect to have a thing for bad boys—oof!" He gasped as Zoe drove an elbow into his ribs, trying to get him to stop talking.

I gave him a warning glare as well. Even though Erica and I were dating, she was still wary of opening up. There were plenty of things she had never fully explained—notably her relationship with Joshua. I suspected she had only mentioned it now because she was trying to calm my fears of being ambushed—and so I was worried that Mike's response would make her clam up again.

Thankfully, she didn't. In fact, she completely ignored Mike's response and explained, "He was three years older than me, and he hadn't turned evil yet. In fact, he was easily the best of the other spies-in-training at the academy when I got there. And he was also really . . ." She trailed off awkwardly before finishing the sentence, but I knew the word she had just avoided was "handsome."

I had met Joshua only once in his pre-cyborg form. It had been brief and the lighting wasn't great, as it was in an abandoned coal mine and I had been slightly distracted by the fact that a nuclear missile was about to launch and blow up several world leaders, but even then, it had been evident that Joshua was good-looking.

"Anyhow," Erica went on. "He was nice to me, and I took it as romantic interest, but it probably wasn't. I was just a silly first-year student and, let's face it, he was probably already plotting to turn evil and only faking an interest in me so that he could trick me into giving up classified information."

I thought about denying this. I'd once had a conversation with Joshua where he'd indicated that his feelings for Erica had been genuine. But seeing as Joshua had already tried to kill me twice that day, I decided against saying anything that might make him seem like a better person.

"So . . . no," Erica concluded. "I never told Joshua about this tunnel. Or any of my family secrets. I think that even though I liked him, I still must have had an inkling there was something untrustworthy about him. Not that it made me feel any better when I learned that he'd betrayed me—and everyone else, for that matter."

"Obviously, you've gotten much better at picking boyfriends," Mike noted. "Because Ben would never—oof!" He wheeled on Zoe. "What was that one for? I was being supportive!"

"Sometimes it's best to just keep your mouth shut," Zoe told him.

That seemed to be good advice. I knew that Erica had felt badly betrayed by Joshua, although I was unsure if she had ever told anyone until that moment. I wasn't sure what to say in response, so I just took her hand in mine and gave it a reassuring squeeze.

Erica had never been much for holding hands—unless she was arm wrestling. But this time, she seemed to appreciate the gesture. She didn't pull away, and actually kept my hand clasped in hers as we continued through the tunnel.

However, now that we had been discussing Joshua Hallal, something occurred to me.

"Why didn't Joshua jump off the train today?" I asked.

"Because . . . ," Mike began, then looked at Zoe guardedly. "Is it okay to talk now . . . or am I going to get another elbow in the gut?"

"It's okay," Zoe told him.

Mike heaved a sigh of relief, then said, "Because jumping off a train is crazy. The only reason to do it is if someone's trying to kill you. Or if you're a professional stunt person."

"Or if millions of dollars are on the line," I said. "If Joshua truly thought I had jumped off the train, and he really wanted the reward for killing me, don't you think it would have been worth jumping? If we had actually jumped and he'd followed, I wouldn't have been able to get away. I would have been an easy target in the middle of the bay."

"So maybe he realized you hadn't really jumped," Zoe suggested. "And that only the others had."

"Then why didn't he come up onto the roof of the train to look for us?" I asked. "He *must* have thought we'd jumped. It was just chance that he spotted us getting off the train later."

"Sorry about that," Erica said. "I should have had us get off earlier."

"You were the only one who even thought that we should get off before the station," I pointed out. "So no need for apologizing."

Erica didn't say anything else, but it was clear she was still annoyed with herself.

Zoe said, "Joshua must have decided that jumping wasn't worth the risk. He's had a couple of falls from great heights before and lost several limbs as a result."

"Yeah," Mike agreed. "Maybe he figured that if he had one more accident, he'd lose something *really* important, like his head."

I had to admit that argument made sense, and yet, it still felt as though it wasn't the real answer.

"Do you think Chip and Jawa are all right?" Zoe asked. "They *looked* all right. But we were moving so fast, I couldn't tell."

"They were safe," Erica assured her. "And so was the principal."

"How do you know for sure?" Zoe pressed.

"I saw all three of them come back up again after they went in the water," Erica replied. "They looked perfectly fine to me."

"But we were on a train that was rocketing away from them," Zoe went on. "Your eyesight couldn't possibly be that good . . ."

"It is," I said. "Erica has better eyesight than anyone I've ever met. If she says they were okay, they were okay."

"But I bet they're gonna be seriously annoyed the next time we see them," Mike mused. "Not only did Erica trick them into being decoys, but Jawa and Chip are now stuck out in the middle of nowhere with the principal. And wet underwear. That's not exactly a recipe for a good time."

"No, it's not," I agreed. Although I would have been

happy to trade places with them. Being damp and stranded with the principal was still better than being on the run from conspiracy theorists and assassins.

A loud rumble suddenly echoed through the tunnel. The ground around us trembled ominously. It felt as though we were in the intestine of a giant with irritable bowel syndrome. I clenched Erica's hand more tightly, worried.

"Don't panic," she said. "It's just the subway. We're getting close to the Market Street Line."

Since we were underground, I couldn't tell exactly what direction we were heading, but I was able to make a good estimate of how far we had traveled. I knew my usual walking speed and how long we had been moving, so I figured we had gone a fifth of a mile, or about two city blocks.

The glow of the oil lamp revealed the end of the tunnel ahead of us.

Another set of stone steps headed upward, built in the same way as the ones we had descended from Independence Hall. They led to a wooden ceiling with a hatch built into it, which was held closed by a centuries-old slide bolt.

Erica held the oil lamp close to inspect it. The metal was silver and encrusted with tarnish—although the latch appeared extremely well crafted.

"Let me guess," I said. "Paul Revere made this."

"Don't be ridiculous," Erica said. "Revere lived all the

way up in Boston. And he had his hands full building the hardware for all the secret passageways up there. This was probably forged by Franklin himself." She shoved the bolt sideways. Due to the tarnish, it gave some resistance, but ultimately slid into place.

Erica hung the oil lamp on a hook near the hatch, then blew out the flame, plunging us into darkness.

I immediately felt fear grip me again.

Erica pushed the hatch up. The centuries-old hinges groaned in the creepiest way possible, which made my sense of fear get even worse.

Since I was still below Erica on the steps, I couldn't see what the hatch opened into. But the air was quiet and still, indicating that the exit led into a building, rather than emerging outdoors.

Erica scoped out her surroundings, then said, "Coast is clear," and climbed out.

I followed right behind her.

We were in a small colonial building with windows that fronted a major street. The interior of the building was dark, save for the light that spilled through the windows, so everything around us was cast in shadow. On either side of me were large, sturdy wooden structures. In the near darkness, they looked somewhat like giant mutated armchairs with machinery where the seats should have been. At the top of each, six wooden beams splayed out in different directions until they met the ceiling, forming braces. The whole place had a strangely familiar smell that seemed vaguely metallic but also comforting.

I recognized the smell, then immediately understood what the structures were. "That's ink," I said. "And these are colonial printing presses."

"Benjamin Franklin's presses," Erica clarified. "This is his old print shop. It's also part of the National Park Service. The presses still work."

That explained the wooden braces. Old-fashioned printing presses had a lot of moving parts. The braces would prevent them from rocking about wildly while they were running.

Mike and Zoe emerged through the hatch and gasped in amazement. Once again, we had found ourselves in a place of historic importance. Franklin's fame and fortune were a result of his success as a printer. I found myself drawn to the press closest to me. It was evident that the Park Service still used it, probably in demonstrations for tourists. I could see wet ink gleaming on the metal plates of the press, while fresh reprints of Franklin's *Pennsylvania Gazette* hung on the nearby wall to dry.

"Ooh," Mike said, looking at them wide-eyed. "Caslon. I love this font."

"Me too!" Zoe squealed happily. "It's one of my favor-ites!"

Mike and Zoe were both huge fans of typography—or, as they preferred to call themselves, "font-natics." They had bonded over this, forming their own club at spy school. Now they shared an excited grin and performed an elaborate secret handshake.

Meanwhile, Erica lowered the door of the hatch back into place. It fit so snugly and blended in with the rest of the floor so well that, once it was closed, it was almost impos-sible to see.

And then, I noticed someone in the darkness behind Erica.

The person had been lurking there, waiting for us to arrive. Now they stepped from the shadows, closing in on Erica from behind.

I quickly snatched a heavy iron printer's plate off the closest press and sprang toward the attacker while yelling, "Erica! Look out!"

I swung the plate at the attacker's head, intending to brain them with it.

But before I could connect, the attacker raised their own weapon, a long wooden stick, parrying my assault. The ink-slicked plate flew from my hands and clattered across the floor. The attacker then caught my arm and effortlessly flipped me over their shoulder. I landed on my back so hard, it knocked the wind out of me.

My opponent leaned over me. I cringed, expecting a heavily scarred and scowling assassin.

Instead, I found myself looking into the face of an elderly woman.

She was at least seventy, with half-rimmed eyeglasses, a shawl that she appeared to have knitted herself, an amused smile, and a twinkle in her eye. The long wooden stick she had parried my assault with turned out to be a cane.

"You could use a little work on your sneak attacks, young man," she observed.

Erica came and stood beside her. She didn't look worried about the woman at all. Instead, she appeared thrilled to see her.

"Hi, Grandma," she said.

COUNTERATTACK

Poor Richard's Sandwich Shoppe
Center City, Philadelphia
June 11
1745 hours

A half hour later, we were ensconced at the back
of a nearby sandwich shop, using the free Wi-Fi to put Zoe's
plans into action and wolfing down cheesesteaks.

Erica's grandmother was treating. Her name was Mary
Hale, and it turned out that she had worked for the CIA as
well—although she was quick to point out that she had been an
analyst, rather than a field operative. I had learned, a little too
late, that Erica had arranged for Mary to meet us at the northern terminus of the secret tunnel in Ben Franklin's print shop.

"I thought we could use some backup," Erica had explained.

Under other circumstances, I might have questioned what protection a seventy-year-old woman could provide against a horde of assassins, but seeing as Mary had greeted me with a perfectly executed Whirling Dervish move, I realized that, at the very least, she had better martial arts skills than me.

Which Mike was never going to let me forget.

"You know how, when someone wants to razz you, they say, 'You couldn't even beat up my grandmother'?" he asked. "Well, now we know for a fact that you *can't* beat up Erica's grandmother."

"I doubt you could have done any better against her," I shot back.

"Well, I certainly couldn't have done *worse*."

"Could you two keep it down?" Zoe snapped. "I'm trying to save Ben's life over here."

She was hunched over a laptop computer, typing furiously. The computer belonged to Mary, who claimed that no decent analyst ever traveled without one. (Mary, being a member of the Hale family, had come prepared with emergency supplies ranging from pepper spray to dynamite, although she carried hers in a fashionable purse, rather than a utility belt.)

"How's it going?" I asked.

"So far, so good." Zoe had already downloaded the information she needed, much of which was in her own account on the spy school mainframe. She had plenty of photos of Murray stored there, mostly taken from before anyone knew he was secretly evil, although there were a few of him from after that time as well. Zoe had also recovered several documents that were supposed to be classified and was now working as fast as she could to manipulate everything into "evidence" against Murray.

Meanwhile, Erica and Mary were posted near the front window, where they could keep an eye out for trouble—although Mary was using the opportunity to catch up with her granddaughter. I had plenty of questions for Mary myself, seeing as Erica had never mentioned her. (For most people, this would have been strange, but Erica's reasoning made sense, as there were security issues with sharing information about her family; she hadn't even told me that she had a *sister* until six weeks before.) But for the moment, it made sense to let Erica and Mary have some alone time, and besides, there was other work to do.

Erica had originally balked at the idea of putting Zoe's plan into action, as she felt we ought to be trying to get out of the city as fast as possible, but Mary had talked her into it. "Thanks to your reckless driving, this city is crawling with police on the hunt for you," she had pointed out, "not to mention conspiracy theorists and assassins. So it might be in your best interests to lie low for a bit while I arrange a more clandestine way out of town. In addition, I'm guessing that all of you could use some dinner."

That was true. We were all starving, having missed lunch and been on the run constantly ever since. (A constant state of fear burns a staggering number of calories.) So we ducked into the closest restaurant to Franklin's print shop, which had turned out to sell cheesesteaks. That wasn't surprising, as it was hard to throw a rock in Philadelphia without hitting a place that sold cheesesteaks. What *was* surprising was that Erica ate one. Erica generally only consumed exceptionally healthy food to keep her body in peak physical condition, while cheesesteaks were possibly the least healthy food ever invented by humanity. But Erica was ravenous too, and there wasn't a vegetarian restaurant in sight.

The cheesesteak place was called Poor Richard's, in reference to Benjamin Franklin's pseudonym, and because it was in a colonial part of the city, it seemed to be required by law to call itself a "shoppe" rather than a "shop." The walls were bedecked with Philly sports team banners, tourism posters, and plaques bearing Franklin's most pithy sayings. Meat, onions, and peppers sizzled on the grill, and the whole place smelled of grease. There were several other customers, but they didn't appear to be conspiracy theorists—or if they were, then they weren't particularly observant ones. No one had noticed me, although to ensure that didn't happen, I was sitting with my back to everyone else and had my baseball cap pulled down low over my eyes.

Zoe finished doctoring a classified document and grinned proudly. "All right, we're good to go. I fudged this to say that the CIA has concrete evidence that Murray Hill is the king of Flumbo—"

"But don't all these conspiracy theorists distrust the CIA?" I interrupted.

"Yes," Zoe said. "Which is why I've fabricated proof that the CIA is in league with the Flumbonians and has tried to hide all the evidence at Area 51 in Nevada. See?"

I looked over her shoulder at the computer screen. Zoe had done a fantastic job. The fake document looked very official, as all the redactions, the CIA letterhead, and the "Classified" stamps were legitimate. The text of the document was lunacy, but as far as I could tell, the crazier a theory was, the more likely the conspiracy theorists would be to accept it.

"Looks great," Mike said, impressed. "What site are you going to upload to first?"

Zoe opened a website on the browser. "This seems to be Murray's go-to for spreading conspiracy theories. So I think it's our best bet."

Her screen displayed The Truth, the same site where angry red-baseball-cap man from the subway had uploaded the video report of his encounter with me. It was surprisingly rudimentary for a website with such a large reach, with crummy graphic design and a lousy interface. The homepage was simply the words "The Truth" followed by a short screed with abundant misspellings. The gist was that everyone in power was lying to the American people—the government, the media, scientists—and that only the people who ran The Truth could be trusted. The irony, of course, was that everything on the site was a lie.

There was now a page on the site devoted entirely to me, with an exceptionally unflattering photo at the top. (It was from my yearbook, back when I had gone to normal middle school, and showed me after an extremely unfortunate haircut.) The rest of the page was simply a thread of comments from conspiracy theorists, which were pouring in almost as fast as I could read them. Even as I watched, I was accused of manipulating a mayoral election in Poughkeepsie, New York, guiding a wave of illegal immigrants across the border in El Paso, Texas, and somehow ruining the entire cantaloupe harvest in Muscatatuck, Indiana. Each accusation was followed with several comments by fellow conspiracists, thanking them for the information.

"How do all these people think I'm doing all these things

in so many different places at once?" I asked, incredulous.

"I'm guessing they think you've cloned yourself," Mike suggested. "That, or you have some alien teleportation technology."

The only good news about the constant flow of disinformation was that it made it almost impossible for people to figure out where I actually was. The claims that I was still at large in Philadelphia were drowned by claims that I was in hundreds of other places.

"With all these comments, do you think anyone will even notice what you're about to post?" I asked Zoe.

"Only one way to find out," she said, and then set about sharing it. The first thing she had to do was create a profile, choosing CIAInsider007 as her screen name. We had already worked out an introductory statement to post, where she claimed to be a disgruntled CIA operative who had spent the last few years secretly uncovering *the truth* about the Agency's connection to Murray Hill and the Flumbonians. We then stated that, as a brilliant puppet master, Murray had set me up to look like the leader of the cause, leaving him free to lurk in the shadows and undermine our freedoms. To make our statement look legitimate, we had misspelled many words and used an abundance of exclamation points. Now Zoe posted it under the heading *HUGE NEWS: THE REAL THREAT ISN'T BEN RIPLEY!!!!* and then began uploading the evidence against Murray: the fake CIA document, followed by a series of incriminating photographs. Some of these were doctored, like one showing Murray at Area 51, hanging out with some lizard people, but many were legitimately incriminating, such as a selfie that Murray had taken of himself, posing proudly next to a stolen nuclear missile. Zoe also uploaded a photo of Murray and me in my first weeks at spy school; we were simply hanging out in the student lounge at our dormitory, but Zoe claimed that it showed Murray in the process of selecting me as a patsy.

After all the evidence was posted, something astonishing happened: The comment thread stopped. The conspiracists either were taking their time to sift through all the new information—or they were stunned into silence.

Then Truther2034, one of the more aggressive commenters, wrote: *Holy cow. This looks kind of legit.*

This was followed by a flurry of other responses, some backing the evidence (*I KNEW there had to be a mastermind behind this all along!*) and some questioning it (*How do we know CIAInsider007 is the real deal?*).

And then came a series of comments that caught us by surprise.

They were from Murray Hill himself.

Although he wasn't posting as Murray Hill, of course. He was posting as X.

DON'T BELIEVE THIS! the screed began. *CIA-INSIDER007 IS A FRAUD!*

This person is in league with Ben Ripley himself and has posted false evidence to distract you from the real threat he poses to our planet.

I have expected a fabricated attack like this for some time.

The Murray Hill she is referencing is an innocent victim—albeit an extremely handsome one.

For I know the true identity of CIAInsider007. It is none other than Zoe Zibbell, a fellow Flumbonian; I have seen her in her human form with Ben Ripley.

Then Murray posted a photo of Zoe and me from school.

Zoe gasped in astonishment, stunned by both the speed of Murray's counterattack—and the fact that she, too, had now been outed as part of the conspiracy.

Mike was similarly flabbergasted. "How did he know so quickly that we were posting this?"

"He must have a computer monitoring the feed on this site," Zoe replied. Her eyes had gone wide in fear.

As X, Murray was continuing to post photos of Zoe and me. He had taken a great deal over the years, probably because he had a crush on Zoe. Together, all the photos made a powerful statement that Zoe and I were close.

Zoe gaped at them all, overwhelmed by Murray's attack.

"I have to counter this," she said meekly. "What do I do? What should I say?"

"Nothing," said Erica. To our surprise, she was standing behind us, watching the screen over our shoulders. "Log out! Murray's probably tracking you through the connection! If he hasn't already done it."

Her words jolted Zoe into action. She quickly logged out of the account.

But it was too late.

Comments continued to come in from X.

I'm betting that Zoe is with Ben Ripley right now. Along with two other associates, Mike Brezinski and Erica Hale.

And they are currently at Poor Richard's Sandwich Shoppe at 104 Market Street in Philadelphia.

"Uh-oh," Mike said.

Erica slapped the laptop closed and whisked it off the table. "We have to go. Now."

"Right," I said, heading for the front door.

Erica caught my arm. "Not that way. Murray just gave the address of this place to every screwball in Philadelphia." With that, she dragged me into the back of the restaurant.

"Hey!" yelled the guy making cheesesteaks. "You can't go in there!"

We didn't listen to him.

Since the cooking was all done at the grill, there was no

kitchen in the rear, only a storage room with a pair of walk-in refrigerators and shelves lined with industrial-size containers of Cheez Whiz. Zoe, Mike, and Mary followed on our heels as we hustled through it all and barged out the back door.

We emerged onto a cobblestone alleyway, a remnant left over from colonial times, although the cobbles were the only quaint touch remaining. We were surrounded by dumpsters, bags of garbage, and rats the size of small dogs.

"This way," Mary ordered, and strode down the alley with the speed of a woman a quarter her age. She whipped out a phone, dialed a number, and said, "Are you close? We need extraction immediately."

There were major streets at both ends of the alley. The sidewalks were full of workers heading home at the end of the day and tourists wrapping up their sightseeing. I was overcome by the feeling that all of them were conspiracists who Murray had sent to find me.

Which wasn't true, of course. That was just paranoia.

Only a few of them were conspiracists who Murray had sent to find me.

"That's them!" someone yelled from the end of the alley behind us.

I glanced back to see three burly young men in fraternity shirts. One was pointing our way.

We ran in the other direction.

"From now on, let *me* make the plans," Erica told Zoe. "Seeing as mine actually work."

"This was a perfectly good idea," Zoe replied heatedly.

"Except for the part where it completely backfired," Erica said.

"How was I supposed to know Murray would respond within seconds?" Zoe asked. "The guy's in prison! He's not supposed to have that much freedom! It made complete sense to try to play his own game against him. Fight fire with fire."

"Why would you fight fire with *fire*?" Erica shot back. "Then all you get is a bigger fire. You're supposed to fight fire with *water*. Or industrial-strength chemical flame retardants."

"Erica!" Mary snapped. "Here's a piece of advice: If you don't have something nice to say . . ."

". . . then say it directly to the person who screwed up so they won't make the same mistake again," Erica finished. "Yeah, I know it."

"Er . . . not quite." Mary reached the end of the alley and hooked a right turn onto the sidewalk. "The saying is actually: If you don't have something nice to say, then don't say anything at all."

"That doesn't make any sense," Erica said. "How is anyone supposed to learn if you don't tell them what they did wrong?"

Mary sighed. "This is already a stressful situation. Your friends need support at this time, not criticism. Otherwise, the entire mission will go to pieces."

"It's already going to pieces," Erica stated, slaloming through pedestrians.

"Then help get it back on track," Mary said sharply. "Don't make it worse."

With most people, Erica would have argued the point, or simply ignored the advice, but things were different with her grandmother. Erica looked somewhat ashamed of her behavior.

I hustled along the sidewalk behind the Hales while trying to keep my head down. There were people all around us, and I didn't want anyone else to recognize me. For all I knew, dozens of other conspiracy theorists were racing to the address Murray had given. And it would only be a few seconds before the frat boys emerged from the alley behind us.

As we reached the next corner, a recreational vehicle suddenly pulled to the curb in front of us, blocking our path. It was a large one, nearly the length of a city bus, with the evidence of many miles on it.

My heart sank. The RV looked like the sort of vehicle that a conspiracy theorist trying to stay off the grid might live in, and I expected that a horde of anti-Flumbonians was about to leap out of it and subdue me.

But then the door flew open, revealing Cyrus Hale, Mary's husband—and Erica's grandfather.

I froze in surprise. Cyrus was one of the most decorated spies of his generation, and the last place I had ever expected to see him was behind the wheel of an RV. I found myself wondering if an assassin had disguised themselves as him in order to lure me into a mobile torture unit camouflaged as a Winnebago.

"What are you waiting for, an engraved invitation?" Cyrus snapped gruffly. "Get your butt in here, pronto."

It was definitely Cyrus. The man was crustier than week-old bread.

I piled into the RV along with Erica, Mary, Mike, and Zoe.

Cyrus hit the gas and veered into traffic.

I glanced out the window and spotted the frat boys exiting the alley onto the crowded sidewalk. They scanned the crowd desperately, wondering where we had gone, but didn't seem to consider that we might have hopped aboard the RV.

And then, I saw something even more unsettling.

Down the street, Joshua Hallal, Ashley Sparks, and Warren Reeves emerged from Poor Richard's Sandwich Shoppe. All three appeared angry that we had given them the slip once again; Joshua was so livid, he punched a lamppost with his bionic arm, hitting it hard enough to dent it. None of them picked up on the RV either—but just to stay safe, I shied back from the window to avoid being seen.

Even though we were getting away, our situation was far worse than it had been only an hour before. Zoe's plan had backfired terribly. The assassins were still after me, the conspiracy theorists hadn't been deterred—and now, thanks to Murray's latest maneuver, Zoe, Mike, and Erica had been outed as fellow aliens.

A look at their faces told me they were just as upset about all of this as I was.

So far, this mission had been a complete failure.

REUNION

State Route 663

Southeastern Pennsylvania

June 11

1930 hours

Despite everything that had gone wrong, there was one piece of good news: The RV was a nice way to travel.

It was a deluxe model and, although it had been used a lot, the Hales had taken extremely good care of it. It was also very spacious, offering plenty of room for us to move around inside, with a breakfast nook, a kitchenette, a small bathroom, and a master suite at the rear. The breakfast nook could convert into an extra sleeping area, but for the time being, we needed the seating. Cyrus was at the wheel while

Mary sat in the passenger seat. Erica, Zoe, Mike, and I were in the nook with a map of southeastern Pennsylvania spread out on the table before us.

The Falcon Ridge penitentiary was located in an abandoned coal-mining area in the middle of nowhere, because nobody wants a supermax prison filled with dangerous criminals built anywhere near their home. It was two and a half hours from Philadelphia, although there was no direct route. We were cruising along a winding, two-lane state road. The countryside around us was beautiful in the late spring evening. The hills were rolling and forested, and the farms were straight out of storybooks, with red barns, green fields, and cattle grazing contentedly.

We had been driving for nearly two hours without any incidents. No assassins or conspiracy theorists had come after us. Either we had given them all the slip—or no one suspected that we'd be traveling by RV. With the added protection of the elder Hales, I found myself more relaxed than I had been all day. I wasn't *completely* relaxed, but I was at least at ease enough to join Zoe and Mike in questioning Mary about her career.

"So you never went into the field?" I asked.

"The *field*," Mary responded dismissively, saying the word the same way other people might say "head lice" or "incontinence." "That's not where the *real* work gets done.

Analysts are the true heroes of the CIA, but you never hear about all the amazing work they do. Instead, everyone thinks that field operatives are a big deal. Probably because the field operatives can't shut up about it. They're always going on about how they've been defusing bombs and dangling from helicopters and escaping bad-guy lairs full of trained piranhas. Most of that's a load of hooey. Just a bunch of field ops trying to make themselves sound impressive and justify their expense accounts."

"*I* was a field operative!" Cyrus reminded her.

"Oh, I know," Mary said, rolling her eyes. "And I'll admit, you were good at it, darling. You had plenty of successes. But be honest, you would have been lost without us analysts. No mission would ever succeed without our help. But you never hear a peep about us. We do the lion's share of the work and get a mouse's share of the credit."

I wasn't surprised to hear any of this. The tension between analysts and field operatives played out at spy school as well. Field operative was the glamorous career. Most students dreamed of that, while regarding analysis as a boring dead-end desk job, even though it was extremely important. The issue was exacerbated by agents like Alexander Hale, who boasted of their daring exploits in the field, many of which hadn't actually happened. Personally, I had a soft spot for the analysts; since my math and reasoning skills were exceptional while my self-defense skills were pathetic, I certainly would have ended up as an analyst if I hadn't repeatedly been thrust into action.

Mary caught my eye in the rearview mirror. Her gaze immediately softened. "Benjamin, just so you know, even though I'm an analyst, that doesn't mean I can't handle myself in the field."

"Oh, we already saw that," Mike said, amused. "When you kicked Ben's butt back at the print shop."

Mary smiled at this. "That was only a little taste of what I'm capable of. And you know that Cyrus and Erica can handle themselves as well. We're all here to help. After today's events, you deserve to be as nervous as a long-tailed cat in a room full of rocking chairs. But I assure you, you're safe with us. Plus, I haven't noticed anyone following us since we left Philadelphia."

Mary's words, delivered in her charming, grandmotherly voice, were certainly calming. And yet, fear still niggled at me.

"Maybe no one's following us *now*," I said. "But someone's going to guess we're headed for Falcon Ridge, right? It's no secret that Murray's being held there."

"That's true," Mary admitted. "Which is part of the reason we're traveling incognito like this. And we'll keep a low profile the rest of the way."

"But we still have to go to the prison," Zoe reminded her.

"The place is probably going to be crawling with assassins, waiting for Ben."

"Don't worry about that," Cyrus said. "I have a plan."

Mary gave him a sharp look. "Don't you mean '*We* have a plan'?"

"The point is," I said quickly, before an argument could erupt, "that what we're doing here is risky and"—I glanced warily at Erica, knowing she wouldn't appreciate what I was going to say next—"it might all be a wild goose chase."

I was right. Erica didn't appreciate my comment at all. "I already told you it won't be," she snapped. "So why are you bringing it up again? Are you hoping that my grandparents are going to overrule me?"

"No," I replied, even though that was *exactly* what I'd been hoping.

"Why would this be a wild goose chase?" Mary asked.

"Ben thinks that maybe Murray Hill isn't at Falcon Ridge," Erica told her.

Cyrus took his eyes off the road just long enough to give me a nasty glare. "Of course Murray's at Falcon Ridge! I delivered him there myself! Are you suggesting that I can't be trusted to do my job?"

"Of course not," I conceded. "It's just that, well . . ."

Mike jumped in, loyally backing me up. "Murray has a

history of getting out of prison. And we're worried he might have done it again."

"First of all, that's impossible," Cyrus said tartly. "And second, what would you geniuses have us do *instead* of going to the prison? Seeing as your last plan to thwart Murray worked so well."

"Er . . . ," I said. Which was as far as I got. Because I *didn't* have another plan. Even though I had been racking my brain to come up with one.

Mike drew a blank as well.

"Rule number one for any mission," Cyrus declared. "If you don't have something constructive to contribute, then keep your trap shut. I know what I'm doing here, and it's going to work. Speaking of which, we need to make a pit stop." He suddenly veered across the road into the parking lot of a gas station and brought us to such a sudden halt that everyone in the breakfast nook was nearly thrown from our seats.

The gas station didn't fit in at all with the picturesque countryside we had been traveling through. It was a squat, ugly box set on a slab of concrete. We had passed a few local restaurants along our route, all of which were charming, family-owned businesses, often with freshly baked pies in the windows. Meanwhile, the gas station had a dingy food mart displaying hot dogs that looked as though they were nearly as old as I was.

But then, we weren't there to eat. Or even to get gas. Cyrus had only been stopped for a second before a shadowy figure slipped out from behind the food mart, slunk across the concrete, and then climbed into the RV.

It was Trixie Hale, Erica's younger sister.

Trixie was clever, cheerful, and kindhearted—and yet, she had caused a great deal of trouble for me. Shortly after meeting her, Mike and I had accidentally spilled the beans that everyone else in her family was a spy. The resulting security risk would have been bad enough, but Mike and Trixie had also fallen for each other, which many of the Hales seemed to somehow consider my fault as well. It had taken me a while to patch things up with the family, although they had still done their best to keep Mike and Trixie separated. Until now.

Trixie was thrilled to see Erica—but when she spotted Mike, her happiness ratcheted up to a whole new level. She shrieked with excitement and threw her arms around him. "I didn't know you were going to be here!" she exclaimed. "Why didn't anyone tell me?"

"That was classified information," Cyrus said, giving Mike and me a stare hard enough to cut glass with. "And some of us know how to keep a secret."

This was the first time I had seen Cyrus since letting word of his identity slip to Trixie. It was clear that he still hadn't forgiven me for it. He also obviously didn't like seeing Mike and Trixie in a romantic clutch one bit.

I knew Mike was excited to see Trixie, but he was even more scared of Cyrus. He wriggled away from her grasp and held her at arm's length. "What are you doing here?" he asked.

"I was wondering the same thing," Mary said, then shifted her gaze to Cyrus. "What, exactly, is the bright idea behind bringing our granddaughter who has no survival training along on a life-or-death mission?"

"What was I supposed to do?" Cyrus asked sharply. "Take her back to boarding school? Her identity is compromised, thanks to Tweedledee and Tweedledum back there." He jabbed a finger toward Mike and me. "The way I figure it, she's safer with us than she is without us."

"Grandpa!" Trixie snapped. "That's not fair! Mike and Ben didn't compromise my identity. *You* did. You're the ones who are spies. I just figured it out."

Cyrus huffed. "You figured it out because those two weren't careful."

"And you are?" Mary asked him. "You just left Trixie waiting for us out here at a gas station in the middle of nowhere!"

"Would you have preferred that I bring her into the city to rescue everyone from a horde of assassins and nutjobs?"

"I would have preferred that you not bring her at all. Why didn't you tell me you were doing this?"

"Because I knew this was how you would react, and I was trying to put it off as long as possible."

"So you knew it was a bad idea all along." Mary's brow creased with concern. "Why aren't we moving?"

"I need to use the toilet." Cyrus got up and squeezed past us to head for the tiny bathroom. "I've been sitting in the driver's seat for three hours straight, and my bladder's about to burst."

Mary promptly slid into the driver's seat and floored the gas. The RV's tires squealed on the pavement before we shot back onto the road again.

Cyrus nearly toppled into the tiny kitchen. "Hey!" he yelled. "I'm the driver here!"

"Not anymore," Mary responded.

Cyrus seemed to be grappling with whether to argue or use the toilet, but his full bladder won out. He slipped into the bathroom and locked the door behind him.

With her grandfather temporarily distracted, Trixie now felt comfortable enough to snuggle up next to Mike in the breakfast nook. "I've been so worried about you today! Are you all right?"

"I am now that you're here," Mike said.

Behind his back, Zoe mimed vomiting in disgust.

"Actually, we're not all right at all," Erica said solemnly. "Things are getting worse by the second." While her grandparents had been bickering, she'd been using Mary's laptop. Now she turned it around so that the rest of us could see it.

She had been looking at The Truth. In the time since we had last been on the site, thousands of new comments had poured in.

The Truthers were now just as focused on Erica, Mike, and Zoe as they were on me. And the rumors they were spreading about us had spiraled even further out of control. The four of us—along with our fellow Flumbonians—were accused of all sorts of outlandish schemes: plotting to replace every world leader with a shape-shifting lizard, using our space laser to slowly heat the planet so that we could make money selling alien air-conditioning technology, and secretly seizing control of the global zinc supply.

Not every comment was about us, but they were all equally deranged. One Truther was convinced her neighbors were secretly Flumbonians who had eaten her goldendoodle. Another posited that Flumbonians made up over 50 percent of the population of San Francisco. And yet another suggested that Flumbonians had bulletproof hides, so if you really wanted to kill one, you'd need either a few sticks of dynamite or a flamethrower.

As upsetting as the comments were, I couldn't stop

reading them. I was at once astonished by what people could believe and devastated that my friends had now been lumped into the conspiracy with me. Even though Murray was behind it, I still couldn't help but feel as though everything was my fault.

I was so engrossed, it took me a few moments to notice that the general mood inside the RV had changed. Everyone had stopped speaking and was looking out the windows, staring at the road behind us with concern.

"What's wrong?" I asked.

Mary said, "It appears I was right: Bringing Trixie along was a really bad idea."

"Why's that?"

"Because some hired killers are following us."

DEFENSIVE DRIVING

State Route 663

Southeastern Pennsylvania

June 11

2000 hours

I ran to the bedroom at the rear of the RV. It was small, designed to take advantage of every inch of space. There was a couch along the back wall that converted into a bed at night. I stood on it and looked through the rear window.

In the dusky evening light, a sports car was hurtling down the road toward us. It was too far away for me to see who was behind the wheel, or to even determine what make of car it was. But there was definitely something menacing about the vehicle. I felt as though I was treading water and had just spotted a shark bearing down on me.

Zoe, Mike, Erica, and Trixie joined me at the window.

"Mary!" Zoe shouted. "Step on it!"

"I'm trying!" Mary yelled from the driver's seat. "But Bertha here is built for comfort, not speed!"

"Bertha?" Mike asked, confused. "Who's Bertha?"

"The RV," Trixie replied, looking embarrassed. "My grandparents name everything: the cars, their house, their guns . . ."

It wasn't surprising that the RV couldn't go very fast. After all, it weighed several tons and was as aerodynamic as a cinder block. Still, I had been hoping that Cyrus had secretly modified the vehicle to give it more power—although that obviously wasn't the case. I could hear the engine straining through the floor beneath us. It sounded as though it might blow a gasket at any second. And yet, the RV had barely added any speed. Meanwhile, the sports car was quickly gaining on us.

"Why did you bring this RV if it's so slow?" I asked, failing to keep the fear out of my voice.

There was a flush from the tiny bathroom and then Cyrus emerged, zipping his pants. "Bertha might not be fast, but she has other assets." He flipped a switch, and a portion of the bedroom wall slid aside, revealing a small arsenal of weapons. Plenty of guns were mounted on racks inside, although there were also several larger, less common weapons, like a grenade launcher and . . .

"Is that a flamethrower?" Trixie asked, stunned.

"Darn straight," Cyrus replied. "An XT-80. Top-of-the-line Russian army surplus."

"I'm guessing that's not a standard feature for a Winnebago," Mike observed.

"No." Cyrus beamed proudly. "I installed this myself. C'mon, kids. Help me get Penelope ready to go."

"Er . . . ," I said, confused. "Is Penelope the flamethrower?"

"Of course not!" Cyrus said, like I was a fool. "Penelope's the grenade launcher! What kind of dimwit names a flamethrower Penelope?"

I had no answer to that. Instead, I did my best to help prep the grenade launcher—which wasn't much, really. I didn't have a lot of experience with them—and neither did Mike or Zoe; we weren't scheduled for Introduction to Heavy Artillery until our fourth year of spy school. And yet, we had at least seen grenade launchers up close before. Trixie hadn't. She just stood to the side, dumbfounded by the idea that her grandparents were tooling around the country in a Winnebago armed with military-grade weaponry—and that her sister knew how to use it.

Erica and Cyrus had Penelope ready to go within only a few seconds, which was an exceptionally fast time—and yet, as far as I was concerned, it still wasn't fast enough. The sports car was almost upon us. Out the rear window of the RV, I could now see that there were two assassins in the car, one driving and one in the passenger seat. Both wore black masks and bodysuits, which made it impossible to make out any of their features. As the sports car came closer, the passenger stood up, poking the upper half of their body through the sunroof, and aimed their own grenade launcher at us.

Theirs was bigger than ours. Big enough to rip the RV in half.

"They've got one of those things too?" Trixie exclaimed. "Was there a sale on them?"

"Get her out of here," Cyrus told Mike. "It's too dangerous."

Mike didn't question orders. He grabbed Trixie by the hand and led her toward the front of the RV.

Cyrus shouldered Penelope and aimed it toward the rear window.

"Should we open that?" Zoe asked. "So you don't blow it up?"

"There's no time," Cyrus replied, then shouted, "Fire in the hole!"

Erica, Zoe, and I ducked away.

Cyrus pulled the trigger.

There was a tremendous blast that shook the entire RV. A rocket-propelled grenade tore through Bertha's rear wall, vaporizing the window and a good section of the back end of the vehicle as well. The kick from the weapon lifted Cyrus off his feet and lofted him through the bedroom door into the kitchenette. He slammed into the cabinets so hard that they burst open and rained cookware down on his head.

Fortunately, the sudden attack caught the assassins by surprise. One second, they were behind an unassuming Winnebago, and the next, a grenade was screaming toward them. However, the driver had incredible reflexes. And veered out of the way at the last second. The RPG screamed past the sports car and obliterated a billboard advertising shoofly pie.

Still, the sudden evasive maneuver had caught the second assassin by surprise. The grenade launcher slipped from their grasp, clattered into the road, and discharged. The shot went well wide of us, nearly barbecued some cows in a pasture, then detonated in a pond, sending a geyser of water and startled trout into the air.

The cows didn't seem to notice anything unusual had happened. They continued grazing, unfazed, while fish plunked down around them.

The assassins weren't done yet, though. The driver regained control of the sports car and dropped in behind us once again. The shooter ducked back through the sunroof and came up with a machine gun. This was much smaller than a grenade launcher, but still capable of doing plenty of damage to the RV—or, more importantly, to *us*.

Meanwhile, our own grenade launcher was out of commission. Cyrus was struggling to get back to his feet and fire it again, but the weapon had somehow gotten jammed lengthwise in between the kitchen cabinets and the refrigerator. "Mary!" Cyrus shouted desperately. "Give them the slip!"

"Done!" Mary dutifully pressed a button on the RV's dashboard.

There was a hiss from the undercarriage of the Winnebago, and then two jets of oil spurted out from the rear bumper, coating the road behind us—as well as the windshield of the sports car and the shooter, whose top half was still sticking out of the sunroof. While the shooter spluttered and spat, the driver lost control of the car in the slick and skidded off the side of the road. The car smashed through a barbed-wire fence and plunged into a ditch, coming to such a sudden stop that the shooter launched out of the sunroof and plopped into a pig wallow.

We continued on down the road, unharmed, save for the gaping hole in Bertha's rear end.

At the front of the RV, Trixie looked frightened,

exhilarated, and terrified all at once. She had the wide-eyed appearance of someone who couldn't quite believe what was happening to her. "Whoa," she said with a gasp. "That was intense. I can't believe we got through that safely!"

Everyone else in the RV turned to her angrily. Including me.

Trixie grew confused. "What'd I do?" she asked.

"You just violated Twomey's Rule of Premature Gloating," Mike informed her. "When you say you're out of a situation too soon, you jinx it."

Trixie laughed. "You're all spies and you still think jinxes are real? What else do you believe in? Leprechauns? Fairies? Unicorns?"

At which point, another group of assassins attacked.

Gunfire burst from the side of the road. Luckily, spy school had trained us well for a situation exactly like this. All of us instantly dropped to the floor inside the RV—except Trixie, who Mike tackled. A line of bullets perforated the sides of the vehicle above our heads. Thankfully, none of us was hit, although the microwave in the kitchen was mortally wounded.

"Now look what you did!" Cyrus barked at Trixie angrily.

"This is not my fault!" she yelled back, curled in a ball on the floor. "There's no such thing as jinxes! This is just *really* bad luck!"

An engine roared, and a pickup truck jacked up on enormous tires trundled out of the woods and then swerved into the road behind us, taking up the chase. More gunfire erupted from it, peppering Bertha's rear end.

"I got this!" Mary announced, then hit the button for the oil slick again.

This time, a sickly wheeze came from the undercarriage of the RV, followed by the sound of something bursting. Instead of spurting out through the jets in the bumper, all the oil dropped into the road beneath us.

"They must have hit the oil repository!" Erica announced, bracing herself against the kitchen cabinets. "Hold on!"

Sure enough, the wheels of the RV skidded in our own oil slick. They lost purchase on the road, and the big, lumbering vehicle went into a spin. Our back end came around to where the front end should have been and then kept on going. It was like being on a merry-go-round that had broken loose from its moorings and was now careening down the road. The centrifugal force of the rotation flung all of us against the walls.

Meanwhile, the truck with the assassins was closing in on us, and Cyrus still couldn't free Penelope from where she was jammed between kitchen appliances. It didn't look like the weapon would be of any use . . .

Until I suddenly had an idea.

The RV continued spinning. In another few seconds, it was going to be sideways on the road.

I quickly made some mathematical calculations while scrambling into the kitchen. It was a struggle to move against the centrifugal force, but I made it to Cyrus and Penelope just in time.

"Look out," I warned Cyrus, and then pulled the trigger.

The grenade launcher discharged, blasting the entire refrigerator out of the RV. One second, the appliance was there, and the next, there was only a gaping hole in the side of the vehicle.

I was never very good with weapons. My Arms and Armaments professor had given me a D minus on my last exam, along with the comment that she wouldn't even allow me to use a stapler. It's extremely hard to fire a weapon accurately. Even if you're adept at calculating *where* to aim it, as I was, that doesn't guarantee you can hit the target. In spy movies, the good guys are always casually picking off bad guys without ever accidentally hitting anything else, like hostages or random passersby. That's not the way it works in real life.

Although things change when your weapon is a refrigerator.

It was like having a catapult instead of a bow and arrow. If I'd been at a medieval siege with a bow and arrow, I probably wouldn't have been able to hit my enemies at all. But if I'd launched a giant object with a catapult, not only was I more apt to do some damage, but I'd most likely scare the pants off anyone who saw it coming.

Which was exactly what happened with the refrigerator. I didn't really need to hit the assassins with it. All I needed was for them to *think* it might hit them. When you see a very large appliance heading for you at great speed, your general response is to get the heck out of the way.

Sure enough, the assassins took evasive action.

The refrigerator smashed into the road in front of them, leaving a divot the size of a bathtub, then cartwheeled onward like an enormous rectangular tumbleweed, shedding mechanical parts and food as it went. The freezer door flew into a tree while a family pack of frozen pizza rolls impaled itself on the horns of an extremely confused bull. The refrigerator clipped the rear end of the truck, ripping off the tailgate and sending the vehicle into a skid. Still, the assassin at the wheel was a skilled driver and might have wrestled the truck back under control if a value-size jar of mayonnaise hadn't slammed into the windshield. The jar exploded on impact, coating the window with a giant splotch of white goo; it was as if a bird the size of a 747 had suddenly pooped on the car. Blinded, the driver steered off the road, smashed through a fence, and plowed into a cornfield.

The RV spun around once more and finally came to a stop in the middle of the road.

We sat there for a moment in the battered vehicle, taking stock of our situation. Bertha was in bad shape; in addition to the huge holes torn in her sides, the engine was wheezing asthmatically. The road behind us was slicked with oil and strewn with evaporators, cabbages, and frozen dinners, while the crumpled hulk of the refrigerator lay on the shoulder, where some cattle regarded it curiously.

Still, we were alive.

"Nice going, Ben!" Zoe exclaimed.

"Yeah!" Mike chimed in. "You finally hit something with a weapon!"

"Don't get too excited yet," Cyrus said grumpily, then pointed through the gash where his refrigerator had once been.

The assassins were climbing out of their truck. They were dizzy and dazed but still otherwise all right.

"Grandma," Trixie said. "Get us out of here."

"I'm trying," Mary replied. She stomped on the gas, but nothing happened. "The fuel line must be busted."

"I've got this," Erica assured us, and grabbed the flame-thrower, which had tumbled out of the secret armory onto the floor.

But before she could even strap it on, a minivan skidded

to a stop on the road near the wrecked pickup. Erica and Trixie's parents, Alexander and Catherine Hale leapt out, aiming guns at the assassins.

"Put your hands in the air!" Alexander shouted dramatically. "You're under arrest!"

The assassins did as ordered.

I heaved a sigh of relief along with everyone else in the RV, thankful the ordeal was finally over.

Except Cyrus, who glowered at me and said, "You owe me a new refrigerator."

QUESTIONING

Kozy Korner Kampground

Southeastern Pennsylvania

June 11

2200 hours

Cyrus Hale was a decent mechanic and a staunch
believer than anything on earth could be fixed with duct tape.
The RV had two entire drawers full of it, along with plenty
of other tools. (It was notable that the kitchen drawers in
my house held useless junk like old batteries and chargers
for electronics we no longer owned, while the Hale family's
drawers held things like hand grenades and plastic explosives.) It didn't take Cyrus long to patch up the fuel line and
get Bertha running again—although the vehicle still was in

bad shape. It limped along the country roads, creaking and groaning, until we found a place to camp for the night.

That was the Kozy Korner Kampground, an RV park so run-down that even on a beautiful spring evening, almost no one else was using it. Although the surrounding area was forested, most of the trees on the property had been cut down to allow for as many RVs as possible, making it feel as though we were camping in a parking lot. There was a small food mart, a duck pond coated with a thick mat of scum, and a sewage disposal system that smelled as though it hadn't been serviced in at least a decade. The campsite entertainment was a literal dumpster fire; each night, all the guests' garbage was gathered and set ablaze. This event drew the attention of most of the other campers as well as what appeared to be every raccoon in the county.

Still, we appreciated the fire, because it distracted the other guests from the fact that we had prisoners.

In addition to the two assassins in the pickup truck, Alexander and Catherine had also captured the two with the sports car. The Hales had planned all along to rendezvous with us, but while trying to catch up to us, they had discovered that we'd left a trail of killers along the road. "Like Hansel and Gretel leaving breadcrumbs," Catherine observed, "only much more deadly." Fortunately, Catherine was extremely competent at trussing enemies (another good use of duct tape), and the minivan was spacious enough to hold all four prisoners comfortably. "We could even fit another two assassins in here," Alexander noted, then thought to add, "Not that we want another attack, of course."

We found a spot at the back corner of the campground and parked so that the RV shielded us from the view of the other sites. Then the Hale family arranged the prisoners in folding chairs around a campfire and set about interrogating them.

Before that day, I had met each of the Hales except Mary, but I had never seen them all together. I had tried to imagine what a family event like Thanksgiving or the Fourth of July might be like in a family full of spies, without much success. It was hard to picture them doing anything normal, like carving a turkey or playing Scrabble.

However, they were all in their element having a family interrogation.

Even Trixie, who had no spy training at all, seemed to be enjoying the show. She sat with Mike, Zoe, and me at our campsite's wobbly picnic bench, watching with rapt attention as her relatives got our captives to spill their guts.

It didn't take long. Cyrus, Mary, and Erica handled the questioning while Catherine made dinner. Since the only appliance that was still working in the RV was the toaster oven and all the fresh food had been lost along with the refrigerator, we had to settle for frozen pizza; Catherine bought every last one from the camp store. It was a crummy discount brand, but she worked some magic with spices and made up the dining area nicely with candles and sprigs of daisies.

Meanwhile, Cyrus, Mary, and Erica laid out an array of potential torture devices. These were really just tools, like socket wrenches and Phillips-head screwdrivers, or kitchen implements such as potato peelers and pizza cutters, but in the flickering light of the campfire, they looked menacing. The Hales would never have tortured anyone—Catherine wouldn't allow it—but even she wasn't above letting the assassins *think* that it might be done.

The two assassins from the sports car didn't look very concerned at first. The driver was a woman while the shooter was a man. They were athletic, stylishly dressed, and exuded both competence and disdain for us at once. Except for having their arms and legs bound with duct tape, they had the haughty, refined look of people at an art gallery filled with paintings they didn't like.

The assassins from the pickup truck appeared far more uneasy. They were both men, burly and imposing, wearing jeans and T-shirts. One had a thick, bushy beard while the other had really sunburned arms. As each kitchen implement was placed on the picnic table, the men grew more and more skittish. They shared worried looks and shifted about nervously.

Once the last of the "torture devices" had been laid out, Cyrus brandished a meat tenderizer and glared at the assassins through the fire, making sure that he was lit from below in the scariest way possible. "Here's how things will go tonight," he said in his most sinister voice. "I'm going to ask you some questions. You can make things easy on yourself and answer them right away. Or you can do it the hard way and hold out. But I promise you, I'll still get my answers—and your night isn't going to be any fun at all."

"I'm not saying anything," the well-dressed woman sneered defiantly.

"Neither am I," said the well-dressed man.

"What do you want to know?" asked the bearded guy.

The well-dressed assassins shifted their disdainful glares toward him.

"That's all it took to make you crack?" the well-dressed woman asked angrily.

"I don't want to get hit with a hammer!" Bearded Guy exclaimed.

"It's not a hammer," said Well-Dressed Man. "It's only a meat tenderizer."

"Which is basically a hammer," Bearded Guy said. "And it'll hurt!"

"You could at least try to hold out for more than thirty seconds," Well-Dressed Woman sniffed. "Where did you do your training?"

"Hey!" Cyrus snapped. "*I'm* the one asking the questions here!" He wheeled on Bearded Guy and Sunburned Guy. "Who are you working for?"

"Just ourselves," Sunburned Guy replied. "We're freelance. This is our first assassination."

The well-dressed assassins now looked even more disgusted. "You're amateurs?" the man asked in the same tone of voice other people might have asked, "You stepped in what?"

"Well, you have to start sometime, right?" Sunburned Guy shot back, sounding offended. "Everyone has a first day on the job." He returned his attention to Cyrus. "Me and Earl here have always been handy with guns . . ."

"Earl and I," Catherine corrected.

"Mother," Erica hissed under her breath. "There are more important things right now than proper grammar."

"Sorry," Catherine apologized. "Force of habit. But you know I hate it when people butcher the King's English."

"That's not nearly as bad as the fact that they tried to butcher *Ben*," Erica pointed out.

"Point well taken," Catherine said, then looked to Sunburned Guy. "Please proceed."

"Right," Sunburned Guy said. "So me and Earl . . . I

mean, Earl and I . . . have always been handy with guns, although we've never killed no humans before . . ."

Catherine cringed. I noticed Erica quickly put a hand on her arm, signaling her mother not to correct his grammar again.

"But we've killed plenty of animals," the bearded man, who we now knew was named Earl, added proudly. "Like deer and rabbits and squirrels and such. One time, in Montana, I even bagged a bighorn sheep! And then, this afternoon, we got word that there's a kid with a twenty-million-dollar bounty on his head . . ."

"How?" I blurted out, unable to control myself.

Cyrus gave me a hard stare. "Could I *please* conduct this interrogation without interruptions?"

"Sorry," I said. "Although it is *my* head that has the bounty on it. And I was just wondering how these guys found out."

"Benjamin does have a valid point, dear," Mary Hale said.

Cyrus sighed heavily. "Fine. How did you learn about the bounty?"

"The internet," Earl replied. "It's all over social media. Like *everywhere*. I mean, first, we heard that the kid over there was an alien-lizard thing, and then word came across that anyone who took him out would get twenty million bucks. So we figured, hey, we shoot lizards all the time! This isn't any different. The lizard's just bigger and evil. So why not do it?"

I groaned, realizing there were now sure to be plenty of other amateur assassins on the hunt for me as well.

The well-dressed assassins groaned too. "It's bad enough that we're up against every other professional assassin for this job," the man groused. "Now we have to compete against every pinhead with a shotgun and an internet connection?"

"I'm no pinhead!" Earl snapped. "I've got a PhD in sociology from Harvard, for Pete's sake!" Then he glared at Cyrus. "Why are you even helping this kid? Are you one of those lizard things too?"

Cyrus stiffened, offended. "Are you calling me a traitor? Because no one has done as much for this country as I have . . ."

Mary coughed conspicuously.

". . . except my wife," Cyrus added quickly, then pointed to me. "That boy is not an alien, and he is not part of any plot against the government. You've been hoodwinked by a con man, and I want the details of how it happened. If I don't get them, I'm gonna get angry." He whacked the picnic table with the meat tenderizer so loud that it spooked a few passing raccoons, which squealed and scampered into the underbrush.

Sunburned Guy and Earl both looked worried as well.

The well-dressed assassins fixed them with icy stares. "Don't tell them anything else!" the woman ordered. "You've said way too much already! And frankly, you're making all of us look bad."

"One more word out of you and I'll duct-tape an opossum to your face," Cyrus said in a tone that indicated he would actually do it.

The well-dressed woman clammed up.

Cyrus turned back to the amateurs and let the firelight glint off the meat tenderizer. "Start talking."

"Okay," Sunburned Guy said quickly. "This person known as X has been posting about Ben Ripley on a website we frequent. X is the one who first claimed that Ripley was a traitor—and for a while, only X seemed to know where he could be found. But now lots of other people are tracking Ripley too. There's Facebook groups and Twitter streams and whole web pages devoted to it."

"How are they keeping tabs on him?" Catherine asked.

"Well, the entire anti-alien community is on the lookout," Earl explained. "If anyone thinks they've seen Ben, they post about it online. And then other folks sift through all the posts and suggest which ones they think are the most trustworthy. Like CalamariLover."

"CalamariLover?" I repeated, thinking that I hadn't heard it right.

"Yeah," Sunburned Guy confirmed. "Calamari. Like fried squid. He's on a site called RipleyTracker that only started up today. He reported that Ben was heading for Philadelphia and put out word to people there to keep an eye out for him. Then someone spotted you getting into a Winnebago around Independence Hall. CalamariLover said that was credible and then suggested you might be headed in this direction. He even thought you might be coming up the very route we ambushed you on. Me and Earl were . . ." He noticed Catherine tense up and quickly corrected himself. "Earl and I don't live far away, so we figured we could catch you by surprise. We just weren't expecting you to lob a refrigerator at us."

"Yeah, that was a surprise to me, too." Cyrus gave me a sidelong glance to let me know he still wasn't happy about that.

"Hold on now," Mike said, his face screwed up in confusion. "How could CalamariLover know the exact route we were going to take out of Philadelphia? There were a thousand different ways we could have gone."

"Maybe there was a mole on our team," Erica said suspiciously.

"Erica!" Catherine exclaimed. "Everyone on this team is either a close friend or a family member of yours."

"You can't trust anyone," Erica replied.

Even though Erica was being ridiculously paranoid, I didn't have a better explanation. After all, we had been betrayed by close friends before.

But then, Zoe said, "CalamariLover is Murray Hill."

"How do you figure that?" Mary asked.

"Because *I'm* Calamari," Zoe replied in a voice thick with disgust. "It was his nickname for me, back when we first met."

"I don't remember him ever calling you that," I said.

"Because I hated it and told him that if he didn't stop, I'd bust his nose. This was before you got to spy school. You know how I like to give everyone nicknames? Well, Murray thought I ought to have one too. And since my eyes are kind of big, he used to joke that I was like a giant squid, because they have the biggest eyes of any animal on earth. Fried squid is calamari, so that's what he called me. And on your last mission, you discovered that Murray's been crushing on me. So that makes him CalamariLover."

"Ugh," Trixie said. "That's the least romantic story of a pet name I've ever heard."

"Murray is as romantic as an intestinal parasite," Zoe said. "It's one of the several thousand reasons I will never date that weasel. The main one being that he's evil, of course."

"But how can Murray be CalamariLover?" Alexander asked, perplexed. "I thought he was X."

"You can be as many people as you want on the internet," I answered. "It certainly explains how CalamariLover knew what route we'd be taking. That road was the most direct path from Philadelphia to Falcon Ridge. Murray must have figured that we're coming for him and put the information online so anyone could ambush us on the way."

Everyone else mulled that over, then nodded agreement.

"That little scoundrel," the professional female assassin growled. "We passed up a perfectly good job in Argentina for this mission, and then Murray open-sources it to amateurs? It's insulting for us to be in contention with these incompetent laymen."

Earl bristled. "Cool it with the attitude, lady. You're no better than we are. You failed to kill the kid too."

"So far," the woman said—and then she lunged at me.

To my surprise, she had somehow sawed through her duct-tape bonds during the interrogation. In half a second, she had knocked Cyrus aside, swiped a steak knife off the table, and was poised to gut me with it.

Luckily for me, she had unwisely chosen to do this in front of the entire Hale family. In the next half of the same second, Erica, Catherine, and Mary Hale all intercepted the assassin at once and knocked her flat on her back. Mary pinned her legs and Catherine secured her arms while Erica wrested the knife from her, then knelt on her chest, placed the blade to her throat, and snarled, "Try anything like that again and I'll rip off your head and feed it to the raccoons."

"Understood," the female assassin said, looking both intimidated and impressed. "You're all in incredible shape. What's your secret? Pilates?"

Erica ignored the question. "Beardy McBeardface told us how he found out where we were. How'd *you* do it?"

The woman hesitated to answer. So Erica grabbed a piece of pizza off the table, then smeared it on her face and called out, "Dinnertime!"

Several raccoons that had been lurking around the campsite perked up eagerly.

"Okay!" the woman shouted. "I'll tell you! We learned about it from a different chat group!"

"This one's called AssassiNation," her accomplice offered helpfully. "It's a clandestine online forum for professional killers, hitmen, and mercenaries where we can discuss things like job opportunities, contract issues, and the best ways to dispose of a body. Someone named MegaBrain posted that you might be taking this road."

"That sounds like Murray too," I said with a sigh. "He always wants everyone to know how clever he is."

The Hale women hoisted the female assassin off the ground and bent her over the picnic table. Erica and Catherine duct-taped her wrists together again while Mary frisked her, quickly coming up with a small razor blade she had concealed in her shirtsleeve. "This is how she cut herself loose," Mary deduced, then used a set of pliers to crumple the razor.

The female assassin started to say something, but Erica slapped a strip of duct tape over her mouth before she could. "If Murray has been spreading the word that we came this way, we should expect more assassins. And soon."

Even though I had already presumed this, her words still made my stomach churn.

"Maybe not," Catherine said reassuringly. "We're a good distance away from that route and quite well concealed back here . . ."

"Still, it makes sense to be prepared for trouble," Cyrus concluded. He cast a gaze over the other three assassins. "I think we've heard all we need to from these scumbags. Gag 'em."

"Sure thing." Erica grinned and tore off another strip of duct tape.

While she muted the assassins—who protested mightily until their lips were forcibly sealed—Alexander said, "I'm still confused. What's the point of Murray having so many personalities online? Why not just have one?"

"Because many people are more convincing than just one person," Mike explained. "If Murray only posts as X, some people might believe him, but a lot of others might not. However, if Murray pretends to be dozens of different people and forms a chorus supporting X, now it looks like a movement is starting. It's like those polar-bear plunges, where people go swimming in freezing water in the middle of winter. No one ever does that on their own. Because it's a terrible idea. They only do it in groups. It's still a terrible idea, but it's a lot harder to say no to something when lots of other people are doing it."

"Very true, Michael," Catherine agreed sadly. "People are much more likely to behave badly when they're part of a crowd than on their own."

"But something still doesn't add up," I said. "To pose as all these people requires internet access and a lot of time online. Plus, within seconds of Zoe posting on The Truth, Murray counterattacked. Which means he must have been on the internet at that very moment. So how is he doing all this if he's in prison?"

"We'll find out first thing tomorrow morning," Cyrus answered. "When we see him at Falcon Ridge."

ANTICIPATION

Kozy Korner Kampground

Southeastern Pennsylvania

June 12

0500 hours

I dreamed about zombies.

It was terrifying. They were chasing me all over the countryside, trying to catch and eat me.

I woke up in a pool of sweat.

And then I realized that my reality was even scarier than my dream had been.

It really stinks when your waking life is worse than your nightmares.

As a precaution against assassination attempts, I had not

slept in the Winnebago. None of us had. It was an obvious target and too big to conceal.

Luckily, Cyrus Hale had come prepared. The RV was stocked with camping supplies. There were tents and sleeping bags for all of us, and they had only sustained minor damage in our gunfight. They all had a few holes, but were otherwise usable.

We didn't want our captured assassins around, plotting to escape and kill me in my sleep, so Alexander and Catherine bundled them into the minivan and headed to Harrisburg to drop them off at the FBI office there.

The rest of us tramped a quarter mile into the woods around the Kozy Korner, found a spot on a wooded hill that the Hales felt would be easy to defend in case of attack, and bedded down for the night. Mike and I were given one tent. Cyrus and Mary took another. The three girls crammed into a third.

It had been difficult for me to fall asleep, as I had been on edge after the day's events. Now that I was awake again, shaken from my nightmare, I felt the chances of me getting any more rest were unlikely. I couldn't help but imagine that the woods were full of assassins. And I was also experiencing Hogarth's First Rule of Camping: Once you are nice and warm and comfortable in your sleeping bag, you will immediately have to pee.

Beside me, Mike was sleeping peacefully, cuddling his pillow with a blissful smile on his face. "Ooh!" he murmured. "I've always wanted a baby panda!"

Taking care not to wake him, I quietly unzipped my sleeping bag, pulled on my sneakers, and slipped out of the tent. The late spring night was still warm, and the air had the lovely scent of pine trees. A thousand fireflies danced through the trees, blinking on and off. If I hadn't been terrified for my life, the moment might have been magical.

I went a good distance away from the other tents, did my business—and suddenly had the feeling that I was being watched. I tensed, listening to the world around me. I could hear thousands of crickets, the gentle flow of a breeze through the trees, and Cyrus's raucous snoring, which sounded like a bear being strangled.

And then, only a few feet behind me, I heard a footstep.

I whirled around, saw a dark shape right behind me, and went on the attack, using Nook-Bhan-San. First, I performed the Wily Monkey Feint, followed by Duck Like the Wind, and then a sudden shift into the Hundred Fists of Fury.

My opponent immediately responded with the Lightning Foot Sweep, knocking my legs out from under me. I landed flat on my back, and then the assailant dropped onto my chest and slapped a hand over my mouth before I could scream for help.

"It's a good thing you have the rest of us around to protect you," Zoe told me. "Because you stink at fighting."

"I know," I said, although it came out more like "Mly ppphhlow," because Zoe's hand was over my mouth.

Zoe took her hand away and helped me to my feet. "What were you doing out of your tent?"

"I couldn't sleep—and I had to pee."

"Hogarth's First Rule of Camping. Me too. I went the other direction. I was coming back when I saw you over here."

"Why didn't you just say hi?"

"I didn't want to startle you. I thought coming up to you quietly would be the better thing to do."

I rubbed my aching neck. "It wasn't."

"Yes, I see that now. Are you going back to sleep?"

"I don't think that's likely. And it's going to be daylight soon anyhow." I pointed to the east. The sky was lightening ever so slightly.

"Good point. Might as well watch the sunrise." Zoe found a nice, mossy log beside a maple tree, sat down, and waved to the spot next to her.

She smiled pleasantly, but it looked faked to me. I took the seat next to her and asked, "You're upset about being dragged into all this, aren't you?"

"Well, sure. It's no fun to have every conspiracy theorist in the world think you're an alien."

That all made sense, but I had the feeling that Zoe was holding something back. "What else is wrong?"

"Nothing," she said quickly.

"You can tell me. I'm your friend."

Zoe averted her eyes, like she was ashamed. "It's dumb, really. Especially compared to all your problems. I mean, it's not like anyone has targeted me for assassination."

"That doesn't mean it's not important."

Zoe sighed. "It's just that, everyone on this mission is in a couple except me. You're with Erica now, Mike and Trixie are a thing, and then there's Cyrus and Mary and Alexander and Catherine . . ."

"Alexander and Catherine aren't together anymore."

"Oh please. They've obviously patched things up. Didn't you see how they looked at each other while they were apprehending the assassins?"

"Er . . . no."

"Trust me, they're back together. Which means I'm like the ninth wheel here. Meanwhile, the people who *do* like me are all jerks like Murray Hill and Warren Reeves." Zoe flicked a pebble with her finger, sending it flying into the night. "Why can't someone who's not evil ever like me?"

"Technically, Warren Reeves fell for you while he was still good," I pointed out. "In fact, the whole reason he became evil was because you liked me instead of him."

Zoe shot me an annoyed look. "That's really not helpful."

"Sorry." I plucked a few blades of grass, feeling awkward. My relationship with Zoe was complicated. I had always liked Erica, and Zoe had always liked me. A few months earlier, when Erica had told me that she didn't think spies should have relationships, I had considered starting something with Zoe. Zoe had told me to figure things out, and then Erica had changed her mind and we had become a couple. Zoe and I had never discussed that—largely because I had done everything possible to avoid the subject.

"You're a really great person," I said finally. "You're smart and funny and much better at fighting than me . . ."

"There are asthmatic goldfish that are better at fighting than you."

"I'm sure that someone's going to notice all that about you someday. Someone who isn't evil."

Zoe nodded, then looked at me with her big, beautiful eyes. "If Erica didn't exist, though, we'd be a thing, right?"

I hesitated before answering, uneasy with the question. "Er . . . I guess. Although if Erica didn't exist, I would have been dead fourteen times over already. So I wouldn't really be a very good boyfriend."

"I suppose I owe her thanks, then. Because without her, I wouldn't have my best friend." Zoe smiled sadly at me.

"Aw, gee, Zoe, that's really sweet of you to say," I said.

"It sure is," Erica agreed.

Zoe and I both screamed in surprise and practically leapt out of our skin.

Erica emerged from the shadows only a few feet away from us.

"How long have you been hiding there?" I asked, clutching my heart in fear.

"All night. I wasn't about to go to sleep while there's assassins trying to kill you."

"But . . . ," Zoe stammered. "Last night, you went to sleep in the tent . . ."

"I only acted like it. To throw off any assassins who might be eavesdropping. Then I slipped out and stood watch."

"And you've been standing there on guard all night?" I asked.

"Most of it. I did a few patrols of the perimeter. I chased off some raccoons that were trying to steal our Doritos. And I captured those three assassins." Erica pointed into the darkness. Sure enough, there were three unconscious people, laid out on the ground, their arms and legs bound with duct tape.

Zoe gaped at them, then looked to me. "Apparently, Erica's saved your life *seventeen* times over."

There was a sudden yelp from back by our tents, followed by a howl of pain.

Zoe and I wheeled around, startled, although Erica didn't seem particularly concerned.

"What was that?" I asked worriedly. "Another assassin?"

"No," Erica replied. "That was Mike."

I quickly got to my feet and hurried back, followed by the girls. We found Mary Hale pinning Mike to a tree, one hand clenched around his neck, the other holding a machete. She noticed us arriving and said, "I caught this scoundrel trying to sneak into Trixie's tent."

"It was an accident!" Mike protested weakly. "I got up to pee and then got confused as to which tent was which."

"Don't give me that malarkey," Mary snapped. "I know exactly what you were doing."

Trixie emerged from her tent, alerted by all the commotion, still tangled up in her sleeping bag. "Grandma!" she exclaimed. "Please don't strangle my boyfriend!"

"I'm not gonna kill him," Mary assured her. "I'm just letting him know he'd better watch his step around my family."

"I get the picture," Mike gasped. "Can you let go of my neck now?"

At this point, Cyrus appeared from his tent as well, roused by all the noise and extremely irritated. "Keep it down, everyone!" he demanded. "Do you want to alert every assassin in the country that we're here?"

At which point, the RV exploded.

Even though we were a quarter mile away, the fireball was big enough to light up the night. And it was loud enough to startle all of us into silence. There was a great burst of flame, which sent what remained of the vehicle and its appliances careening into the sky.

"Bertha!" Mary exclaimed. She released Mike, who sank to the ground, clutching his neck.

Trixie ran to his side and cradled him in her arms.

In the distance, the RV was blazing, its twisted hulk silhouetted against the flames. A thick column of smoke rose into the predawn sky.

"What just happened?" I asked.

"Looks like some assassins found Bertha," Cyrus reported. "Good thing I booby-trapped her."

Mary turned on him, upset. "You blew up our camper?"

"No," Cyrus said. "I only rigged it to explode in case of trouble. The assassins blew it up." Mary started to argue, but Cyrus quickly cut her off. "I'm not happy to lose Bertha either. She was a good RV. But let's face it, after today, she wasn't in great shape. We were gonna have to put the old girl down."

Mary lowered her head sadly, as if in mourning.

A scorched and twisted hubcap fell through the trees and landed, smoking, on the ground between us all.

Mary said, "I don't know this Murray Hill character, but I'm gonna make him pay for all the trouble he's caused."

"Sounds good to me," Cyrus agreed. "Let's go see him."

INFILTRATION

Mockingbird Motor Lodge/Falcon Ridge Federal Penitentiary

Southeastern Pennsylvania

June 12

0800 hours

Cyrus was the only one who went to Falcon Ridge.

There were two reasons for this. First and foremost, it was dangerous. If Murray had tipped off his network of professional and amateur assassins that I was heading to the penitentiary, then it followed that at least some of them would be staking it out. So it was in my best interest to stay as far from the place as possible.

Second, Falcon Ridge was a supermax prison with high security. "If I show up with a bunch of kids in tow, it'll raise eyebrows," Cyrus explained. "They're not gonna buy the 'It's Take Your Family to Work Day' routine at this place."

Catherine and Alexander had returned from Harrisburg shortly after Bertha exploded, but it still made sense to send Cyrus in. He had high security clearance, while Catherine, a British MI6 agent, did not. He had field experience, while Mary, an analyst, did not. And he had competence, while Alexander, a screwup, did not. Plus, he had delivered Murray to Falcon Ridge in the first place, so he was known there.

The rest of us piled into a cheap motel from which we could monitor Cyrus's mission remotely. The Mockingbird Motor Lodge was a rickety two-story L of rooms that hooked around a murky swimming pool, sixteen miles from Falcon Ridge. Even though the place was run-down, it was still fully booked, as an air show at the local airfield had drawn plenty of tourists.

That wasn't a problem. We had never planned to officially check into a room anyhow. That would have drawn the attention of the motel staff. Instead, we "borrowed" a room. We staked out the motel from the minivan until we saw a tourist family leave for the day. It was evident they were going to the air show, as everyone was wearing T-shirts featuring planes, and we could tell they had the room booked all day, because they left their bags. Five minutes after they left, Catherine easily jimmied the lock on their door, and we all slipped inside.

Zoe hung the DO NOT DISTURB sign on the doorknob. "To keep the maid service from coming in," she explained.

"I don't think we have to worry about that," Erica said, casting a wary eye over the room. "Looks like maid service here is about as common as a solar eclipse."

I had to agree. The furniture was all chipped and scarred, cobwebs dangled from the ceiling, and the carpet was threadbare and stained. Meanwhile, the tourist family's clothes were strewn everywhere, as though each of their suitcases had exploded. Dirty T-shirts, shorts, and underwear covered the unmade beds, the chairs, and much of the floor.

Still, the room served our needs. There was a decent Wi-Fi connection and just enough space for all of us. We set up Mary's computer, and then Cyrus headed off to Falcon Ridge in the minivan.

The plan was simple. Cyrus would use his security clearance to gain access to the prison and meet with Murray. Then he would get Murray to call off the assassination and refute all the conspiracy claims he had made as X.

Of course, I still had my doubts that Murray was actually there. But it was evident that the Hales thought otherwise and were tired of hearing me question them. So I kept my mouth shut and hoped that they were right. It was certainly possible that I was just being paranoid; after all, Cyrus had seen Falcon Ridge for himself, whereas I hadn't, so if he said it was impossible to escape, then perhaps it was. Still, if I had learned one thing in the spy game, it was that missions rarely went according to plan. While I tried to look calm and supportive on the outside, I was nervous and jittery on the inside.

Normally, Cyrus would have allowed us to keep tabs on his mission by wearing a small radio microphone in his ear. But this time, he was using his phone. The idea was for him to make a video call and covertly film everything. He also wore Bluetooth earbuds so that we could feed him questions. The earbuds were cleverly designed to look like hearing aids. However, this didn't work quite as well as we had hoped.

Like many grandparents, Cyrus wasn't adept with technology. He kept accidentally switching the view on the phone, so that instead of filming what was in front of him, he recorded things like the palm of his hand, his shoes, or worst of all, the interior of his very hairy nostrils. Erica was tasked with coaching him through this, as he was less likely to get annoyed with her than anyone else. Even so, he still was repeatedly defensive and curt as he arrived at Falcon Ridge.

I had seen some ugly places in my life, but the supermax penitentiary had them all beat. It was like a black hole that had sucked all the ugly out of the surrounding states and concentrated it in one spot.

For starters, it had been built in a ghastly location, a flat plain of dirt a half mile across that was devoid of any plant life whatsoever; not a tree, not a bush, not even a blade of grass. I had never seen anywhere so lifeless.

Then, the penitentiary itself was a complex of exceptionally unattractive, blocky brown buildings. These were surrounded by two separate imposing metal fences spaced ten feet apart with nothing but a stretch of barren ground between them. Every hundred yards along them was a guard tower. The fences were both topped with electrified razor wire.

I couldn't tell any of this from Cyrus's video, though, because Cyrus had the camera oriented in the wrong direction once again, showing the minivan's cup holders as he pulled into the parking lot. Instead, I was looking at photos of Falcon Ridge that Alexander had brought up on his phone.

"Uh, Grandpa," Erica said, "could you change the view on your phone so we can see where you're going?"

"I *am* showing you where I'm going," Cyrus replied testily.

"Er . . . no you're not," Erica told him. "We're looking at the cup holders."

"What? Dang phone must be on the fritz." Cyrus parked the van and then fiddled with the phone for a bit. "Is this better?"

"No," Erica answered. "Now we're looking at your ear."

Cyrus cursed, then fiddled with the phone some more, aiming the camera at the steering wheel, the sky, and up his nose again before finally managing to get it pointed in the right direction. He then exited the van and started across the parking lot.

"Looks like we made the right call not bringing Benjamin here," he reported. "There's a sniper positioned on the hill way up yonder. See?" He attempted to show us with the phone, but accidentally flipped the camera view again.

"Sorry, but we don't," Erica told him. "You're filming your hand."

"No I'm not."

"You *are*, Grandpa."

"This darn phone is defective."

"You need to switch the camera direction again."

"There. Is that better?"

"No. Now all we can see is the ground."

Cyrus cursed some more. Then he randomly poked at his phone, which resulted in him raising the volume to deafening levels, sending Erica a text that said "mazgblreg," and ultimately, accidentally hanging up on the call.

Erica sighed heavily. "This is not going well."

"This is *nothing*," Trixie told her. "I've been with Grandpa for the last few weeks. You should see him try to work the TV remote. It can take him half a day to change the channel."

"Your grandfather has never been very good with technology," Mary recalled. "He was a great spy, but hopeless with electronics. The first time he ever had to use a microfilm camera, every single photo was just a blurry view of his thumb."

"How'd he ever get by?" Mike asked.

"It was a different time," Mary answered. "Electronics weren't as important back then. It was common for Cyrus to go undercover for months without making so much as a phone call."

"That must have been rough on both of you," Zoe observed.

"It certainly was," Mary agreed. "But while technology does have many advantages, there are plenty of problems with it as well. A conspiracy theory like the one being used against all of you would never have spread so quickly before the internet existed. When the internet started, everyone thought it would be an incredible way to share information. But almost no one realized how well it could be used to spread *disinformation*, too."

Erica managed to reconnect with Cyrus, who grumbled as he struggled to operate his phone. "We didn't need all this newfangled gadgetry in my day. The only things I needed to be a successful spy were my wits, my smarts, and a lot of gumption."

"And I'm sure everyone at the CIA was very proud of you," Erica said diplomatically. "Try pressing the icon at the bottom right of your screen."

Cyrus must have done this, because the view from the camera switched so that it was facing the proper direction. "How's that?"

"Very good," Erica told him. "Now place the phone in the breast pocket of your jacket so that the camera will record everything that you're seeing."

The image jumped around nauseatingly for a bit, but eventually steadied as Cyrus got the phone situated properly. Finally, we had a decent view of the front gates of the prison across the parking lot.

"That's perfect!" Erica said. "Keep the phone right there! Don't touch it again!"

"I'm not a child," Cyrus snapped. "I know how to use a phone."

Trixie rolled her eyes at this.

Cyrus continued toward the gates. The camera jostled as he walked, but continued to display Falcon Ridge and its barren surroundings.

"What happened to that place?" I asked. "Did they cut down the entire forest when they built the prison?"

"No," Mary replied. "The coal industry had already razed it. In fact, there used to be a small mountain where that prison sits. The miners shaved the top right off it. That's why there's no longer any ridge at Falcon Ridge. Or falcons, for that matter. After they were done, there was just a big, ugly, denuded strip of land polluted by coal runoff. It was the perfect place to build a prison. No one else wanted anything to do with it."

"The builders also saw the lack of trees as an asset," Catherine explained. "They prefer clear lines of sight around a prison, so if anyone manages to make it past the fences, there's nothing for them to hide behind."

Cyrus was now approaching the double set of fences, so we had a good look at the ten feet of desolate ground between them. It was all sand, raked into neat furrows.

"What's the deal with the raking?" Mike asked.

"It's obviously a Zen garden," Alexander said knowingly. "Like the Chinese use. Very clever of them to surround a prison with one. They're very calming. I bet it helps prevent prison-yard fights and riots."

"Not quite, dear," Catherine said in the tone a mother would use with a kindergartner who had just botched reciting the alphabet. "It's not a Zen garden. And those are from Japan."

"It's to display footprints better," Trixie said. "So the guards can tell if anyone got past the first fence somehow."

"Ah," Alexander said, looking embarrassed.

Mike grinned at Trixie, impressed. "How'd you know that?"

"I know a lot of stuff," Trixie informed him. "Just because I'm the only one in my family who's not a spy doesn't mean I'm dumb."

"I know you're not," Mike said. "And I like that you're smart."

"Aww," Trixie cooed. "You're sweet."

"Ick," Erica and Zoe said at the same time.

Cyrus arrived at the front gates of the penitentiary, where a guard was posted inside a large security booth. The gates were great big iron-barred structures, each twelve feet high.

While Cyrus might not have been skilled with new technology, his espionage skills were immediately on display.

The first thing about him was his demeanor. Cyrus carried himself in a way that demanded respect. The guard at the gate snapped to attention upon seeing him and immediately tried to serve his needs.

The next thing Cyrus did was project confidence. He flashed his badge and announced, "Agent Cyrus Hale, Central Intelligence Agency. I'm here to see prisoner Murray Hill."

The guard immediately checked the logbook and grew concerned. "I'm sorry, Agent Hale. I don't have you scheduled here for today."

"Of course you don't," Cyrus said. "This is a top secret operation."

"What's its purpose?" the guard asked.

"If I told you the purpose, then it wouldn't be top secret, would it?" Even though I couldn't see Cyrus, I knew he was giving the guard one of his patented icy stares.

The guard withered under his gaze. "I suppose not, sir."

"Feel free to run my ID and make sure I'm on the up-and-up," Cyrus told him. "Then send me through the metal detectors and frisk me down. I'm unarmed—and I'm not here to break Murray Hill out. In fact, I'm the one who brought him here in the first place. Feel free to verify that. I want that son of a gun to grow old and gray in here. But it's of national importance that I speak to him right now. So it'd be wise of you to not make any waves."

"Of course," the guard replied. "Hold on, sir."

He took Cyrus's identification, ducked back into the booth, and made a call. He was gone for two and a half minutes, and when he returned, he looked ashamed and embarrassed. "I'm sorry, Agent Hale, but I can't allow you inside."

The feeling in the motel room grew tense.

"Why the heck not?" Cyrus snapped. "You checked out my credentials, didn't you?"

"Y-yes," the guard stammered. "And they're fine . . ."

"Then why aren't you letting me in? I'm here on a crucial mission!"

"The warden's coming out to explain."

"The warden?" Cyrus repeated, confused.

A sinking sensation was growing in my gut—and it appeared that everyone else in the room was feeling the same way. Except Alexander, who seemed to have lost focus on the mission and was distracted by the landscaping of the prison.

"Maybe that isn't a Zen garden," he observed. "But it's still very calming. I think I may put one of those in the yard."

On the feed from Cyrus's phone, a red light flashed in the guard booth. "The warden's coming now," the guard said, looking extremely relieved that someone far senior to him was on their way.

Beyond the front gates, it looked to be about fifty yards to the first prison building. The path was a bland corridor of asphalt, flanked by more fences. A stout, florid man emerged from the guarded doors of the building. He wore a three-piece suit that gave the impression of authority and had an official badge clipped to the lapel. He walked the length of the corridor until he arrived at the gates, but he did not pass through them. Instead, he stayed on the other side and spoke to Cyrus through the bars.

"Hello, Agent Hale," he said. "It's good to see you again."

"Drop the fake friendly act, Warden," Cyrus snapped. "And let me in to see Hill."

I got the sense that he was leveling another one of his icy stares, but the warden appeared immune to it. "That's simply not possible."

"Of course it is. And you're going to see to it that it happens right away . . ."

"No I'm not. I can't. It's not possible for you to see Murray Hill because he's not here."

"I knew it!" I exclaimed before I could stop myself.

Everyone in the room wheeled on me at once. There were a wide variety of emotions. Mike, Zoe, and Trixie looked concerned. Erica, Mary, and Catherine looked somewhat embarrassed. Alexander looked confused, as though I had just interrupted the mental planning of his Zen garden.

On the video, Cyrus spoke brusquely to the warden. "What are you saying? That Hill escaped?"

"Certainly not," the warden replied. "No one has ever escaped from Falcon Ridge. Murray Hill was never here in the first place."

"Of course he was! I brought him here myself!"

"That's what the official records say, of course, but . . . sometimes the records aren't completely accurate." The warden gave Cyrus a loaded stare. It seemed he wanted Cyrus to understand something without him saying it.

Erica grasped what he was getting at. "Oh no," she said.

"Where's Murray Hill?" Cyrus demanded.

"I have no idea," the warden replied. "And even if I did, you know I couldn't tell you. Sorry that this has been a waste of your time." With that, he turned away and headed back to the prison.

Cyrus called after him. "You have to give me more than that! National security is at stake!"

The warden ignored him and kept on walking.

I sat on one of the sagging motel beds, overwhelmed. "I knew it," I said again, softer this time. "I told all of you, but you didn't believe me. Murray Hill can weasel himself out of anything." I knew I wasn't being a good team member by pointing out that so many of the others had been wrong, but I couldn't help it. For the first time in my life, I had really been hoping that I wasn't right. And now that I *was* right, I was terrified. Without Murray's help, I was a goner.

"I don't understand," Mike said. "The warden just admitted that Cyrus brought Murray to Falcon Ridge. So why isn't Murray there?"

"Perhaps he was abducted by aliens?" Alexander suggested. "The government would definitely keep that hushed up."

"No," Erica said. "Isn't it obvious? Murray cut a deal with the government. He must have turned over evidence to avoid going to jail."

Mike blinked at her, stunned. "They put that jerk in the Federal Witness Protection Program?"

"Looks that way," Catherine said sadly.

"Then how do we find Murray now?" Zoe asked.

Catherine and Erica shared a look of concern.

"I don't know," Erica said.

ANALYSIS

Mockingbird Motor Lodge

Wickham, Pennsylvania

June 12

0830 hours

"Can't we just ask someone in the Federal Wit-ness Protection Program where Murray is?" Mike asked.

"Unfortunately, no," Alexander replied. For once, he appeared to know what he was talking about. "The whole point of the program is to provide safety and security for the people in it. That means their locations and new identities can never be given out, not even to other members of the government, and not even for national security issues."

"That doesn't make any sense," I said heatedly.

"Your own parents are in the program," Alexander reminded me. "Would you feel safe if any government employee could learn of their new identities?"

"No," I admitted. "But this is different. My parents are in the Witness Protection Program *because* of people like Murray. Murray shouldn't be entitled to the same protection that they are. He's a jerk." I slumped on the bed, stewing angrily.

Everyone else in the room seemed similarly frustrated—except Mary Hale. She appeared strangely excited, despite everything that had happened.

"Now, don't fret, Benjamin," she said. "Despite the warden's sentiments, this mission wasn't entirely a fool's errand. I suspected that something like this might be the case."

I sat back up on the bed and gaped at her. "You agreed with me that Murray might not be there?"

"Well, I certainly hoped that wouldn't be the case. But a good agent must be prepared for any eventuality."

"Why didn't you say you agreed with me, then?" I asked.

"It would only have upset you. I mean, look at you right now. You're practically having a heart attack, you poor dear. I didn't want to put you through that."

"But I'm going through it *now*," I pointed out.

"Yes," Mary admitted. "And if Murray had been at Falcon Ridge, you would have been spared this. Sadly, that didn't turn out to be the case. But let's see if we can do something about that." She turned her attention back to her computer.

Cyrus was still recording, although now his video feed showed the parking lot of Falcon Ridge as he stormed away from the penitentiary. We could hear him grouching about how many nincompoops there were in the government.

"Cyrus, dear," Mary said. "Did you get his identification?"

"Of course I did," Cyrus replied. "You think I'm gonna come all this way for nothing?" He held up the warden's ID card. Apparently, he had nicked it off the man's lapel while he was at the gate.

Mary laughed. "Ooh! I love it when you're devious. Hold that up to the camera so that I can get a screenshot of it."

It took Cyrus a little while to do this. Instead of just holding the ID card in front of the camera, he tried to hold the camera over the ID card and thus ended up filming his chin, some garbage in the parking lot, and the zipper of his pants. But eventually, he managed to get Mary what she needed: a clear shot of the warden's ID and all the information on it.

"Thanks, darling," Mary chirped cheerfully. "Hurry back. Time is of the essence."

Then she went to work at the computer, her fingers dancing across the keyboard.

Trixie turned to her, intrigued. "Grandma, can you really find out where Murray is?"

"Watch and learn," Mary replied. "When things get tough, that's when you need an analyst."

We all gathered around to see what she was doing. She was obviously far more adept with technology than her husband was. She was also far more adept than me—and possibly any of my fellow spy school students. She was opening screens and entering information faster than I could follow, although I caught glimpses of few log-in pages, a directory of federal employees, and the home page for the US Marshals Service, which ran the Federal Witness Protection Program.

I began to feel somewhat hopeful again, although it was still annoying to think that the very person who was causing so much trouble for me was being protected by my own government, rather than being punished for his crimes. "What information do you think Murray gave up to get into witness protection?"

Erica said, "They wouldn't have let him out of jail unless he gave up plenty. And given that Murray is a skunk with no loyalty to anyone but himself, I'm sure he was happy to rat out every person he ever worked with. He probably gave up anyone involved with SPYDER, the Croatoan, and any other evil organization he's worked for."

Zoe added, "Knowing Murray, I'll bet he made up a few other evil organizations just to have extra info to give away."

"Hmm," Mary said suddenly. She had stopped typing

and was studying a web page that looked like a bunch of random gobbledygook to me. It seemed to make sense to Mary, though.

"Is there a problem, Mom?" Alexander asked, concerned.

"Only a slight hiccup. I think I've got a workaround." Mary grabbed her phone and dialed the number of someone in her contacts. When they answered, Mary spoke pleasantly. "Annie? It's Mary Hale. How are the grandkids? . . . Oh, mine are too. Growing like weeds. Listen, I'm doing some freelance work and I need a little bit of info. I've got a form 36C-97 here that has a blank space on it. . . . I know sometimes that's done on purpose, but I really think this is a mistake. I have authorization from Warden Moore at Falcon Ridge supermax to track it down. Here's his official ID number . . ." She rattled that off, along with several other pieces of information that were probably supposed to be classified.

There was a screech of tires in the parking lot, followed by a chorus of annoyed and angry voices.

Alexander, stationed by the window, peered through the slats of the blinds and gasped, "Good gravy! The family's back!"

Everyone immediately sprang into action. We couldn't head out the door, as that led to the parking lot, where the family would see us—so there was only one other option. We scooped up all our gear and crammed into the bathroom.

Mary was still on her call, although she lowered her voice to a whisper and continued talking without missing a beat. "All I need is that missing location. . . . Sure, I can wait a few minutes. I'm not going anywhere. Take your time." She slipped into the bathroom with us.

The tiny space would have been cramped for a single person. With eight of us, there was barely room to breathe. Thankfully, the Hale family was an unusually pleasantly scented family, even after a night in the woods, so being in close quarters with them wasn't too bad. The bathroom itself, however, was rather pungent. It reeked of mildew, cheap body spray, and disinfectant that had completely failed to take care of the mildew.

The three adults clambered into the small bathtub, Zoe perched atop the toilet, and Erica, Trixie, Mike, and I wedged ourselves between the door and the sink. I pulled the door shut and we all held our breath.

A second later, we heard the front door to the room open, followed by the heavy footsteps and grumblings of an extremely annoyed father. "Which one of you knuckleheads put the 'Do Not Disturb' sign on the door?" he shouted, as though yelling back to the car. "No one's gonna clean the room if this sign's on the door!"

This was followed by some distant voices all denying their guilt.

The father stormed around the room, roughly moving things about, muttering the whole time. "I can't trust anyone else to do *anything*. I say, 'Do you have the tickets?' She says, 'Of course I have the tickets.' Then we get to the air show and she doesn't have the freaking tickets!" He suddenly bellowed at the top of his lungs, "Candace! Where'd you leave them? I don't see them anywhere!"

I glanced at the bathroom counter. There, between a gutted tube of toothpaste and the can of noxious body spray, were five tickets to the air show.

It wouldn't be long until the father ran out of places to search in the tiny motel room, checked the bathroom, and found us all suspiciously jammed inside.

At that very moment, I heard Mary's contact Annie return to the call. "Okay, Mary, I've got that info you needed. Hello? Mary? Hello?"

Luckily, Mary had the volume turned down as low as possible. But of course, she couldn't respond. And she didn't want to risk the father hearing anything. So she reluctantly turned the phone off.

I snatched the air show tickets off the counter, bent down—which required quite a bit of contortion in the packed bathroom—and shoved them under the gap at the bottom of the door. If the father saw them suddenly appear, he would know something was wrong, but I didn't have many other options.

Fortunately, he didn't see them slide out onto the carpet, but it was close. Only two seconds passed before he spotted them. "Oh for Pete's sake," he muttered. We heard him trudge to the other side of the door and snatch the tickets off the floor. There was a pregnant moment where he seemed to be debating whether or not to use the bathroom, but then he turned around and stormed back out of the room. "They were on the floor by the bathroom!" he shouted, then slammed the door to the motel room behind him.

All of us would have heaved a sigh of relief, but we didn't have enough room to breathe so deeply. I opened the bathroom door again, and we all burst back out into the motel room like a bunch of snakes popping out of a fake can of peanuts.

There was a screech of tires in the parking lot. Someone was in a big hurry to return to the air show with the tickets.

Alexander raced to the window and peered through the blinds. "They're gone," he reported.

His mother was already redialing her phone. "Hey Annie, it's Mary. Sorry I lost you. The call just dropped. . . . You've got the info? Amazing. You're a lifesaver. Fire when ready." She grabbed a pen, found a flyer for the air show, and jotted down an address. "I owe you big. Next time you're in town, Cyrus and I will have you and Herman over for pot roast."

She said a few more pleasantries, hung up, and held out the paper so we could see it. "This is where the Feds have placed Murray Hill."

We all gathered around to look at the address.

It was in Florida.

"Of course," I said. When my parents had been placed under protection, I had been told that there were whole towns in Florida that were almost entirely federal witnesses. My parents had been sent there themselves. "Does anyone know where in the state this is?"

Catherine was already looking it up on her phone. "In the south," she said. "Near the Everglades."

I felt a wave of relief. My parents were in northern Florida, near the east coast. Far away from Murray.

It was also nice to know where Murray *really* was. It put us a step closer to getting him to call off his assassins. "Thanks," I said to Mary.

"My pleasure," she replied. "I told you, kid, the analysts are the real heroes of this agency."

"Sadly, I don't think we should celebrate quite yet," Catherine said, having now mapped the route to Murray on her phone. "That address is twelve hundred miles away from where we are right now. That's a long way to drive, given how many people Benjamin has after him."

"True," Alexander said, calculating on his own phone. "But if we leave right now, averaging sixty miles an hour, it should only take us eight hours to get there."

"Twenty hours," Erica corrected. "Who taught you math?"

"Oops," Alexander said. "Well, that's certainly longer, but we can still make the best of it. I'll download some audiobooks, we can sing show tunes, maybe I can even find a place around here that sells Travel Bingo . . ."

"The issue is Benjamin's safety," Catherine said. "We can do our best to keep him out of sight, but Murray has already told every assassin on the planet that we were headed to Falcon Ridge. There's probably dozens of professional killers on their way here, if not hundreds, and they're all going to be watching the roads leaving this area. If anyone spots us, we won't be able to outrun them in a minivan."

"Plus we lost the arsenal when Bertha blew up," Mary said sadly.

"Maybe Ben shouldn't go," Zoe suggested. "He could lie low somewhere around here, with a team to protect him, while everyone else heads south to find Murray."

"I'm afraid that staying here might be even more dangerous than trying to leave," Catherine cautioned. "If we're moving, we can at least lead our enemies on a chase. If we're staying put, it's easy for them to trap us. Plus, I'm not crazy about splitting up the team. And I think it'd be best to have Ben with us in Florida. Murray might have more tricks up his sleeve, and Ben knows him better than anyone. After all, he was the only one who suspected that Murray wouldn't really be here."

Mary coughed conspicuously.

"Except for Mary," Catherine added. "The rest of us were caught with our knickers down."

As she said this, I noticed Erica avert her eyes, looking ashamed.

Trixie suddenly piped up. "If we're in a big hurry to get to Florida, why don't we just take a plane? The flight would only be a few hours."

"Oh, Trixie," Alexander said patronizingly. "We can't possibly fly to Florida. There's no way we could get Benjamin through a commercial airport without being spotted. Or purchase tickets without tipping off our enemies. Some of them are certainly monitoring the airlines, and they'd know exactly where we were heading. I appreciate that you're trying to help, sweetheart, but why don't you leave the planning to the professionals here?"

Trixie narrowed her eyes angrily, annoyed by his tone. "I never said we should use a commercial airport," she said coldly. "And I didn't say we should buy tickets. I said we should *take a plane*."

Erica turned to her, intrigued. "You mean, like steal one?"

"Exactly," Trixie said. "One of these." She pointed at the flyer for the air show.

Catherine beamed proudly at her youngest daughter. "That might just work," she said.

TRANSPORT

Zamperini Airfield

Near Wickham, Pennsylvania

June 12

0915 hours

Once Cyrus returned from Falcon Ridge, we all piled into the minivan and headed directly to the air show. It wasn't hard to find. It was only a mile from the motel, and all we had to do was follow the smell of jet fuel.

The event was located at a municipal airfield that normally only handled small private planes. There were two runways, some hangars, a control tower, and a tiny museum that housed a few aircraft from World War II. The air show was the major event of the year for the entire county; according to the kindly woman who sold us our tickets, more people visited the airfield on this one day than the rest of the year combined.

The whole community had come together to put on a delightfully pleasant festival. Hundreds of booths had been erected in a grassy field alongside the runways. In them, artists displayed paintings, pottery, and handmade furniture; farmers hawked everything from house-cured bacon to locally made honey; the Elks Club was running a pancake breakfast, and the Lions Club was selling the most mouthwatering array of homemade pies I had ever seen. There were also carnival rides, bouncy castles, a petting zoo, and a shooting arcade.

But of course, the big draw was the airplanes. The museum had wheeled out its collection, while dozens of other planes had been flown in. It turned out that a lot of people restored vintage aircraft and then spent the summer flying them to air festivals around the country. While most planes were merely on display, a good number of owners were selling rides. For a few hundred dollars, you could go up for fifteen minutes in a variety of biplanes, World War II trainers, helicopters, and even a crop duster. Despite the bucolic setting, there was a constant whine of propellers and roar of engines as planes took off, landed, and taxied on and off the runways.

However, all of those aircraft were too small for our needs. Each was only designed for two passengers at most. Except one.

"That's what we're here for," Trixie said excitedly, pointing it out. "A Douglas C-47 Skytrain. Military transport modified from the civilian DC-3 airliner to move troops, cargo, and wounded soldiers. Over ten thousand were produced in two years. Two Pratt and Whitney R-1830 Twin Wasp air-cooled engines. Twelve hundred horsepower. Maximum elevation twenty-two thousand feet. It's not cushy inside, but there's plenty of room for all of us and it has a sixteen-hundred-mile range."

Zoe and I were both astonished by Trixie's wealth of knowledge—although her family didn't seem surprised. Meanwhile, Mike stared moon-eyed at her, completely smitten.

"How do you know so much about planes?" he asked.

"I've just always found them fascinating," Trixie replied, then flashed a coy smile. "I told you I knew a lot of stuff."

"You're incredible," Mike told her.

"Ick," said Zoe and Erica at once.

Rides were being offered on the C-47, for up to ten people at a time. The plane was the pride and joy of the local museum, which had beautifully refurbished it. It was significantly larger than the other planes at the air show, with a much wider body, but it was still streamlined and aerodynamic. It sat at the edge of the tarmac, surrounded by a group of Air Force veterans, who were all eagerly talking to guests about it. The ground crew was just finishing gassing it up for a day of flights, which explained the tang of jet fuel in the air.

Trixie looked to her family. "Can any of you fly that?"

"I can," Alexander answered.

"Really?" Trixie looked to Erica and Catherine for confirmation. It hadn't taken her long to realize that Alexander wasn't particularly competent.

"Really," Catherine said. "Your father might not be the most capable agent, but he's a talented pilot."

"Aw, thanks," said Alexander, not having realized that the statement wasn't entirely complimentary.

Trixie stared across the tarmac, carefully observing the C-47. "Taking the plane by force on the ground looks like it would be tricky. But if we all go up as passengers, hijacking it might not be too difficult. There's only three members of the flight crew, and from what I've seen, you ought to be able to easily overpower them."

Everyone looked to one another, then nodded agreement.

"Good thinking, munchkin," Catherine told Trixie, then headed off to buy tickets.

The rest of us went to get pancakes.

These were served under a large tent between the petting zoo and the artisans' booths. Several men from the Elks Lodge were working at big outdoor griddles, serving up stacks of pancakes smothered in powdered sugar and maple syrup. We each got a plate, then found an empty picnic table.

The pancakes were fantastic.

Normally, I might have enjoyed the air show. I liked aircraft, even though in the past few months I had been forced to parachute out of—or crash-land in—quite a few of them. Plus, the food was good and the festival was charming.

The problem was, I no longer felt comfortable being around people.

Even though we had arrived early, the festival grounds were already getting crowded, which meant there was an increasing chance of someone recognizing me and then either accosting me for being an alien or outright trying to kill me. I was doing my best to lie low, with my baseball cap pulled down to shade my face, but I still couldn't shake the feeling that everyone was staring at me.

And if that wasn't bad enough . . .

Erica had only a few bites of pancake left when she froze, sniffing the air cautiously. Then she frowned as though she realized she had just stepped in dog poo. "Do you smell that?"

"What? The jet fuel?" Mike asked.

"No. The *other* bad smell."

"The pig pen at the petting zoo?" Zoe guessed.

"No. Even worse."

"What's worse than a pig pen combined with jet fuel?" Trixie asked.

"Joshua Hallal," I said. I couldn't smell him myself, but I couldn't think of anything else that would concern Erica so much.

"Yes. He's here." Erica scanned the crowded cautiously. "And Ashley is too. I can smell her hairspray."

"What about Warren?" Zoe asked.

"I don't smell him," Erica reported. "Or see him. But then, he's rarely easy to see."

Mike had spent much of the last night trying to bring Trixie up to speed on who all our enemies were. Now she tried to recall what was pertinent. "Ashley's the evil gymnast who had a crush on Ben, Warren's the weasel who turned to the dark side because Zoe didn't like him, and Joshua's the evil guy who Erica had a thing for, right?"

"It wasn't a 'thing,'" Erica said quickly. "I just thought he was handsome. And I didn't know he was evil at the time. No one did."

"Sure," Trixie said, obviously not believing this. "Point is, everyone's relationships at spy school are a mess."

Catherine arrived at our table. "I have nine tickets for us on the C-47's very first flight of the day. They originally weren't planning to start until ten a.m., but I got them to give us an earlier flight."

"How?" Alexander asked.

"I can be very convincing when needed." Catherine flashed a devastatingly attractive smile that would have reduced most men to jelly. "And also, I paid them an extra thousand dollars."

"A thousand dollars!" Cyrus exploded. "That's most of our emergency reserves!"

"And this is an emergency," Catherine reminded him. "Plus, thanks to Trixie's brilliant plan, we're still only spending a fraction of what it would cost to fly there on a commercial plane."

"We're not out of this yet," Erica said, snatching a few tickets from Catherine's hand. "Joshua Hallal is onto us. We'll meet you at the plane in five minutes." With that, she grabbed my hand and yanked me away from the picnic table.

"Where's Joshua?" I asked as she led me out of the pancake tent. "Is he close?"

"I still haven't seen him," Erica admitted, sounding annoyed at herself. "He's being cautious this time. So it's better to be on the move. You're too much of a target sitting still." Then she led me into the city of booths.

We were no longer as exposed as when we'd been seated at the picnic table, but there were still tourists all around us. I did my best to scan the crowd, but there were just too many people. Joshua, Ashley—and Warren in particular—could have been anywhere.

Erica was scanning everyone as well, her eyes darting about wildly. Normally, Erica was cool and calm under pressure, but now she seemed unusually skittish and uneasy.

Then she suddenly stopped. "Ashley's ahead of us."

I didn't see her. I only saw a crowd of airplane enthusiasts.

We were directly beside a booth that sold wooden duck decoys. In theory, they were for hunters, but it seemed that a lot of people used them as decorations, too. Erica quickly grabbed one to use as a weapon. While it probably would have been better to find ourselves next to a booth that sold actual weapons, like maces or tomahawks, I knew that Erica could defend herself with almost anything.

The crowd parted before us, and I finally got a glimpse of Ashley Sparks.

To blend in with the crowd, she wasn't in her usual spangled leotard, but instead wore a T-shirt and leggings—although she still had glittery eye shadow.

Erica whipped the duck at her.

It whizzed through the crowd like a boomerang, heading right for Ashley, whose eyes widened in surprise . . .

And missed her.

Instead of clonking Ashley on the head and knocking her unconscious, the duck sailed past her, and bounced harmlessly off the thick hide of a llama in the petting zoo.

I gasped in astonishment. I had never seen Erica miss before. It was like spotting something mythical, like a UFO or the Loch Ness Monster. For a few moments, I presumed that Erica must have missed on purpose—that her plan was to spook the llama into knocking down the gate of the petting zoo and releasing a stampede of barnyard animals that would trample Ashley.

But Erica looked just as stunned that she had missed as I was. Maybe even more.

"Hey!" the woman who ran the petting zoo shouted. "Who's throwing ducks at the llamas?"

Ashley smiled cruelly and attacked.

Ashley always fought with a combination of martial arts and gymnastics that had been specially designed for her. Rather than running at us, she cartwheeled—and she did it with surprising speed, a blur of arms and legs. She finished it off with a backflip that shifted into a roundhouse kick.

I dove into a nearby booth for cover.

Erica deftly sidestepped Ashley as she sailed past, then steeled herself for another attack.

Only, the attack never came.

Before Ashley could launch it, Zoe emerged from the decoy booth and flung another wooden duck. Unlike Erica, her aim was spot-on. She nailed Ashley right between the eyes.

Ashley staggered, spun around, and passed out onto a table full of homemade pies, splatting face-first into a strawberry rhubarb.

Erica turned to Zoe. Both of them looked slightly thrown by the turn of events. We all knew Zoe was a highly competent fighter, but still, we were used to Erica doing the rescuing. After a few seconds, Erica said, "Thanks."

"Sure thing," Zoe replied.

I clambered out of the booth I had taken refuge in, and only then noticed what group it was for. This particular booth hadn't been rented to a local artisan or a farmer, but an organization looking to spread its message and attract followers: the Servants of The Truth.

A large homemade sign proclaimed this location to be the Booth of Truth, while many smaller signs declared things like HEAR THE REAL STORY BIG MEDIA AND THE GOVERNMENT DON'T WANT YOU TO KNOW and YOU CAN'T TRUST ANYONE— EXCEPT US. The booth was staffed by a middle-aged couple who looked quite normal, except they were handing out flyers filled with the same nonsense that was trumpeted on The Truth's website.

A photograph of my own face was on the flyers, sandwiched between an article claiming that the Masons had built a hidden crypt beneath the US Capitol from which they secretly controlled world events and another claiming that the metric system was a European plot to destabilize our government.

The Truthers looked from me to their flyers, then back to me again.

Then they shrieked and recoiled in terror.

"Please don't suck our faces off!" the woman cried.

"Oh for Pete's sake," I groaned. "I'm not a lizard. I'm a normal human being."

"That's exactly what a Flumbonian lizard would say!" the man responded.

I considered trying to talk sense into them, but it was evident that probably wouldn't work. Plus, I had a plane to catch.

And Joshua Hallal had just arrived on the scene.

He strode into the row of booths with a snarl on his face, priming his bionic arm for an attack.

Erica and Zoe had the same idea at once. Each grabbed a pie from the booth behind them and flung it in Joshua's direction.

Erica missed yet again. She hit the petting zoo llama once more, coating it with banana cream.

"Oh come on!" she exclaimed.

Meanwhile, Zoe's aim was dead-on. She hit Joshua square in the face with a blackberry pie, temporarily blinding him. While he struggled to wipe the gunk out of his eye with his one good hand, we fled the scene.

Luckily, the Truthers didn't try to stop me. Instead, they backed away, terrified that I would consume their faces. But once I was a safe distance from them, they implored other fair guests to apprehend us.

"Someone grab that kid!" the man yelled. "He's Ben Ripley, the alien who's trying to destroy our country!"

"And that girl is cruel to llamas!" the petting zoo manager added, pointing to Erica.

Quite a few people tried to block our escape. I couldn't tell which were Truthers and which were llama rights activists, but they all made things difficult for us. Zoe, Erica, and I fended them off with a few extra pies the girls had swiped, smashing them into our opponents' faces as we dashed past. Erica's aim wasn't an issue in close quarters, and even I could hit someone with a pie from two feet away. We left behind a trail of people smeared with rhubarb, blueberry, and lemon meringue, although several others joined the chase.

Still, Erica, Zoe, and I outran them. The girls moved fast because they were in top physical shape, while I was having a fear-fueled adrenaline rush. We arrived at the airfield and saw Catherine, Alexander, Cyrus, Mary, Mike, and Trixie waiting to board the C-47, looking about anxiously for us. The plane was ready to go, its engines roaring and propellers whirring.

The angry mob was a good distance behind us, but they were still a concern. We raced out onto the tarmac toward the plane. "We have to go!" Erica shouted. "Now!"

Several of the Air Force veterans were clustered by the open door of the plane, in charge of taking tickets and ensuring passenger safety. "What's going on?" one asked, concerned.

Erica pointed to the approaching mob. "That's a group of Truther conspiracy theorists. They were telling us that the US military is secretly in league with the Russians. We said that was a bunch of lies and things got out of hand."

The veterans all grew upset, as though their honor had been insulted. I got the feeling that this wasn't the first time they had heard of the Truthers bad-mouthing them. "Get on board," the first vet said. "We'll take care of those anti-American radicals."

"Thanks so much," Zoe told him.

We handed over our tickets and filed onto the plane.

The veterans quickly closed the door behind us, then formed a phalanx to stop the Truthers.

The interior of the C-47 hadn't changed since World War II. It was mostly empty space, which would have allowed for transporting large amounts of supplies or big items like jeeps and trucks. The only furnishing in the passenger cabin was a row of jump seats along each wall and a wooden box full of emergency supplies. Another hundred people could have joined us inside, and there still would have been plenty of elbow room. Every single thing was painted olive green.

Two pilots were in the cockpit, which was open to the rest of the cabin. A young woman was stationed by the door to serve as our flight attendant.

With the propellers going, it was extremely loud inside. I could only faintly hear the crowd on the tarmac.

"You just let Ben Ripley on board that plane!" the man from the Booth of Truth was shouting. "He's a Flumbonian who is part of a secret alien plot to overthrow our government!"

"And he's got something against llamas, too!" the petting zoo manager added.

"The people on that plane are honest, law-abiding Americans," one of the veterans replied. "Why don't all of you go find someplace else to spread your crackpot theories?"

"My goodness," said our cheerful flight attendant. "It seems you all have already had some excitement here today. But I promise you, this flight will be even more exciting! You're about to take to the air for fifteen minutes aboard a working vintage C-47."

"This flight's going to be far more exciting than she realizes," Mike whispered to me.

Outside the plane, the ground crew removed the chocks from under the wheels and we began taxiing onto the runway.

We all took seats as the flight attendant went over the safety instructions. There weren't many of them, as the C-47 had none of the safety features of a modern passenger plane, like emergency oxygen systems or seat belts.

There were no bathrooms, either.

I looked out a window as we readied for takeoff. The small mob of Truthers was squaring off with the veterans at the edge of the tarmac. The veterans had been joined by more people who seemed to have an issue with the Truthers, so their crowd was much larger. There was a lot of shouting back and forth.

It was a relief for me to see that there were far more people who didn't believe I was an alien-lizard creature than who did. And yet, I was still unsettled.

It wasn't only because I had been attacked and unjustly accused once again. I felt like something else was going on, something that I wasn't quite comprehending. I had the sense there was an important piece of information right under my nose that I had missed.

"Everyone get ready!" the flight attendant announced. "We're about to take off!"

The propellers spun faster, making the entire plane vibrate. We began rolling down the tarmac.

Erica took my hand and squeezed it.

Out the window, I caught a glimpse of Joshua Hallal, standing by the edge of the runway. His face was still smeared with pie, but he had removed enough of it so that he could see. He watched the C-47 rumble past him and then lift into the air.

Given the vibration of the plane and the amount of blackberry pie on Joshua's face, it was hard for me to get a really good look at him, but it seemed to me that he was smiling. It was a devious smile, like he knew something that I didn't.

I kept my eyes locked on Joshua as the ground dropped away beneath me, until he was only a tiny speck. Everything below was a beautiful patchwork of forest and farms, spread out over river valleys and gently rolling hills—except for the Falcon Ridge penitentiary, which looked like a big brown scab on the landscape.

After a few minutes, our attendant said, "We have reached our cruising altitude of twenty thousand feet. If you'd like, you are all free to move about the cabin."

Cyrus, Catherine, and Alexander immediately sprang to their feet and approached the cockpit.

The attendant moved to block them. "Sorry, but I can't allow you to go in there."

"Actually, we're the ones who should be sorry," Catherine replied, sounding genuinely upset about what she was about to do. "I'm afraid we need to commandeer this plane."

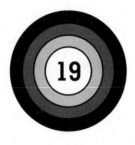

SELF-DOUBT

Somewhere over southern Florida

June 12

1215 hours

All things considered, the hijacking went quite pleasantly.

The crew of the C-47 didn't put up a fight. At first, they had thought all of us were joking. But then Catherine explained the situation. She didn't tell the crew everything, but she made it clear that national security was at stake while Cyrus, Mary, and Alexander all flashed their CIA badges. As usual, Catherine was abundantly charming and convincing. At the end, she gave the crew the option of either surrendering without a fight or being knocked unconscious, and they quickly went with the first option. They allowed us to duct-tape their wrists and ankles together—which Catherine was extremely apologetic about ("It's only for security reasons, you understand")— and even radioed to the air show to falsely claim that the C-47 had suffered an engine malfunction and been forced to make an emergency landing two counties over, which meant no one would notice the plane had been stolen for a few hours. (We hoped.)

While Cyrus and Alexander took the controls, Mary and Catherine invited the crew to sit with us in the passenger area. They seemed very excited to be part of a CIA mission and truly regretful that there weren't any snacks available for us. ("It was only supposed to be a fifteen-minute flight," the attendant explained, and then offered to share the pack of gum in her pocket.)

Overall, our hostages were in much better spirits than Erica, who appeared sullen and downcast. I kept trying to engage her, but each time, she said she wanted to be alone. So I spent most of the flight with Mike, Zoe, and Trixie, playing cards or trying to spot landmarks out the windows as we headed south.

However, I still couldn't shake the feeling that I was missing something. That, along with Erica's dour mood, kept me on edge. As we neared the end of the flight, I couldn't take it anymore. I went to where Erica was seated by herself, glumly staring out the window, and sat beside her.

"You're upset because you missed Ashley and Joshua when you were trying to protect me, aren't you?" I ventured.

Erica kept her eyes locked on the landscape below us. But she finally spoke to me. "I'm supposed to protect you—and I failed."

"Everyone makes mistakes."

"Not me."

"That's not true. You've made mistakes before."

"Not many. And not like this. Your life was in danger—and I missed. *Twice.* I've trained my whole life to be prepared for situations like this. So I won't crack under pressure. And then I did."

"It happens. I miss my targets all the time!"

Erica turned from the window and looked at me with pity. "Is this what it feels like to be you? Ugh. This is terrible."

"Er . . . Well, I wouldn't say it's *terrible.* . . ."

"Really? Because you have the worst aim of anyone I know. I don't even remember the last time you hit a target . . ."

"I hit that truck just yesterday!"

"With a *refrigerator.* I could have done that when I was in kindergarten."

"You weren't a normal kindergartner."

"I suppose." Erica seemed to realize that the way she had

put things hadn't exactly implied understanding. "Sorry, Ben. I didn't mean to sound insulting."

"I know. It's no secret that I stink at self-defense . . ."

"But you have other talents. Whereas self-defense is supposed to be my specialty," Erica said, then thought to add, "Along with strategy, tactics, decoding, breaking and entering, surveillance, counterintelligence, bomb defusion, bomb construction, foreign languages, reconnaissance, evasive action, criminology, psychology, and mustelids."

"Mustelids?" I repeated.

"Yes. The family of mammals that includes weasels, skunks, badgers, wolverines, and otters. They're fascinating. And adorable. That's really more of a hobby, but you never know when it will come in handy."

"Of course," I said, once again stunned by how much I still didn't know about Erica.

Erica sighed heavily. "The problem is, where self-defense is concerned, I'm getting into my own head too much. I used to just aim and hit my target without thinking about it. It was automatic. But earlier, when I was trying to take out Ashley and Joshua, I suddenly found myself worrying about what would happen to you if I missed. Which threw my focus off, so of course, I missed. And now that I know I *can* miss, I'm worried that I'm going to do it again. Which means that I probably will. And then the next time, I'll be even more worried about missing, so I'll miss again and again and again . . ."

I realized she was spiraling and took her hand to calm her. "That's not going to happen."

Erica searched my eyes with hers. "How do you know?"

"Because you're Erica Hale."

A smile flickered briefly on Erica's face, then went away. "I'm serious about this. The air show wasn't the only place I've failed to protect you on this mission. I was also off my game back on the train in Philadelphia. And I was completely wrong about Murray being at Falcon Ridge."

"But Falcon Ridge wasn't a dead end. Cyrus had to go there to get the information about Murray being in the Witness Protection Program."

"I should have guessed Murray would trade evidence for his freedom long before that. I should have listened to you. You're the smart one on this team."

I shook my head. "I know Murray. You know everything else."

"I *don't*. And even worse, I was so set on my wrongheaded plan that I got annoyed when you tried to argue against it. Like I said, I'm making one mistake after another. Which would be bad enough on a normal mission, but on this one, your life is on the line. What would have happened if Zoe hadn't been there as backup at the air show? Joshua would have killed you."

"I'm not so sure about that."

"Of course he would have! Do the math, Ben. You were right out in the open, and my counterattack had gone wide and hit a llama."

"True, but . . . I don't think Joshua *was* trying to kill me."

Erica looked at me curiously. "Sure he was. Just like when he tried to kill you on the train yesterday."

"I don't think he was trying to kill me then, either." Everything that had been bothering me about Joshua's attack the day before was now starting to come together in my mind. "Think about it: When he thought we had jumped off the train, he didn't follow us. . . ."

"Because jumping off a train is nuts. You only do it when someone is trying to assassinate you."

"He still could have taken a shot at the guys in the water. That cannon in his arm has a long range. But he didn't do it. Why not?"

"Maybe he wasn't sure we had really jumped and he didn't want to kill innocent people."

"Joshua once plotted to flood half the earth just so he could make money off real estate. Do you really think he'd care about some innocent people's lives when twenty million dollars was on the line?"

Erica pursed her lips thoughtfully. "I'll admit that's strange. But then he came after us in Philadelphia."

"Yes, but he never took a shot at us. He only yelled at us to stop—and then chased us when we didn't. He didn't try to shoot us at the air show, either. Even though he had a clear shot at this plane when it took off. He could have blown this thing right out of the sky."

"That doesn't make any sense. Joshua *hates* you. He holds you responsible for thwarting all his plans. As far as he's concerned, you've destroyed his career—and a significant portion of his body. Now he has the chance to kill you—and make millions of dollars for doing it—and he doesn't take the shot? Why not?"

I didn't have an answer. I only had a blurry image in the back of my mind, an idea that I couldn't fully comprehend. It was intensely frustrating.

Erica looked equally exasperated. And then, she suddenly grew concerned.

"What's wrong?" I asked.

"I heard something," she said, then pressed herself against the window, trying to look behind our plane.

I hadn't heard anything myself. It was hard enough to hear Erica over the loud thrum of the C-47's propellers, and she was right beside me. But I was used to Erica being able to do plenty of things that normal humans couldn't. So I pressed myself up against a window too.

We were approaching the southern tip of Florida. On the left side of the plane was the urban sprawl of Miami, stretching for miles along the Atlantic coast, while on the right side was the vast expanse of the Everglades.

And directly behind us was a vintage P-41 Mustang. I recognized it from the air show. It was part of the museum's collection; a docent had boasted that it had been completely refurbished to the exact same condition as when it had rolled off the assembly line, right down to the machine guns. It appeared that someone had stolen it and finally caught up to us, although the plane was too far away for me to see who was in the cockpit.

"Dad!" Erica yelled. "Get ready for some evasive action! We've got a bogey on our tail!"

"I'm sure it's nothing to worry about!" Alexander shouted back. "Looks like it's just another pilot out for a joyride!"

At which point the Mustang opened fire on us.

AERIAL MANEUVERS

20,000 feet above Miami, Florida

June 12

1230 hours

Bullets tore through the fuselage, leaving a line of holes in the side of the plane.

Everyone inside yelped in surprise.

"Don't you ever get tired of being wrong?" Erica shouted to her father. "Get us out of here!"

"Roger," Alexander said, and immediately banked to the left, veering toward downtown Miami.

"Don't head into the city, dimwit!" Cyrus barked at him. "Head toward the Everglades!"

"Dad, I know what I'm doing!" Alexander insisted.

"That'd be a first," Cyrus said tartly.

Alexander's feelings were obviously hurt, but he didn't give in. Instead, he shoved the stick forward, taking us into a dive. "This is going to get hairy!" he shouted back to us. "Everyone buckle up!"

"We can't!" Catherine reminded him. "There's no seat belts back here!"

"Oh," Alexander said. "Then hold on tight!"

The sudden dip of the plane had tilted the floor at a steep angle. Everyone had to cling to their seats to keep from sliding into the cockpit. This was extremely difficult for our captives, given that their hands were bound, but they were managing.

Still, Alexander's evasive maneuver had worked for the moment. It seemed to have caught the pilot of the Mustang by surprise. A few seconds passed before the smaller plane corrected its course, which gave us a slight lead on it for the moment. However, we all knew that wouldn't last long. The Mustang was designed to be much faster and more agile than the C-47. It quickly began to close the gap on us again.

In addition, we had no way to fight back. The C-47 had no weapons. Between the dive and the aerial assault, everyone on board seemed worried—although Trixie looked particularly bad. Somehow, she had gone pale with fear and green with airsickness at the same time, leaving her the color of lemon-lime Gatorade.

"Remember when I was jealous because all of you got to be spies and I didn't?" she asked, on the edge of panic. "I'm not jealous anymore! This is no fun at all!"

"Where are the parachutes?" Mike asked the flight attendant.

"There aren't any," she replied. "We normally only use this plane for short tourist flights. And most people don't know how to use parachutes."

"Really?" Mike asked. "Because we use them all the time."

Despite everything else that was going on, the attendant gave Mike a look of astonishment. "How often have you bailed out of a plane?"

"Twice since spring break," Mike answered. "And once, we just crashed in a lake full of crocodiles."

Through the front windshield, we could see the ground approaching disturbingly fast. The buildings of downtown Miami were growing bigger and bigger.

"Pull up!" Cyrus yelled at Alexander. "Or you'll crash!"

"Not yet," Alexander said.

"If you wreck this plane and kill us, I will never forgive you," Cyrus told him. "You're doing this all wrong!"

Alexander gave him a wounded look. "For once in my life, it'd be nice if you gave me a little less criticism and a little more support." He suddenly yanked back on the stick, leveling the plane so quickly that the g-force flattened us into our seats. The C-47 creaked and groaned under the strain. A few rivets popped, flying loose from the fuselage and ricocheting around the cabin.

Once again, the sudden move caught the Mustang's pilot off guard, and the smaller plane dove right past us, leveling off only seconds before it plowed into the streets of Miami.

We were now flying so low that the skyscrapers of downtown loomed directly in front of us.

"Now look what you've done!" Cyrus screamed. "You're going to hit a building!"

"Dad, please," Alexander begged. "I could really use some positive input right now."

"What you could use is a crash helmet," Cyrus muttered. "To protect the few brain cells that you have. Why aren't you turning?"

"There are too many other buildings around," Alexander said with surprising authority. "We'd only end up on a collision course with one of them. So we have to perform a trick I learned in flight school. Everyone, hold on to your seats again. This is going to be a little rough!"

The Mustang had returned to our altitude and dropped in behind us, while the skyscrapers were coming up fast. We heard the rattle of machine guns as the Mustang opened fire again.

Alexander banked violently, nearly turning the C-47 sideways. Everyone on the left side of the plane tumbled down into everyone on the right. There were a lot of screams and moans, along with a strange thud and a yelp from the tail of the plane. But the maneuver worked. The bullets missed us—and we avoided the buildings, threading the gap between two of them with only inches to spare. I actually locked eyes with one old woman, who was watering her begonias on her balcony, as she goggled in dismay while the plane cruised past.

The Mustang had to take a different course, passing on the other side of the apartment building, so that we lost it among the towers of downtown. Alexander kept the C-47 on its side for another few blocks until we passed through Miami and emerged over Biscayne Bay. Then he leveled it out again. Everyone tumbled back to the floor.

There was another thud and a yelp from the tail of the plane.

Erica and I shared a look, realizing what was going on at the same time. Erica sprang toward the back of the plane. Another thump and a yelp followed, these much more pained and whiny. Then Erica stood, clutching something in her hand.

For a moment, it looked like she wasn't holding anything at all. But then, it became apparent that she was gripping the shirt collar of a boy about my age. His entire outfit was the exact same color as the olive-green interior of the C-47, and his skin and hair were painted the same color as well. This excellent job of camouflage had allowed him to blend in so perfectly that we hadn't noticed him for the entire flight.

"Warren?" Zoe said with a gasp.

"Hey," Warren replied, giving us a weak wave. He shot Zoe a glance that was at once ashamed and lovestruck. "It's really nice to see you again."

"What are you doing here?" Zoe demanded.

"Isn't it obvious?" Erica asked. "He's spying on us. While Ashley and Joshua were distracting us back at the air show, he snuck onto the plane."

Behind the C-47, the Mustang suddenly emerged from the maze of skyscrapers and unleashed another salvo of gunfire at us.

"Rats," Alexander said. "I thought I'd lost him."

"Obviously, you thought wrong," Cyrus scolded. "As usual. Now get us out to sea where it's safe to shake him."

"I have a better idea." Alexander dropped the plane so fast that we were all momentarily lifted out of our seats, then leveled out just above the surface of the bay.

"You've never had a better idea than me in your entire life!" Cyrus shouted, then called to the back of the plane.

"Mary! Catherine! Could you get this bonehead out of the pilot's seat so that I can take over?"

Mary and Catherine dutifully approached the cockpit, although it was a struggle to move through the rattling C-47.

"Good," Cyrus said. "It's about time someone on this plane listened to reason."

"Oh, we're not here for Alexander," Mary said. "We're here for *you*." With that, she held up a strip of duct tape, then slapped it over Cyrus's mouth.

Cyrus's eyes went wide in surprise. But before he could do anything, Catherine used more tape to lash his arms to his side and strap him into his chair. "As we've told the children, if you can't say something nice, then you won't be allowed to say anything at all."

Alexander beamed at her. "Thanks."

Catherine gave him a reassuring pat on the shoulder and a supportive look. "Of course, darling. Now shake this assassin for good, will you?"

"I'm on it." Alexander veered to the right with such speed that Warren slipped from Erica's grasp and slammed into the side of the plane with a painful clang.

Once again, we shook the Mustang, but not for long.

Trixie was now so nauseated, she was almost the same olive-green color as the interior of the plane. "I am *really* not enjoying this," she said. "I think all the pancakes I had for breakfast are about to make a return trip."

Mike looked to the attendant imploringly. "You *do* have air sickness bags on this flight, yes?"

"Tons," the attendant replied, then pointed to the box where they were kept.

Mike grabbed one and got it to Trixie just before she blew.

Meanwhile, Erica grabbed Warren again. "What's Joshua up to?" she demanded.

"I don't know!" Warren squealed. "He doesn't tell me anything!"

"That's a lie!" Zoe said accusingly.

"It's not!" Warren gave her the lovelorn look again. "I could never lie to you. You're my everything."

"Ick," Zoe said. "If you keep talking like that, *I'm* going to need a barf bag too."

The Mustang fell in behind us and unleashed another round of gunfire, forcing us to drop to the floor as more bullets punctured the C-47.

Alexander wove back and forth wildly, trying to dodge the attack. The plane sank even lower, until it was practically skimming along the surface of the bay. We buzzed several sailboats so closely that the crews abandoned ship and dove into the water.

A bridge loomed ahead of us, arcing above the bay between the mainland and Key Biscayne. It looked tall enough for us to fit under, but the pilings were awfully close together to accommodate the wings of the C-47.

Cyrus started screaming at Alexander. The tape over his mouth muffled his words, but it was obvious from his tone that they weren't positive.

Despite the support they had given Alexander, even Catherine and Mary looked concerned.

"Are you sure this is a wise idea?" Catherine asked.

"Wise? No," Alexander replied. "But sometimes you have to take risks to get a payoff."

While he was focused on the bridge and the Mustang, my mind was racing with other thoughts. I was starting to understand what Joshua's plan might be. I glared at Warren as I hugged the floor of the C-47. "Joshua told you to get on this plane with us," I deduced. "He wanted you to find out where we're going. Because he isn't after me at all. He's after Murray."

Warren made a telltale gulp.

"Murray?" Mike echoed, still chivalrously holding Trixie's bag full of puke. "Why would Joshua be after him?"

The bridge was coming up quickly. The Mustang was clinging to our tail like a barnacle.

Everyone held their breath. Alexander didn't have much room for error.

Just before we passed under the bridge, Alexander dropped the C-47 a few feet lower. The propellers dipped into the surface of the bay, kicking up seawater, which splattered all over the windshield of the Mustang behind us. It was as though the smaller plane had suddenly flown into a tidal wave.

The C-47 made it between the pilings with only inches to spare on either side. The plane also snagged the lines of a dozen fishermen angling off the bridge, wrenching their poles from their hands.

Normally, the Mustang should have had an easier time passing under the bridge, as it had a much shorter wingspan. But the pilot was flying blind, thanks to the water he'd been doused with. He came through the gap too far to the right and smashed his wing off on a piling.

The Mustang cartwheeled across the water, crashed into the bay, and exploded in a ball of fire.

Everyone in the plane cheered, impressed by Alexander's skills and pleased to still be alive.

Catherine and Mary slapped him on the back while Trixie vomited again in a slightly more positive manner.

Alexander yanked on the stick, and the C-47 lifted back into the air. Wind whistled through the bullet holes in the fuselage. The right engine was coughing smoke, although it still seemed functional enough to work for the next few minutes. A flounder that had been caught by one of the fishermen and then whisked away when the plane snagged its line was flattened against the window closest to me, looking extremely confused.

I turned to Erica and resumed explaining my theory. "Before we were attacked, you said Joshua hates me. Which may be true. But he hates Murray even more. Murray hasn't only betrayed *us* plenty of times; he's betrayed Joshua, too. He helped us thwart SPYDER in Mexico and then showed us how to defeat the organization once and for all. So I'm sure Joshua wants revenge." I looked at Warren. "Am I right so far?"

Warren averted his gaze.

"Answer him," Zoe ordered.

"You're right," Warren told me, then returned his attention to Zoe. "You smell really great, by the way. What perfume is that?"

Zoe said, "It's called None of Your Business, You Creep."

Warren cringed, looking mortified.

Erica angrily pinned him to the wall of the plane. "So what's the plan now? Were Joshua and Ashley in the Mustang we just took down?"

"No," Warren whimpered. "They stole a different plane from the air show to track you."

"All right. We can deal with that." Erica dragged Warren

to the door of the C-47 and explained her plan to the rest of us. "Joshua knows we're in southern Florida, but he doesn't know Murray's exact location. So all we have to do is throw this wretch into the swamp so he can't tell them." She reached for the latch that opened the door.

"No!" Warren yelped. "Don't! It won't do you any good!"

There was something in his voice besides desperation, as though he wasn't only saying this to get out of being tossed from the plane.

Erica sensed it too. She stared Warren in the eye and asked, "Why not?"

"Because Joshua already knows where Murray is."

"That's not possible," Erica told him. "We only learned of Murray's location this morning, and we've all kept it a secret."

"Not quite." Warren reached into his pocket and removed a crumpled piece of paper. "I found this on the floor of the plane."

My heart sank as I recognized what it was: the scrap of paper from the motel that Mary had written Murray's address on.

Zoe snatched it out of Warren's hands. "You sent this information to Joshua?"

Warren withered under her gaze. "I texted it to him right after I found it."

Mike looked to me, concerned. "Murray's the only one who can call off the hit on you. Or tell his followers that we're not aliens. And if Joshua gets to him first, that doesn't happen."

I nodded, having realized this myself. I wasn't sure how far behind us Joshua was, but we had definitely lost some time in our dogfight over Miami.

We had to get to Murray before Joshua did. And it was going to be close.

CONFIDENCE

Homestead, Florida

June 12

1330 hours

No one took responsibility for dropping the scrap of paper with Murray's address—although I was pretty sure that Cyrus was to blame. He had asked to see it when he returned to the motel from Falcon Ridge. Standard protocol was to take a photograph of anything written on paper so that it couldn't fall into the wrong hands—or better yet, simply memorize it—and then destroy the original, but Cyrus had his issues with modern technology. It was only a guess that he was guilty, though, and there wasn't much point in throwing around accusations. We had enough to be stressed about as it was.

Besides, we were all responsible for the bigger security failure: not noticing that Warren was aboard the plane.

The spacious interior of the C-47 was deceptive. It didn't look like there was any place to hide at all, which made it perfect for someone with Warren's camouflage skills. As we had learned in our Avoiding Observation class, it was often best to hide in plain sight, because even professional spies rarely thought to look there. The tail of the plane might have been empty, but it was also dimly lit and full of shadows. Warren had snuck aboard while everyone was distracted by the chaos at the air show, then spent the flight crouching in the farthest corner, while the rest of us had been clustered toward the front, near the cockpit, where the seats were. None of us had ever thought to case the C-47 for stowaways.

No one was more upset at themselves for this than Erica. She looked even more distraught than she had been at the start of the flight. She didn't even help hogtie Warren with duct tape, which she usually enjoyed. Instead, she kept to herself, brooding.

Catherine located a place for us to land on the outskirts of Homestead, Florida, not far from Murray's address. Below us, the urban sprawl of Miami gave way to a patchwork of suburbs and farmland. Our wounded engine was coughing and sputtering, but Alexander stayed calm and made a textbook landing.

The airstrip was a small, rural one primarily used by locals with small planes and crop dusters. Given its shoddy maintenance and tropical climate, it felt very similar to one we had encountered in Panama only a few weeks earlier. The runway was cracked asphalt with weeds growing through it, fringed by some hurricane-battered hangars. One had actually collapsed and never been removed or repaired; it was just a jagged pile of rusted aluminum siding.

The afternoon humidity was thick and oppressive. It roasted the C-47 as we rolled to a stop, so all of us were sweating before we even stepped out onto the broiling tarmac. There was no breeze at all, although some dark clouds loomed ominously on the distant horizon.

There were no other vintage airplanes at the airport. "Looks like we beat Joshua here," I said hopefully.

"That doesn't mean we're ahead of him," Catherine cautioned. "There are plenty of other airstrips in this area. Or, if Joshua has a small enough plane, he could simply land it in the street in front of Murray's house."

That was something we couldn't do with the C-47—although it had been considered. The plane was just too large.

The Everglades began abruptly right across the street from the airstrip. A chain-link fence ran along the shoulder, and on the other side of that was wilderness.

The Everglades is often referred to as a "river of grass." In most places, rainwater runs downhill until it finds a river-bed and then heads toward the coast. But Florida is so flat, there's virtually no downhill, so all the water flows across an extremely wide swath of land at the southern end of the state. In this unusual ecosystem, a difference in height of only a few inches can create an entirely different habitat: Forests of trees grew on the drier "high ground" while the "low ground" was home to vast flooded plains of grass.

"What's that fence for?" Mike asked. "To keep us from getting into the Everglades?"

"Actually, I think it's to keep alligators from getting over here," Zoe replied.

"Then it's not working." Mike pointed to the end of the runway, where three alligators the size of linebackers were basking in the sun.

Two cars were parked by the hangars that were still stand-ing, most likely left there by people who had taken their planes out for the day. It took less than a minute for Cath-erine and Cyrus to break into them and get them started. (Mary had removed the duct tape from Cyrus's mouth after he had promised to only say positive things about his fellow spies.) Cyrus had to hot-wire his car. Catherine found the keys to hers in the center console; the owner was either extremely forgetful or extremely trusting of people.

We freed the crew of the C-47, cutting the duct tape off their wrists. We didn't need hostages, and there was no room for them in the cars—not that they wanted to go anywhere with us anyhow. "People are trying to *kill* you," the flight attendant said. "We'll be much safer walking to town." With that, they waved good-bye to us and headed off.

The cars were like ovens after sitting in the heat for so long, but we didn't hesitate to pile inside. There was no time to lose. With Cyrus and Catherine driving, we raced toward Murray's home. There was little traffic out on the fringe of civilization. We saw more alligators than other cars; most were lurking on the shoulder by the Everglades fence, although some were splayed right in the middle of the road like living speedbumps.

Erica and I rode with Catherine and Alexander—as well as Warren, who we had kept bound and gagged with duct tape.

We hadn't gone far before Erica said, "When we get to Murray's, I'm going to stay in the car and let all of you handle things."

"What?" the rest of us asked all at once, equally surprised. Even Warren asked it, although with his lips taped together, it sounded more like "Mmmmthpfl?"

"Why would you do that?" I added.

"I'll only mess things up," Erica explained. "I keep failing you. I missed that Warren was thirty feet away from me the whole flight!"

"So did everyone else," I told her, trying to be supportive. "He's extremely good at camouflage. And who would have ever thought someone would be hiding on our plane?"

"*I* should have," Erica replied bitterly. "I should have sensed him. I smelled Warren yesterday from two train cars away!"

"The whole plane reeked of diesel fuel," I said. "And it was so loud, there could have been a rock concert in the back and we would barely have heard it."

"That's right," Catherine agreed. "You can't be so hard on yourself, sweetheart. Everyone has bad days now and then."

"I've had thousands," Alexander said. "But I never quit. Even when I probably should have."

"That's not really an argument for staying on the mission," Erica pointed out, then added, "And besides, Dad, you've actually been doing things right today. Unlike *me*. You handled that air battle like a pro. While I've just screwed up one thing after another."

"That's not true," Catherine argued, swerving around a dozing alligator.

"It *is*," Erica countered. "And if I keep making mistakes,

it will jeopardize the mission. So I think it'd be best if I sat the rest of this one out. You can deal with Murray, and I'll just listen to a podcast or play a game on your phone. You know, like a normal person."

I caught Catherine's eyes in the rearview mirror. She looked worried. I was too. Erica had sometimes lost her cool on a mission—but she had never lost her confidence.

"You can't sit this out!" I told Erica. "You're *not* a normal person. You're the best spy I know! There's no way I can do this without you."

"Yes you can," Erica said. "You're not that bad a spy— anymore. And you'll have the whole rest of the team helping you. You guys don't need me."

Before I could dispute this, Catherine announced, "We're here."

She turned off the main road into a small subdivision. It was called Whispering Oaks, even though the nearest oak tree was at least a hundred miles away. The homes looked relatively new, but cheaply built. They were all nearly identical, indicating that the construction company had simply used the same plans over and over. Each was two stories tall with a garage in front and a small yard in back. The yards were completely enclosed by screens to keep out mosquitoes, which made sense as the whole neighborhood sat directly next to the swamp. For many homes, the Everglades were right out their back door. I could see dark swarms of insects roaming the neighborhood like tiny storm clouds.

We parked in front of a house two blocks from the entrance, across the street from a small community recreation center, where a group of older residents was doing aquarobics in the pool. At first glance, the house looked like every other one in Whispering Oaks, with the exact same landscaping, right down to the fake pink flamingos jammed into a small patch of lawn. There was nothing to indicate that my nemesis was living there, and for a moment, I feared that we had come all this way on a wild goose chase. But then I got out of the car and heard the telltale noise.

The air was still. The neighborhood was so quiet, I could hear a dog barking several blocks away. So it was easy to pick up on the loud hum of electrical wires overhead.

While every other home in the neighborhood had one electrical wire strung between it and the closest utility pole, this one had five.

Zoe noticed me staring at them as she got out of her car. "This house is using a huge amount of power," she observed. "Like someone's doing a lot of computing."

"Be on the alert," Cyrus warned, warily eyeing the plastic flamingos. "There might be booby traps. For all we know, those flamingos could be armed with lasers."

Mike threw a rock at one, smashing it. It turned out to

be a completely normal lawn flamingo. "That one's clean," he reported.

"Fan out around the house in standard siege formation," Cyrus ordered. "Once we have determined the coast is clear, we'll all go in at once. Erica—you, Catherine, and Benjamin take the back—"

"Actually, I'm going to pass," Erica said. She was still standing by the car. "You guys have fun."

Catherine looked back to her, pleading, "Please come with us. We could really use your help intimidating Murray."

"Someone has to stand watch in case Joshua shows up," Erica said. "I'll call for help if he does."

Zoe and Mike looked at me, incredulous. "Call for help?" Mike whispered. "When has Erica ever asked anyone for help?"

"Or passed on intimidating Murray?" Zoe added.

"Her confidence is shaken," I explained. "She says she's off her game. And we don't have time to argue with her. We have to get Murray to call off his assassins as fast as possible."

"I'll stay out here with her," Trixie offered. "I'm not really trained for this anyhow." She trotted over to Erica's side.

Catherine, Alexander, and Mary all looked torn between tending to Erica and finishing the mission. However, as agents, they knew the mission came first.

Cyrus laid out our attack plan and we went into action. I was sent around back with Catherine and Mike.

Murray's place was one of the homes that backed right onto the Everglades. A canal full of murky brown water ran along the edge of all the yards. Several of the homes—including Murray's—had small docks on the canal with airboats tied to them.

You can't use a normal boat throughout most of the Everglades: It's too shallow for an outboard motor, and the propeller will constantly get jammed with grass. Instead, you need an airboat, which looks somewhat like an enormous cookie sheet with seats and a giant fan bolted to it. The fan blows the boat forward, making it skim across the surface of the water. Without propellers, airboats can operate in water less than an inch deep. Murray's still had the stickers from the dealer on it, indicating that it was brand-new and had possibly never been used.

The swamp was quite beautiful; certainly, it was far more attractive than the housing community, or the airstrip, or any other man-made place we had just come through. On the far side of the canal was a great tangle of mangroves, and beyond that was a stand of trees draped with Spanish moss. Scarlet ibises roosted in the branches, white egrets stalked through the shallow canal, and turtles basked on the banks.

I could have done without the mosquitoes, though.

As we approached Murray's back porch, a plague of them descended on us. I was bitten dozens of times in the space of a second. I swatted them off as fast as I could, but more were ready to take their place.

"Ugh!" Mike groaned, swatting at them as well. "Let's get inside before these little jerks siphon us dry!"

"Wait," Catherine advised, even though she was also being mobbed by mosquitoes. "The screens are alarmed. And possibly electrified."

Upon closer inspection, I realized this was true. The entire screen around the back porch was crackling with energy. We could feel the heat coming off it. Beyond the screen, the windows of the house were shrouded with thick drapes. Whoever was inside didn't want anyone to see in.

The porch wasn't being used as a porch at all. There was some new patio furniture, but it was all buried under stacks of cardboard boxes, which someone had been too lazy to break down and recycle. There were over a dozen empty computer boxes, as well as many larger ones for televisions. Scattered among them were smaller boxes for pizza, dough-nuts, and bulk orders of soda and chips.

"This definitely looks like Murray's place," I remarked. "Murray eats more junk food than everyone else I know put together."

We weren't surprised that the porch screens were electri-fied. In fact, we had come prepared for it. Cyrus was waiting to cut the power at our signal.

Over her phone, Catherine reported, "We're good to go."

"So are we," Cyrus confirmed. "In three seconds. One, two . . ."

The feeling of heat suddenly left the screens. Catherine immediately kicked one, tearing through it. Mike and I quickly followed her through the hole, then across the porch and past the tower of pizza boxes to the back door.

The screens began to crackle again, and the loose ends around the hole sizzled.

"He's got a backup generator," Catherine observed, then casually picked up a patio chair and heaved it through a sliding glass door, which shattered into thousands of pieces.

We pushed through the blackout curtains and found ourselves in what should have been a normal living room, but which instead looked like a homemade version of NASA's mission control. Twenty computers were arrayed on a circle of card tables, while five flat-screen TVs were mounted on the walls; each was flickering back to life as the power resumed. Ten different mobile phones were charging, and another dozen were scattered about the room. Power cables snaked across the floor like tree roots. The air conditioner was running at full force to counteract the heat generated by the electronics, making the house feel like a meat locker. Under each card table was a wastebasket stuffed to the brim with fast-food takeout wrappers and empty soda cans.

Murray Hill sat in the midst of it all, wearing a food-smeared sweatshirt to stay warm in the frigid house. The fast-food diet had taken a toll; in the few weeks since I had last seen him, he appeared to have gained twenty pounds. Noise-cancelling headphones were clamped over his mop of unruly hair, and his attention was riveted to one of the computers. He hadn't even heard us smash the sliding glass door, and so he was slow to react to us storming the room.

The first thing he seemed to notice was that the light had changed as a result of us moving the curtains aside. He considered that for a moment, confused, then turned around, saw us, and completely freaked out.

Murray tried to run, but forgot to take his headphones off first. The cord connecting them to his computer snapped taut, pulling the headphones down across his face and yanking him off his feet. He fell backward on the floor and, thanks to his newfound bulk, struggled to get back up again, like a turtle that had been flipped onto its shell.

The rest of our team came in through the front, having knocked that door off its hinges. We all surrounded Murray within seconds.

I was never quite sure how Murray would behave each time I saw him. As a con artist, he often faked friendliness in order to dupe his enemies, although the last time we had been together, back in Panama, he had been so frustrated by my thwarting his plans that he'd let his real self show, displaying the anger and frustration that had ultimately led to his trying to have me killed.

This time, he went with the fake-friendly persona. He flashed a weak smile and made a lame attempt at innocence. "Hey, guys! What a surprise. What brings all of you here?"

"Can the nice-guy act," Mike said. "And call off the hit on Ben."

"I don't know what you're talking about," Murray replied.

"What if I drop one of these computers on your face?" Zoe asked. "Will that jog your memory?"

"Oh! That hit!" Murray said quickly, then sat up and flashed Zoe his best smile. "It's really good to see you again. That outfit looks great on you."

"Ick," Zoe said, looking even more disgusted than she had when Warren had hit on her. "Get it through your thick skull, sleazeball. I don't like you."

"There's no sense staying hung up on Ben," Murray said petulantly. "He's with Erica now. Oh, and he's also going to be dead soon. Because I'm not calling off the hit."

"We don't have time to play games," Catherine said sternly.

"Yes, but *I* do." Murray flashed the self-satisfied grin of someone with an ace up his sleeve. "Take a look at the TV mounted over the fireplace."

We all turned that way. Now that the power was back on, the TV was up and running again. And what I saw on it made my heart sink.

While the other screens were all tuned to internet news channels, this one displayed the feed from one of the Whispering Oaks security cameras. It showed the pool at the recreation center across the street, where the aquarobics class was underway.

Directly in the front row of the class were my parents.

"That pool is rigged with enough explosive to send Ben's folks and the rest of the gang into orbit," Murray said. "So I guess I'm calling the shots here, not you."

EXPLANATION

Whispering Oaks Estates

Homestead, Florida

June 12

1415 hours

I was so overwhelmed with questions about my parents, I forgot about the one piece of information that might change Murray's mind.

Zoe didn't. She glared at Murray and told him, "The reason we don't have time for your games isn't to save Ben's life, you moron. It's to save *yours*. Joshua Hallal is on his way here right now to kill you. If we don't get you out of here, you're dead."

Instead of reacting with fear, Murray burst into laughter.

"That's the best lie you can come up with? Last I heard, Joshua was trying to kill *Ben*."

"He was only following me, hoping I would lead him to you," I explained. "And that's exactly what happened. Ask Warren."

"Warren's here?" Murray said, surprised. "I didn't notice him. But then, when did anyone ever notice him?" He sat up, realized that Cyrus had brought Warren inside with us, and made a face of disgust. "Hey, Chameleon. Olive green is not your color, pal. You look like a giant fleck of vomit."

Cyrus brought Warren forward and yanked the duct tape off his mouth so he could finally speak.

"They're telling you the truth," Warren informed Murray. "Joshua's coming. He'll be here soon. You should run. Although, before you go, do you have anything to drink? I'm parched after being gagged for so long."

"So they have you in on this scam too?" Murray asked skeptically. "I get it. They caught you, so you need to pretend to play ball with them. Been there. Done that." He picked himself off the floor. "I've got plenty of drinks. Anyone else want one? I'll just pop into the kitchen." He started that way, but Alexander caught his arm.

"You're staying right here," he warned.

"I can blow up Ben's parents anytime I want," Murray threatened.

Alexander looked to all of us, unsure what to do. Finally, Catherine said, "Take him to get the drinks."

The kitchen was attached to the computer room, so we could all see right into it. Alexander went in with Murray.

"How *did* my parents end up here?" I asked, unable to keep the question inside any longer. As worried as I was for my own safety, I was even more concerned about theirs.

Murray grinned proudly, as he often did when he was about to explain how brilliant he was. "As you can imagine, that took quite a bit of planning. Obviously, it's pretty common for federal witnesses to be sent to Florida. In fact, this entire community is people in the program."

"Every single person?" Zoe asked, surprised.

"You think all these people *want* to live on the edge of a swamp?" Murray responded. "We've got alligators the way some people have rats, and I lose like three gallons of blood a day to mosquitoes. Plus, look how cheaply this place was built." He knocked on the door of a kitchen cabinet, denting it. "This isn't even wood. It's *cork*. The government pays bottom dollar for our housing, so the developers spent like ten bucks on materials."

"It's still nicer than prison," Mike reminded him.

"True." Murray opened the refrigerator. It mostly contained soda, except for a single vegetable so moldy that it looked like a Chia Pet. "Any takers on drinks besides

Warren?" When no one responded, he added, "It's not poi-
soned. I promise."

Still, no one accepted the offer.

"I'll take a Coke," Warren said.

"Sure thing." Murray tossed Warren a can, although,
with his usual terrible aim, it went two yards wide. It hit one
of the plasterboard walls and left a small crater in it. "What'd
I tell you? Cheap." Murray cracked open a soda for himself
and returned to the living room. "Anyhow, when everyone
in the community is a federal witness, people tend to let
their guard down. No one's supposed to talk about who they
were before they came here, but sooner or later, they all do.
The Johnsons to the left of me ratted out the Indianapolis
branch of the Mafia. The Johnsons to the right of me spilled
the beans on some big-shot drug runners. And the Johnsons
across the street ran an illegal pangolin smuggling operation,
but then turned in all their clients to keep from going to jail
themselves."

"Everyone's last name is 'Johnson'?" Mary asked.

"They let you pick your new name," Murray explained.
"But most of these folks aren't that creative. Unlike *me*. I
chose an awesome pseudonym: Nick Danger." He looked to
Zoe expectantly, as though hoping she would be impressed.

She wasn't. None of us were.

Mike even snickered. "Really? Nick Danger?"

"It's cool!" Murray protested.

"It's not," Mike told him. "It sounds like the warning label on an electric razor."

Murray turned back to Zoe, his feelings hurt. "You don't like it either?"

"Sure I do," Zoe said diplomatically, realizing that the last thing we needed at the moment was for Murray to go into a sulk. "It's really cool. What were you saying about Ben's parents?"

Murray beamed, pleased by her praise. "Right! My brilliant plan! Well, as you may recall, I had some business dealings with a corrupt agent at Witness Protection, so I knew that Ben's parents wanted to be sent to Florida when they joined the program—although I didn't know where. So I put feelers out into the community, and it didn't take too long to track them down. Then I started an online Floridian federal witness support group and asked them to join. After a couple weeks, we got to be friends . . ."

"You're friends with my parents?!" I blurted, aghast.

Murray grinned, relishing this. "Oh, we're not just friends. Ron, Jane, and I are *close*. They're staying in my guest room this week."

Even though Murray had plotted plenty of terrible things against me, this one nearly made me sick to my stomach. "They're staying *here*?"

"Well, I couldn't invite them down and not offer them a place to stay." Murray sounded slightly offended, as if *I* was the one who had no manners. "They really needed some rest and relaxation, given how bad all the news about you has been this week."

"That's because of you!" I yelled. "You're the one who started the rumors that I'm an alien!"

"Actually, I didn't," Murray said gleefully. "I only said you were a criminal plotting against the government. The internet did the rest—and man, the stuff those conspiracy theorists came up with is golden. I could never have imagined anything as whacked out as that whole Flumbonian lizard-boy thing. But not only do these people believe it, they keep on making it wilder and wilder. Just today, they started a whole thing claiming that you're in league with British royalty to help England conquer France once and for all. It's very complicated, but somehow, it involves three nuclear submarines and a zombie Napoleon." Murray came across some onion rings that appeared to have been lying around for several days and paused to gobble them down.

"The only problem with these folks," he went on, "is that they aren't exactly reliable witnesses. I had this genius idea that they'd serve as my eyes and ears out in the world, reporting where you were, and then I could relay that info to my network of assassins. But for every person who *did* spot you, a thousand mistakenly reported seeing you somewhere else. So I had to make my best guesses as to where you really might be. And even when these loonies got your location right, they got most of the facts wrong. Like, plenty of conspiracists figured you were involved in the dogfight over Miami today, but half said that your plane crashed in Biscayne Bay and the other half claimed it was really a spaceship and you blasted off for Alpha Centauri. Not one of those dingbats managed to report that you'd survived, which is why you caught me by surprise just now. Otherwise, I would've had a welcome wagon full of assassins waiting for you. As it is, they're still going to be a few minutes."

Everyone in the room reacted with astonishment at once. Catherine was the first to respond. "Assassins are coming here?"

"You think I've been spilling my guts this whole time to impress you?" Murray asked tauntingly. "I've been stalling, you dummies."

I looked around the room, concerned, and suddenly understood what Murray had done. All of his computers had built-in cameras; one was on, recording our conversation. "You're livestreaming this?"

"Only to the assassin network, of course. Not to the conspiracy theorists. I don't want to let them know what I really think of them." Murray polished off his soda, crumpled the can, tossed it at a wastebasket, and missed by six feet. "There are hundreds of professional assassins who live in Miami. It's a more popular career there than an orthodontist. It won't take too long for at least a few of them to get here. So if you folks want to keep Ben alive, you should run."

I turned to everyone else, unsure what to do. Our whole plan to have Murray call off the hit on me had been hamstrung by my parents' presence there. It was possible that Murray was bluffing about blowing them up, but I didn't want to take that chance. And now not only was Joshua Hallal en route, but so were an untold number of assassins. We were in a very dangerous situation.

The only option seemed to be reasoning with Murray, which would be a challenge. Murray and sound reasoning were like peanut butter and pickles; they didn't go well together.

Even so, Catherine gave it a shot. "Murray, listen. We are not joking about Joshua being on his way to kill you. We're your only chance to get away from him. But we can't do that if you don't call off the assassins."

"You're going back to this again?" Murray asked doubtfully. "I was really expecting all of you to have at least one more fake story on the back burner."

Erica suddenly raced through the spot where the front door had been, Trixie on her heels, and announced, "Joshua's coming!"

"Whoa!" Murray said, impressed. "You guys worked out a whole skit to convince me? Nice dramatic entrance, Erica, but I'm still not buying it."

"This isn't an act, you nitwit," Erica said. "Joshua's heading straight for your house in a stolen World War Two light bomber."

"It's a Douglas A-26 Invader," Trixie reported. "With what appears to be a thirty-seven-millimeter auto cannon located in the nose, so it can open fire in addition to dropping munitions. Which means we need to get out of here right away."

Murray shifted his attention to Erica's sister, intrigued. "You must be Trixie. Your family and I go way back. It's really nice to meet you . . ." He suddenly trailed off as he noticed the distinct sound of an approaching airplane. He grabbed a remote and aimed it at the TV that was displaying the aquarobics session across the street.

No one was doing aquarobics anymore. They were all looking up at the sky.

That image vanished as Murray flipped through several more security feeds until he found the one he wanted. The camera was obviously mounted on his roof, showing a wide-angle view of the neighborhood.

A vintage airplane was making a beeline for the house. As we watched, it fired a shell from its nose-mounted cannon.

"Uh-oh," Murray said, finally grasping that we'd been telling the truth. And then he hit another button on the remote.

Every light in the house went out. The TVs went blank too. Murray had shut off the generator. We weren't plunged into total darkness, as all the laptops were still running on battery power and the front door was missing, but it was a sudden enough shift that it took all of our eyes a moment to adjust, which was sufficient time for Murray to flee.

We might not have even noticed which way he'd gone if he hadn't slipped on a forgotten glazed doughnut on the way out and banged into the remnants of the glass door to the porch.

Meanwhile, the shell that Joshua had launched was screaming toward the front doorway.

Everyone fled in different directions at once. We scattered into bedrooms and bathrooms. Mike grabbed Trixie and dove through a window with her.

I was closest to the sliding glass door that Murray had fled through, so I followed him out onto the porch.

Erica was right behind me, having paused only long enough to grab one of Murray's laptops.

Ahead of us, Murray had already barged through the hole we'd made in the porch screen and leapt onto the airboat at his small dock.

Erica and I raced after him. Erica was faster than me, as usual, but before she could get to the boat, Murray turned on the ignition and the giant fan on the back roared to life.

The fan was aimed in our direction, and the force of its wind was so strong, we were nearly blown off our feet. We managed to stay upright, but couldn't move forward.

Then Murray's house exploded behind us.

The bomb wasn't strong enough to level it, but it shattered every window at once. The glass blew outward, followed by thick clouds of dust and debris. Roof tiles flew off like popcorn kernels. The entire structure shook and then caught fire.

Joshua's airplane roared past overhead.

And Murray sped off into the Everglades in his airboat, leaving us behind.

HOT PURSUIT

The Everglades
Just outside Homestead, Florida
June 12
1430 hours

Without a moment's delay, Erica ran to the air-boat parked at the neighbor's house. If she was still having a crisis of confidence, she didn't show it.

The airboat had two seats. I jumped into the one beside Erica as she untied the mooring line and hot-wired the igni-tion. The engine roared to life and the fan began blowing. There is no parking brake on an airboat; we instantly rock-eted away from the dock and into the river of grass.

I glanced back at Murray's house. Everyone else had

gotten out of it safe and sound—if a bit singed and startled.

Then I returned my attention to Murray, determined to not let him escape. He had quite a head start on us, but he was among the world's worst drivers, and an airboat is notoriously hard to control. It has no keel or rudder, which makes it less responsive to steering than most other watercraft. Even Erica was having trouble; our initial, sudden burst of speed had taken our boat out of the canal and sent it skimming through the flooded grasslands—but Erica, being gifted at virtually everything she tried, was quickly figuring out how to pilot it.

Meanwhile, Murray was careening about like a toddler on a tricycle for the first time. There wasn't much to hit in the great sea of grass, but Murray still managed to do it. His boat bounced off the side of the canal, ricocheted off a boulder, and then caromed off a large stand of trees, spooking the flocks of birds nesting there into flight.

We were gaining on him, but I worried it wasn't fast enough. In the sky ahead, Joshua was circling around in the Invader for another attack. Murray was an easy target in the open grassland, and if Joshua took him out, then I was in deep trouble.

Erica shouted something to me, but even though I was seated right next to her, I couldn't hear her. Between the growl of the engine and the whir of the fan, the airboat was deafeningly loud. Normally, people on airboats wear earplugs *and* sound-dampening headphones, but we hadn't been able to grab either in our haste. Between the noise and the intense vibration of the boat as it scudded across the water, I felt as though my brains were going to liquefy and dribble out of my ears.

I shouted back to Erica as loud as I could. "WHAT DID YOU SAY?"

She shouted back equally loud. "HANG ON!"

The airboat kicked into high gear, moving so fast that Erica and I were plastered to our seats like insects that had just hit a windshield. We leapt out of the canal and shot across the grass at an angle designed to intercept Murray. I hadn't thought it was possible for the airboat to get louder or vibrate more, and yet, both of those things happened. The giant fan was encased in a metal cage for safety, but it still felt as though we had been plunked into the world's largest blender and were about to be pureed.

The Invader dropped low, bearing down on Murray.

A streak of lightning flickered across the sky.

This was followed almost immediately by a boom so loud, I could even hear it over the airboat. The short span between the flash and the sound indicated that the lightning had struck extremely close by.

It was only now that I noticed the storm that was nearly upon us.

In my defense, I'd had many other things to focus on, but the storm was advancing with astonishing speed. The dark clouds I had seen on the distant horizon earlier were now swallowing up the blue sky. It was as if a cloak was being pulled over the earth. Not far ahead, the rain was falling so hard, it looked like a wall of water. The humidity dissipated almost instantly, and there was a sudden, foreboding chill in the air.

It was dangerous weather to fly in, but still, Joshua kept coming. In the nose turret of the Invader, Ashley Sparks fired the cannon again.

Thankfully, Erica's calculations to intercept Murray were spot-on. We skimmed across the grass and clanged into Murray's airboat as though we were in aquatic bumper cars, shifting his course from one that would have certainly gotten him killed to one that was only extremely perilous. Murray veered into a channel through a cluster of mangroves, and we followed. The munition exploded close behind, creating a small tsunami that drenched us.

Which meant my underwear was going to soon be riding up on me again.

Although I had more pressing problems.

The route through the mangroves was a twisting, coiling labyrinth. Mangroves are some of the only plants in the world that can grow in fresh or salt water, and they did extremely well in the Everglades. Now they formed walls of gnarled trunks on both sides of the channel and a canopy of entwined branches overhead, creating a network of arboreal tunnels. This temporarily shielded us from the sight of the Invader, which continued circling the swamp in search of us—but we were in constant danger of losing Murray in the maze.

The tunnels were only wide enough for one airboat, so we couldn't pull even with Murray. Instead, we had to stay right behind him, even though his fan was blowing hard enough to make our lips flap. Murray did his best to shake us, veering left and right through the tunnels, but Erica stayed on him as tenaciously as a pit bull.

Rain began to fall.

Giant drops punched through the canopy of branches above us. It started slowly, with the drops hitting us every second or two, but the intensity ramped up quickly.

Erica handed me the laptop she had swiped from Murray's house and ordered, "KEEP THIS DRY!"

I crammed it under my shirt as we raced out of the mangrove maze and back into the open again.

That's when the storm hit in full.

I had seen plenty of storms in my life, but those were all drizzles compared to a Florida thunderstorm. The sky had gone completely dark, like someone had turned off the sun, and the rain came down in sheets so thick, we could barely see through it. Within seconds, it had drenched us and filled up the shallow base of the airboat, turning it into a moving pond.

The mangrove tunnels had led us back to the fringe of civilization. We found ourselves along a stretch of road lined with local businesses. I scanned the skies for Joshua's plane, but it had vanished into the darkness.

Now that Murray was somewhat blinded by the storm, he was driving more erratically than ever. He glanced back to see where we were, forgot to watch where he was driving, and slammed into the embankment by the roadside.

To my surprise—and Murray's—the airboat didn't stop. So much rainwater was now covering the ground that the airboat could maneuver across it. It leapt the embankment, landed in the flooded road, and continued going.

Erica didn't hesitate to follow. I held on to my seat for dear life as we jumped the bank and started down the road in our boat as well.

More lightning streaked across the sky above us, immediately followed by booms so close they rattled my teeth. As if we didn't have enough to worry about, the lightning was another major concern. If it struck close by while we were surrounded by water, we could be electrocuted.

Murray raced onward along the road and we stayed right behind him. The rain was coming down so hard that cars had to pull over on the shoulder. I could see the drivers gaping at us in surprise as we boated past.

We only encountered one vehicle that was still capable of driving though the storm: a military-surplus tactical vehicle with a gun turret atop it. It was heavily armored and outfitted with massive tires, which kicked up a curtain of water as we passed it.

The armored vehicle made a sudden U-turn and dropped in behind us.

"OH CRUD!" I shouted. "I THINK ONE OF MURRAY'S ASSASSINS JUST FOUND US!"

"THAT'S NOT ALL!" Erica replied.

Directly ahead of us, the Invader emerged from the storm. It was flying so low, it was practically on the road itself.

I glanced back at the armored vehicle, which was quickly gaining on our airboat. The turret swiveled back and forth, as though someone was inside, trying to get a bead on us.

We were caught between an armored vehicle and a World War II bomber without so much as a peashooter to defend ourselves.

And yet, Erica didn't change course. She kept on driving down the road.

Murray hadn't changed course either. But I figured that was because Murray didn't realize what was going on.

We were directly behind him, getting doused by the rain and the spray coming off his fan. I probably couldn't have gotten wetter if I'd been swimming. I clutched the laptop to my chest beneath my shirt, doing all I could to keep it dry.

The armored vehicle and the plane were both preparing to attack.

"WHY AREN'T WE TURNING?!" I screamed.

"TRUST ME," Erica replied.

In the heat of action, her confidence was back in full force. I could tell she was trying to time things just right, although I really hoped she wasn't off her game again.

Erica pulled up alongside Murray and suddenly slammed into him.

Both our boats veered off the road and into the parking lot of a warehouse store.

A split second later, the armored vehicle and the plane opened fire.

It appeared that, given the bad visibility in the storm, both enemies had been so focused on us that they hadn't noticed each other. Their projectiles passed in the spot on the road that we had just vacated . . . and then each headed right for the other enemy.

The armored vehicle swerved, and the bomb from the plane detonated in the road beside it. The blast sent the vehicle cartwheeling into the swamp.

The Invader banked, but the shell from the armored car sheared its wing off. The plane dropped into the parking lot, skidded across it, and slammed into a row of parked cars.

To my disappointment, it did not explode in a massive fireball.

Both airboats sluiced through the flooded parking lot side by side. Before Murray could figure out how to escape us, I handed the laptop back to Erica and leapt onto his boat. Then I wrestled the controls from his hands and killed the power.

There were no brakes, though, and we were moving fast. We careened onward until we smashed into a pyramid of watermelons stacked outside the front doors of the store. Murray had neglected to buckle his seat belt and I hadn't had time to fasten mine, so we were launched into the pyramid, which promptly toppled. An avalanche of melons tumbled into the parking lot.

Erica expertly brought her airboat to a stop beside ours.

Murray was lying close beside me, surrounded by shattered melons. Half of one was perched on his head like a pith helmet.

Erica leapt from her boat without taking the time to shut it down, held Murray's computer out to him, and shouted over the roar of the fan, "NO MORE GAMES! CALL THE HIT OFF, NOW!"

Behind me, I heard a sudden, high-pitched whine.

I was all too familiar with the sound.

The heart of the storm had already passed. The rain was letting up. It was now only a torrential downpour, rather than a biblical one, which meant we could see all the way into the swamp beyond the waterlogged parking lot.

But what concerned me was much closer.

Joshua Hallal and Ashley Sparks had emerged from what remained of the plane. Both were unscathed, although Ashley seemed a bit shell-shocked after the crash, and her hair looked as though a typhoon had passed through it.

Meanwhile, Joshua glared at Murray Hill with loathing. The sound I had heard was his bionic arm priming for attack. He aimed it toward Murray, ready to destroy him.

Unfortunately, Erica and I were directly in the line of fire.

NEGATION

Boxco Warehouse Store

Homestead, Florida

June 12

1500 hours

There was nowhere for us to run. The entrance to the store was too far away for us to reach safely. We were out in the open.

And we had no weapons to defend ourselves with.

There were only watermelons.

Back in Advanced Self-Preservation class at spy school, Professor Crandall had devoted an entire lecture to using food as makeshift weapons. He had demonstrated that you could pack a serious wallop with a side of beef or a Butterball turkey, but claimed that fruit was generally useless in battle—except for coconuts, which were good for braining your enemies. (The banana peel's reputation for being dangerously slippery was a myth perpetuated by the movie business; if you really wanted to make your opponent fall down, coating the floor in cooking oil or Jell-O was a much better option.) According to Crandall, watermelons were much too heavy and unwieldy to use as weapons, unless you were in a position to drop one off a roof onto your opponent's head.

As I recalled this, I was struck by an idea.

There was a way I could simulate the force of gravity.

Although Murray's airboat was out of commission, Erica's was still running. It wasn't going anywhere, as its bow was buried under half a ton of watermelons, but the fan was still spinning at full power, creating a hurricane-force wind so strong that Joshua had to steady himself against it; Ashley, being much slighter of build, was clinging to his arm to prevent being blown away.

Joshua grinned maliciously as he readied his arm to fire.

"Goodbye, jidiots!" Ashley shouted.

There was no time to work out the math. I had to act.

I grabbed a large melon off the ground and heaved it behind the airboat.

The wind from the fan caught the fruit and blasted it across the parking lot as though it had been fired from a cannon.

Joshua's smug look turned to one of shock as the melon hurtled toward him. He dove out of the way and his shot went wide, blowing a few shopping carts to smithereens.

Erica immediately set Murray's laptop aside and joined the attack, lobbing more watermelons into play. I kept throwing them too.

It was as though we had a watermelon machine gun. It wasn't very accurate, but the sheer volume did the trick. Joshua was struck by several melons, which knocked him to the ground, after which we continued shelling him until he was buried beneath a pile of shattered rinds and red mush. Meanwhile, Ashley was nailed in the solar plexus by an enormous melon, which lifted her off her feet and slammed her into a parked SUV so hard that it knocked the sequins off her leotard.

While we were busy saving his life, Murray repaid our kindness by running away. He bolted across the parking lot in the opposite direction from Joshua.

Erica calmly selected the largest, most perfectly round watermelon she could find, then rolled it toward Murray with the finesse of a professional bowler picking up a seven-ten split. The melon swept Murray's legs out from under him, and he landed flat on his back in a puddle the size of a koi pond.

"Nice," I said. "Although Professor Crandall always told us watermelons made bad weapons."

"Professor Crandall obviously never found himself in this situation," Erica observed. "Go get Murray. I'll make sure the others are out of commission." She turned off the airboat's fan and stalked across the parking lot.

I grabbed the laptop and headed over to Murray. He was lying in the puddle, groaning in pain, the wind knocked out of him after his fall.

"I think Erica broke my back," he gasped. "If she did, I'm suing."

I had zero sympathy for him after everything he'd done to me. "She'll break every bone in your body if you don't call off the assassins. Let's go." I executed a martial arts technique known as the Mangy Dog, which involved grabbing his ear and twisting it as hard as I could, making him howl.

"All right! I'm coming!" He got to his feet while I kept a vise grip on his ear, then let me lead him through the entrance of the warehouse store.

I had been in a few warehouse stores before, but this one was the biggest I had ever seen. The aisles stretched on as far as I could see, and there were thirty separate checkout stations, each with a line of customers waiting. Each customer had at least one shopping cart piled to the brim, if not two or three. It seemed that the store sold almost everything imaginable: bulk cereal in boxes the size of packing crates, wheels of cheese as big as truck tires, actual truck tires, furniture, pianos—and coffins, which I really hoped wouldn't come in handy for me.

Murray and I were now out of the rain, although the air-conditioning was cranked to subarctic to counteract what had been an ultrahumid day not long before. Since we were soaking wet, it was freezing. But I had other concerns. I set the laptop on a pallet of heavily discounted Japanese toilets and demanded, "Call off the hit *now*."

"All right." Murray began typing, but then lowered his voice and said, "Although, I have a proposal for you. I'll call off the assassins and tell all my followers that you're not a bad guy; that was my mistake. But then, instead of turning me over to the Feds, why don't you join me?"

"Why would I do that?" I asked. "You just tried to have me killed!"

"And now I'll make you *rich*. Running scams on the internet is a gold mine—and it's easy! I mean, all those schemes I worked on with SPYDER and the Croatoan and SMASH took years to plan, a ton of coordination, and millions of dollars in start-up money. But you can manage an internet scam from your living room in your pajamas. You barely even have to get out of your chair!"

"Sounds perfect for a sloth like you," I remarked.

"It is!" Murray exclaimed, as though I had flattered him. "You can even pull off a bunch of different schemes at the same time. Setting you up was just a test run. If people will believe you're an alien trying to overthrow the government, they'll believe anything! I've got a hundred ideas for other scams—and these will make us money. *Tons* of money."

"Is that how you got the twenty million dollars you promised all the assassins in return for killing me?" I asked.

Murray gave me a weaselly smile. "Er . . . no. I don't technically have that kind of money . . . yet. When you sank my scheme in Panama, you depleted my reserves."

"You were going to stiff a bunch of assassins for twenty million dollars?" I said, incredulous. "Are you crazy?"

"What could they do about it?" Murray asked. "Get even with me by bringing you back to life?"

"They could kill you, you idiot. They're *assassins*."

Murray paled at the thought of this. "Oh. I never considered that. I was really just focused on getting revenge on you after everything you'd done to me."

Erica raced into the store, pushing an extra-large shopping cart with the unconscious bodies of Joshua Hallal and Ashley Sparks piled in it. Joshua was covered with so much pulped watermelon, he looked like he'd drowned in a smoothie. "How are we doing with cancelling that hit?" Erica asked, sounding worried.

"These things take time," Murray told her. "What's the rush?"

"A few more assassins just showed up." Erica pointed to the parking lot, where four men and women armed with assault weapons were getting out of their cars. Since we were in Florida, none of the other shoppers seemed to consider this out of the ordinary.

"Oh gee," Murray said with mock dismay. "I'm not sure I have time to call the hit off before they get here."

"If they kill me, they're going to expect payment," I reminded him. "Which you don't have."

"I'll hand you over to them myself," Erica threatened. "After I break every bone in your body. Twice."

Murray gulped in fear. "Those are both very good arguments," he conceded, then started typing feverishly.

The assassins were all coming toward the door at once. They were dressed in a variety of ways. One man looked like a ninja, while the other was in the studded leather garb of a Mad Max movie. One woman wore a form-fitting dress that would have looked more appropriate at a charity ball, while the fourth assassin was only in a T-shirt and mom jeans. They all looked slightly surprised to see the others there—and perhaps a bit embarrassed, too. I had hoped that they might all start fighting one another, trying to take out the competition and guarantee the twenty million dollars for themselves before coming after me. But instead, they each hurried for the store, hoping to kill me before the others could.

I ducked behind a display of potatoes, hoping that none of them had seen me yet.

Erica eyed them warily. "Take care of this," she warned Murray.

"It's done." Murray finished typing with a flourish. The computer made the sound of a text message going out.

A second later, the assassins all stopped in their tracks. Each took out their phone to check the message that had just come in. They all frowned, then looked at Murray. All four seemed to know who he was, which didn't surprise me; Murray was rather famous in the evil community, and he'd probably garnered even more notoriety after offering so much money for a single assassination.

"The hit's off?" the man dressed like a ninja called out, sounding very disappointed.

"Yeah!" Murray yelled back. "Someone caught up to Ben Ripley in Poughkeepsie."

The assassins all looked confused. "I thought you said he was here," said the woman in the dress.

"Mistaken identity," Murray said quickly. "My bad. Sorry about that."

"Who got him?" Mad Max asked.

"A young up-and-comer in the assassination world," Murray replied. "You've never heard of her. She's from Canada. Sorry you came all the way out here for nothing, but you know how this business works. Winner takes all."

"Yeah," Mom Jeans said with resignation. "These things happen." She looked to the others. "As long as we're all out here, anyone want to visit the Everglades?"

"Ooh!" the ninja exclaimed. "I know a place near here that has great airboat tours!"

The other assassins all seemed excited by the idea and headed back to their cars.

"Nice seeing you guys!" Murray said cheerfully.

"Let us know if you need anyone else killed!" Mad Max called back.

I heaved a sigh of relief, but remained in my hiding place behind the potatoes. I wasn't about to show myself until the assassins were gone.

"I guess that's that," Murray said, sounding very pleased with himself. "You're welcome—ow!" He yelled out as Erica twisted his ear once more.

"We're not done here," Erica reminded him. "You still have to clear Ben's name."

"Right," Murray squeaked. "That slipped my mind. But

it won't be any trouble at all. Should only take a few seconds. You can feel free to let go of my ear at any time."

"I'll let go once you've taken care of this," Erica told him.

I peeked out from behind the potatoes. The assassins were getting into their cars and driving away.

The rain had moved on. A few rays of light poked through the heavy clouds, signaling clear skies in the near future.

I emerged from my hiding place and watched Murray work.

He logged onto The Truth and typed:

Hey everyone. I made a mistake about Ben Ripley. I was misled by a conspiracy theorist who showed me doctored documents. Turns out, Ripley is not a bad person at all. And he is a PERSON, not an alien. In fact, he is just a normal kid who deserves to return to his normal life. So do not pester, harass, hound, or persecute him anymore. I mean it.

Your fearless leader, X.

He hesitated for a moment before posting it, as if he hated to undo all the trouble he had caused me.

Erica twisted his ear harder.

"All right!" Murray yowled. "I'm doing it!"

He pressed the return key, and the post appeared on The Truth.

A few seconds went by.

Then Truther2034 responded: *RED ALERT: Looks like someone has hacked X and is posting lies under his name.*

More replies immediately followed:

Who do you think is behind this? Ben Ripley?

Obviously. And the rest of the Flumbonians.

I'll bet the British royal family is involved too.

Does anyone know if X is safe?

Within seconds, there were hundreds more, all along the same lines.

"That's not good," I observed.

"Fix it," Erica ordered, clenching her fists.

Murray recoiled from her. "All right. Give me a second." He returned to the computer and typed, *This is really X. I swear. No one has hacked me. I've just realized that I made a mistake. Ben Ripley is not a danger to anyone. THAT IS THE TRUTH. X HAS SPOKEN.*

A few more seconds went by.

Then Truther2034 wrote: *EXTREME RED ALERT. X has obviously been brainwashed by his enemies and can no longer be trusted.*

More responses followed.

I always feared this would happen.

X is now part of the conspiracy as well.

We have to find out who X really is and destroy him.

Stay vigilant! If they can get to X, they can get to anyone.

Murray gaped at the computer in astonishment. "What is wrong with you people?!" he yelled to his followers, even though they couldn't possibly hear him. He quickly posted again:

This is NOT a conspiracy! I am the same X who you have followed all along! No one has brainwashed me!

Truther2034 replied: *That's exactly what I would expect someone who has been brainwashed to say.*

All the other conspiracy theorists backed him up.

Murray was aghast. "No!" he shouted to his followers. "Stop listening to each other! None of you understand anything!"

Erica gave a sharp laugh.

Murray turned on her. "What's so funny?"

"You just did to yourself exactly what Zoe tried to do to you yesterday. You made yourself the bad guy. Although Zoe thought that she had to tell even bigger lies to make that happen, when it turns out, all it took was you telling your followers the truth."

Murray shook his head in dismay. "I can fix this," he said determinedly, then started to type a new message.

Erica placed her hand over the keyboard, stopping him. "Don't bother. Anything else you say will only make things worse."

"There must be a way I can talk sense into them," Murray said.

"I don't think so." Erica was watching the constant stream of comments with resignation. "Sense doesn't appear to be something these people have much of."

"Then how do we undo this?" I asked.

Erica turned to me, looking very concerned. "I don't think we can."

AFTERMATH

Swampland Alligator Farm

Near Homestead, Florida

June 12

1600 hours

"I can't believe Nick Danger was really a bad person," my mother said, stunned. "He seemed like such a nice boy. Terribly messy, but nice."

"You didn't think all those computers he had in his living room were suspicious?" I asked.

"We thought he was just really into coding," Dad replied. "That's a common hobby for people in the Witness Protection Program. It keeps you indoors, where you're less likely to be seen."

"Many of our fellow witnesses spend a lot of time in chat rooms," Mom agreed supportively.

I nodded understanding. I was upset at my parents for allowing Murray to manipulate them, but it wasn't really their fault. Thanks to me, their lives had been uprooted over the past months. They had learned I was secretly a spy-in-training, nearly been killed, and then had to leave all their friends and everything they knew behind to start new lives. It was probably hard for them to know what qualified as normal anymore.

That afternoon was a good example.

None of the team felt it was safe to stay at Whispering Oaks; Murray had compromised the location when he told all his assassins to come there.

So we had regrouped at Swampland Alligator Farm, a rinky-dink tourist attraction just down the road from the warehouse store, right along the edge of the Everglades. It mostly consisted of man-made ponds filled with alligators, which were arranged by age so that the older ones wouldn't eat any of the younger ones. A spindly wooden boardwalk looped around them all. There was also a souvenir shop, a spot where you could be photographed holding a baby alligator, a small concrete arena where an employee would wrestle adult alligators, and a cage full of surly monkeys that repeatedly tried to urinate on the guests. The place wasn't very crowded, which was the main reason we had selected it.

Alexander and Cyrus had taken Murray, Joshua, Warren, and Ashley to Miami to have federal agents figure out what to do with them. I presumed that Murray would be sent back to prison, as hiring assassins to murder someone was a violation of his agreement with the Federal Witness Protection Program—but sadly, it wasn't my call. Catherine and Mary had brought my parents, Mike, Zoe, and Trixie to meet Erica and me at Swampland. Mike and Zoe were currently at the feeding area, where you were allowed to give bits of hot dog to baby alligators. I wasn't sure where the others were; I had been busy with my parents.

Mom and Dad had been very excited to see me, although that had quickly turned to concern when they learned of Murray's evil plans.

The three of us were all standing on the boardwalk, overlooking the pond with the largest alligators in it. The water was the color of iced tea. The alligators were enormous. Most were basking in the sun, although a few lurked in the pond beneath us. Every once in a while, one would suddenly bob to the surface with a quiet blorping noise.

Dad said, "So, it sounds like Nick—"

"Murray," I corrected. "Nick Danger was his alias."

"Right. It sounds like Murray blew our cover. Which means we'll need new identities? And have to move again?"

"I think so," I said, feeling awful about it. "I'm sorry."

"It's not that big a deal." Mom sounded comforting, although I was quite sure she was only trying to make me feel better. "Florida isn't exactly what we were hoping it would be. It's very humid. Look at my hair! It's so frizzy. . . ."

"And the mosquitoes," Dad added helpfully. "I've got so many bites, my skin looks like the Himalayas." He held up a welt-covered arm as evidence.

"Maybe we should give California a shot," Mom suggested.

"Ooh! That'd be nice," Dad agreed, then looked to me. "Do you think they'd let *me* use Nick Danger as an alias? Since Murray isn't using it anymore. It's much cooler than what I came up with last time. And your mother could be Natasha."

"Natasha Danger," Mom said gamely. "I like it."

I said, "You don't have to try to convince me that this is a good thing. I know it's a huge pain in the rear. You were just getting settled . . ."

"And we'll do it again." Mom put her hand on mine. "We're your parents, Benjamin. We'll do whatever it takes to protect you."

Dad put an arm around my shoulders and pulled me close. "We're proud of you, son. Bob Peterson used to think his kid was a big deal because he was the manager at the local arcade. You're a spy! You have airboat chases and dogfights in airplanes! You have a nemesis!"

"Shhh. That's all supposed to be a secret, Dad." I glanced around Swampland to see if any of the other guests had heard, but the only ones I could see were busy complaining to an employee about having been urinated on by the monkeys.

"Sorry," Dad whispered. "It's hard not to boast about it. Like I said, we're proud."

He and Mom beamed at me in a way that made me feel awfully good, given everything that had happened.

Another alligator blorped into view.

Trixie came along, wearing a brand-new Swampland souvenir baseball cap. "Sorry to interrupt," she said apologetically. "My family needs to talk to you."

"I'll be back," I told my parents, then dropped in behind Trixie.

She led me along the rotted wooden slats of the boardwalk. "Your parents are really nice," she said, making conversation. "I wish I could have met them under more normal circumstances."

"Me too," I said. "Although I don't think my life has normal circumstances anymore."

"Yeah," Trixie agreed. "I never thought, when I first tracked you down, that things would end up like this."

"I guess I really screwed things up . . ."

"No you didn't! I mean, I obviously haven't enjoyed every minute of this. Having people try to kill you sucks. But then, so did boarding school. At least I know the truth about my family now. And it's so cool to see Erica in action. She's amazing."

"She is," I agreed.

"Of course, you're pretty awesome at this too."

"No I'm not."

"Are you kidding me? You faced all those assassins—and you and my sister chased down Murray in an airboat while Joshua and Ashley were trying to blow you up—and you took out an enemy vehicle with a refrigerator—and Mike says you've jumped out of planes and been in avalanches and saved the world like ten times. That officially makes you awesome."

I paused, thinking about that. Ever since I had come to spy school, I had been comparing myself to Erica and found myself lacking. But I had never considered what I might look like to other people. "I guess I've learned a few things."

We arrived at a lopsided gazebo at the farthest side of Swampland from the entrance, which made it the most private place in the park. It was set between the edge of an alligator pond and the chain-link fence that served as the border with the Everglades. Mary and Catherine were seated at a picnic table with Murray's laptop in front of them, keeping an eye on the continuous stream of comments on The Truth.

They both looked to me with concern, which I took to mean that there was no good news.

"Has anything changed?" I asked.

"Yes," Catherine said. "It's gotten worse." She waved to a spot beside her at the picnic table.

I sat down and looked at the comment stream. Everyone had turned on X, believing he had been brainwashed—although they still had plenty of anger left at me. Most blamed me and the Flumbonians for the brainwashing, while a few holdouts somehow felt it had been done by the British royal family, the Masons, or the Nobel Prize committee.

"It's like this on every site Murray used," Catherine told me. "Not only did no one believe him, but his telling them the truth actually made them all believe the lies even *more*."

Mary said, "A big part of the problem is, on the internet, people can choose to engage only with people who share the same views. If you only get your news from a site like The Truth, it seems like everyone else agrees with you. Even when it's about something as"—she paused to pick her words carefully—"as *odd* as thinking that shape-shifting alien lizards are secretly plotting to overthrow the world."

"And there's no way to convince these people that they're wrong," I concluded sadly.

"Well, there are no easy solutions," Catherine said, "whereas, on your previous missions, there were. Once you defuse a bomb, or stop a missile from launching, it's no longer an immediate threat. But we're dealing with ideas and emotions here, which are different."

"There's no off switch for hate," Mary said. "Or fear. Or anger. Or racism or sexism or xenophobia. That doesn't mean you can't fight them, but it takes time."

I turned away from the computer and looked through the chain-link fence toward the Everglades, feeling unsettled. On all my other missions, I had felt a huge sense of relief at the end. But this time, I was on edge. Because the mission hadn't been completely successful. Maybe it never would be.

And there were still other problems Murray had caused.

"So my ability to be a spy is compromised," I said. "Not that I'd even be able to keep training. Because spy school has been compromised too."

Mary and Catherine exchanged a glance, as if they had been preparing for this moment. Then they looked back at me.

Catherine said, "You have a decision to make. A very serious decision."

"We've been in touch with many people at the Agency," Mary told me. "And they are all in agreement that you have done more for your country than they ever expected, especially at your young age. Given the trouble Murray has created for you, everyone would understand if you wanted to opt out of any further danger."

It took a moment for me to realize what they were suggesting. "You mean, I could quit being a spy?"

"Yes," Catherine answered. "You'd go into the Federal Witness Protection Program with your parents. Obviously, we'd have to find a relatively remote place to set you up in your new life. A place where you'd have less chance of being noticed by conspiracy theorists. But you'd be well taken care of in return for all your troubles. And you'd be kept under federal protection. You and your family would be safe. The Agency would do everything they could to ensure that. Your life wouldn't be normal . . . but maybe, in time, it could be close."

I took all that in, then asked, "And option two?"

"It's a bit more dangerous," Catherine replied.

"What is it?"

"I'm afraid it's classified. Unless you agree to do it."

"How can I agree to do something if I don't know what it is?"

"I don't make the rules," Catherine said. "I'm only the messenger."

"Take some time to think about it," Mary told me. Then she and Catherine took the laptop and left me in the gazebo.

I stood up and went to watch the alligators in the closest pond. A few blorped to the surface and then sank back out of sight again.

Only a few months before, I had nearly been eaten by several dozen of their relatives in Mexico, after an emergency landing in an airplane due to a missile attack. It seemed as though it had been years since then, during which time I had nearly died multiple times over—in explosions and car chases and jumps from helicopters. I had been shot at, hunted, and turned into a public enemy.

So the idea of opting for a safe life didn't seem like such a bad idea.

I suddenly had the sense that someone was watching me.

"Hi, Erica," I said.

Sure enough, she was standing right behind me. I hadn't heard or seen her approach, as usual.

She came to the railing beside me. "They gave you your options?"

"Kind of. I don't suppose you could tell me more about the second . . ."

"You know I can't share classified information."

"Right." I considered begging her but knew she would never crack. Not even for me. And besides, there was something else I wanted to ask her. "How'd you get your confidence back today?"

"I didn't."

I blinked at her, confused. "When we first got to Murray's house, you stayed by the car, because you thought you wouldn't be any help. But when Murray fled, you didn't hesitate to jump into the airboat and go after him. Even though Joshua and Ashley were trying to kill us. That wasn't you getting over your fear of failure?"

"No. That was me embracing it."

That did nothing to help my confusion. "What do you mean?"

"For as long as I've been at spy school, I've always thought that I had to be perfect. Because I didn't think I could rely on anyone else. But now that's changed. Thanks to you, I'm not in this alone anymore. I have a whole team of people I can rely on. Which means that if I screw up, it's not the end of the world. Literally. I shouldn't have been so upset back at the fair, when I missed hitting Ashley and Joshua with that duck and the pie. I should have been thrilled that Zoe was there to back me up. And I didn't have to worry about going after Murray in that airboat with you, because I knew that I could count on you when the going got tough. I would never have thought to bombard Joshua with high-speed watermelons. That was all you."

"Maybe, but I never would have been able to drive the airboat the way you did."

"We each have our strengths. That's what makes us such a good team." Erica gave me a quick peck on the cheek, then held my gaze. "I'd hate to break it up."

Even though she couldn't explicitly say it, I understood what she meant. She had been given the same choice that I had—and she had already picked the more dangerous option. If I went for the safe one, it was unlikely that I'd ever see her again.

"Hey guys!" Mike raced over with Zoe on his heels. "Sorry if you were about to do any smooching, but the alligator-wrestling show is about to begin. We just talked to the guy who does it. He sticks his head in their open mouths, and they won't bite him or anything!"

"The guy's going to risk death by decapitation for the amusement of ten people?" Erica asked. "Why would someone do something like that?"

"I asked him the same thing," Zoe said.

"And what did he say?" I asked.

"You have to do what you're good at," Zoe replied.

"Come on!" Mike urged. "When are we ever going to get to see something like this again?" He and Zoe hurried back down the boardwalk toward the arena.

Erica grabbed my hand and led me after them.

I ran with her, thinking that this was how people with normal lives behaved, on normal vacations, where they didn't have to save the world and no one tried to kill them. It seemed nice.

However, my real life was a lot more interesting.

I had no idea what option two was, but I was going to accept it.

June 14

From: ███████████ Agent Emeritus
To: ███████████, Head of the CIA
Re: Operation Blazing Phoenix

Dear ███████████,

The events of this week are a dark moment in the history of the CIA. My beloved alma mater—as well as yours, and that of so many of our other fellow agents—has been exposed and nearly destroyed. There is no way we can safely continue educating students there, meaning that a generation of future agents has been compromised.

But it doesn't have to be a total loss. As you requested, I am enclosing my proposal for espionage training to covertly continue for a select few students who have already proved themselves in the field: ███████████ ███████████, and ███████████ I volunteer to oversee the continuation of their studies, along with ███████████ ███████████. ███████████ also volunteered, but I believe he would be a detriment to our students, rather than a boon.)

As this project is to proceed with the utmost secrecy, I would recommend that we relocate to ███████████ and then ███████████ while also ███████████ with ███████████. Plus, we should absolutely ███████████ or else we'll have a real mess on our hands.

Please get back to me on this immediately. My team is ready to go as soon as you give your word.

Sincerely,

███████████

P.S. ███████████ was wondering if she could get your husband's recipe for the potato salad he served when we visited you last month. I know it's classified, but you can trust us. We're willing to trade you our recipe for apple cobbler in return.

author's note

It's no secret to say that this book series was inspired (at least in part) by James Bond. I always loved Bond movies as a kid, but even back then, I knew there were massive plot flaws that it would be amusing to make fun of. And so, in the first nine Spy School books, the evil plots of the bad guys have all been riffs on the sort of ridiculous, over-the-top evil schemes of James Bond villains with their overly complicated logistics, hordes of minions, and questionable financing. (If you can afford to spend a few billion dollars to build a top-secret evil lair in a tropical island, why even bother with an evil plan? Why not just build yourself a nice house there and retire?) But when the time came to think about book ten, I realized that there were actual, real-world issues that would make for good plots as well.

Like conspiracy theories on the internet.

Don't get me wrong. I *like* the internet. It has revolutionized life on earth in thousands of positive ways. And, of course, there were plenty of conspiracy theories before the internet existed. But, as I pointed out in this book, the internet has allowed conspiracy theories to proliferate in astonishing ways. In fact, every time I came up with something bizarre that conspiracy theorists could claim about Ben in this book, I would discover that real-life conspiracy theorists were claiming even more bizarre things. So, I'll admit it: I gave up and adapted actual conspiracy theories. There are really people out there who believe that lizard-people from outer space are trying to destroy humanity. Or that the earth is actually flat. (In fact, I have found evidence that back in Columbus's time, most people *didn't* think the earth was flat. They all knew it was round; they just thought it was smaller than it actually is. Which means that there are more people who believe the earth is flat *now* than there were five centuries ago.)

Obviously, this is a problem.

Admittedly, I have thrown around some goofball conspiracy theories myself in this series. (In *Spy School Revolution*, I claim that the Croatoan was secretly responsible for some major events in American history that they were not responsible for.) But I—and my publisher—make it very clear that these books are fiction. On the internet, that is not always the case.

So, if I might offer a piece of advice that I think will serve you well: Be wary of any information you get on the internet. (Or, for that matter, any information that you hear from a friend who claims to have got it from the internet. Or social media.) There *are* credible sources out there, although it can take a little bit of work to figure out what they are. For help, there are several nonpartisan organizations that study and rank which news sources are the most impartial, and you should know that anything published in most scientific or medical journals must be vetted beforehand by peer review, so those publications tend to be credible.

And, of course, if you really want a credible source of information, you could try good old-fashioned *books*. (Although it still makes sense to take a look at their sources.)

If a website claims that everyone is lying to you except them, there's a very good chance *that* site is not to be trusted. Conversely, if more than 99 percent of scientists and experts on a particular topic agree about something (for example, that climate change is occurring), then there's a good chance that's true.

And finally, the more misspellings in a post, the more likely it is to be factually questionable. (If someone can't even bother to check their spelling, they probably didn't spend much time on research, either.)

The ability to know what is true—and what is suspect— is an extremely important skill in life.

All right, I've said my piece. Go be good citizens.

acknowledgments

It is extremely common for a young aspiring writer to ask me how I get so many ideas. Often, that same young writer will then complain that they don't have nearly as many ideas as I seem to, as if this is somehow a failure on their part.

All you young, aspiring writers out there need to realize something: I've been around a lot longer than you have. That means that I have experienced a lot more things than you, and experience is generally what leads to ideas. In fact, quite often, a single sequence in a book can be based upon several random experiences that took place throughout my life.

For example, take the sequence in this book where Ben and Erica go underneath Union Station in Washington, DC, to get to the train. Here's how I know what that section of Union Station is like: Many years ago, I was taking a train from New York City to Washington, DC, as part of a book tour, when I happened to run into a friend of mine from college: Eve Simon. Eve has multiple sclerosis, and thus, she needed a special cart to drive her from the train platform to the passenger level (a service that was provided by Amtrak, I believe). Eve asked if I would like to join her, so I did, and our route took us through that less-visited area of the station, which ultimately sparked the sequence that I would write many, many years later.

Likewise, many of the scenes that precede the boarding of the train are based upon numerous other trips to Washington, DC, over the years. (I have a lot of good friends there—and I have been invited to do many school visits in the area, thanks to this book series, which plays well in our nation's capital.) Of course, I can't remember everything *perfectly*, so often the details are reinforced by research and many hours poring over Google Earth, but the point is, quite often, a scene in a book is inspired by some completely random set of circumstances that occurred years—perhaps even decades—before I ever wrote it down.

All of which is to say that each book is partially inspired by dozens, if not hundreds, of people.

So then, let me try to make a dent in that list. Thanks to the Washington, DC, crew who have shown me so much of the city over the years: In addition to Eve there's Larry Hanauer, Michelle Kelemen, Sheila Berman, Nani Coloretti, Tracy Soforenko, Yasmin Tuazon, and Miriam Zibbell-Guggenheim. Thanks to the National Park Service rangers who have given me countless tours of Independence Hall and Benjamin Franklin's home and print shop. (For the record, there is no secret tunnel between them.) Thanks to Jon Mattingly, Katie Goodman, Soren Kisiel, Kent Davis, and Jen

Weeks, who joined me on some very ill-fated camping trips in southeastern Pennsylvania many years ago that inspired the Kozy Korner Kampground. Thanks to the wonderful staff and volunteers at the Palm Springs Air Museum, who helped me with all the airplane stuff, took me for a flight in their C-47—and who inspired the WWII aircraft enthusiast in my own home: my son, Dashiell, whose knowledge of those planes proved very helpful for the later sequences in this book. Thanks to John Janke, who first took me to visit the Everglades and so many other areas of southern Florida.

On the professional front, there are many wonderful people to thank at my publisher, Simon & Schuster, as well: Krista Vitola, Justin Chanda, Lucy Cummins, Erin Toller, Beth Parker, Roberta Stout, Kendra Levin, Alyza Liu, Anne Zafian, Lauren Hoffman, Lisa Moraleda, Jenica Nasworthy, Chrissy Noh, Anna Jarzab, Devin MacDonald, Nadia Almahdi, Christina Pecorale, Victor Iannone, Emily Hutton, Emily Ritter, Theresa Pang, and Michelle Leo. Also, thanks to my intern, Paola Camacho, and to RJ Bernocco and Mingo Reynolds at the Kelly Writers House at the University of Pennsylvania for continuing this great program.

Then there's the gang of writers/friends/consultants/ advisors: James Ponti, Sarah Mlynowski, Julie Buxbaum, Max Brallier, Gordon Korman, Christina Soontornvat, Karina Yan Glaser, Julia Devillers, Rose Brock, Jennifer E.

Smith—and my new neighbor, Adele Griffin. And, as usual, thanks must be given to my incredible agent, Jennifer Joel.

Thanks to the home team, Ronald and Jane Gibbs; Suzanne, Darragh, and Ciara Howard; Barry and Carole Patmore; Alan Patmore and Sarah Cradeur; Andrea Lee Gomez; and Emma Chanen.

And last but not least: Dashiell and Violet, thanks for being the greatest kids on earth.